MW00529539

BIRTH OF THE PHOENIX

RISE OF THE PHOENIX, BOOK 1

JESSICA WAYNE

B.A.D.
PUBLISHING

To my Grandmother, who taught me the amazing worlds you can find simply by cracking open the cover of a good book.

This one's for you Grandma Carme.

B.A.D.
PUBLISHING

Birth Of The Phoenix
Rise Of The Phoenix, book 1
by Jessica Wayne
Copyright © 2018. All rights reserved.
ISBN: 978-1-952490-27-9

Edited by Jessa Russo of Russo's Editing Services
Proofread by Dominique Laura
Proofread by Rachel Cass
Cover Design by Fay Lane Graphic Design

CONTENTS

PART II

PART I

"In order to rise from its own ashes a phoenix first must burn." — *Octavia E. Butler, Parable of the Talents*

PROLOGUE

ANASTASIA

Bodies littered the ground before her, their eyes forever unblinking, frozen in fear. The sky thundered and rain poured down, diluting the blood-splattered ground.

"Hello?" Anastasia called, searching for anyone who might have survived. What happened? Why was everyone dead?

Her lungs burned as she ran through the destruction of what had once been her city. Buildings had crumbled to nothing but chunks of brick, and it took nearly all her concentration to make it safely through the rubble.

"Hello?" she screamed as loud as she could, her throat burning from the force. "Is there anyone left?" Her gaze landed on a man lying face down, his dark hair matted with blood. She approached slowly, each step taking her closer to what she prayed wasn't reality.

"Dakota?" she whispered, kneeling beside him. She rolled his body over and cried out. "No!" Anastasia lifted his head into her lap and cradled her best friend. What the hell had happened?

"Anastasia."

She turned toward the sound quickly, raising her fists in the air. A man stood before her wearing a crimson robe. His mouth in a tight line, he narrowed his silver eyes. Dark hair cut short and greying at the temples, he resembled one of the professors at the college, but she didn't recognize him.

"What happened?" she asked.

"You happened."

Her stomach twisted. "What do you mean? I didn't do anything!"

The man snickered. "You did everything!"

"Who are you?" She held her ground, determined to protect Dakota even now that he was no longer breathing.

"I will be your death."

1

ANASTASIA

Anastasia's alarm clock blared to life, and she groaned before rolling over to slap her hand on the snooze button. How is it that she can sleep a full eight hours and still feel exhausted?

Groaning again, she rolled onto her back and covered both eyes with the palms of her hands.

Another day in paradise.

"You good, Ana?" The deep baritone on the other side of the door sent her heart bounding and she jumped out of bed to pull the door open.

Her roommate stood in the hallway, wearing basketball shorts and a short-sleeved shirt, having just returned from the gym. His thick brown hair was matted to the sweat on his forehead. Her stomach flipped as it always did, the sight of him sending her hormones raging. *Damn.*

"You good?" he asked again, eyebrow arched.

"Yeah, great. Thanks." Anastasia forced a smile and took a deep breath. They'd been best friends their entire lives, having grown up living next door to each other.

There were no secrets between them—well—none except the fact that he was the only person who stole the breath from her chest.

"You sleep okay?" All amusement gone from his handsome face, he reached forward and ran both hands up her bare arms in a sweet gesture meant to calm her nerves. "You don't have to see them."

As it always did when they spoke of her parents, her stomach churned with unease. They were coming by for their monthly visit in three days, something she dreaded despite how much time passed.

Her past fears had a sneaky way of burrowing their way into her imagination.

"They help pay the bills, Dakota; I don't have a choice. Besides, things are better now that I'm not living there."

"Yeah, I still think it's bullshit. We can do just fine on our own." He released her and stepped back. "I'm gonna go grab a shower. Want to pick up some breakfast before I head to class?"

She offered him a smile and nodded. "I'll get dressed."

Anastasia stepped back into her bedroom and closed

the door gently behind her. She leaned back against the hard wood and studied the room before her. Her twin bed had been brought from her childhood home, as had the desk, but she'd wanted little else from that place she'd come to hate or those people who haunted her dreams.

Anastasia pulled on jeans and a pale blue T-shirt. Fridays were casual at the used car lot where she worked for her father's golf buddy, and Anastasia took full advantage of enjoying a day without the suffocating uniform of pleated khaki pants and a stiff collared shirt she wore every other day.

She pulled a brush through her long brown hair and wished like hell she'd been blessed with curls—or any sort of volume—rather than the straight, impossible-to-style hair she had been born with.

It had been two years since she'd had to wear makeup, and ever since moving out, she'd chosen to forgo it. It wasn't a luxury to her, as it was to most women. For her, covering bruises had been a matter of survival in high school, and now she chose to show off skin that was no longer marred with black and blue.

After applying a small amount of gloss to her lips, Anastasia stepped into the hall and made her way to the kitchen for a quick cup of coffee before Dakota was ready to go.

Just as she passed his room, his door opened and he stepped out wearing a black T-shirt and a pair of dark blue jeans. She looked up into piercing blue eyes and her mouth went dry. She cleared her throat and gave her head a quick shake. *Why the hell does he have to be so damn attractive?*

Being in love with your best friend was hard enough, but living with him and *seeing* him every day? That was borderline impossible to handle.

Especially when he looked like Dakota Parker.

"Ready?" he asked as he tucked his phone into his pocket.

"How do you take a shower and get ready so fast?"

He flashed a charming smile. "You should know. You practically roll out of bed looking adorable."

Anastasia groaned; she *hated* being called adorable. At five foot four and with no hips to speak of, that seemed to be the male species' favored word for her. Dakota knew it, too, and when he winked, she punched him lightly on the arm.

"Don't be a dick."

Dakota shrugged. "Comes naturally."

That was a load of BS if she'd ever heard it. Dakota was one of the nicest people she knew, and he would be more than happy to give someone the shirt off his back if they needed it.

Perhaps that's why he chose to study and become a doctor like his mother.

"Do you have class today?" he asked as they made their way down the stairs of their apartment complex.

She shook her head. "I have to work a four hour shift at the store today and then I'm headed to the library to work on my paper." Because her parents had refused to help pay for a university—regardless of the fact her father was the ADA for the city of Seattle, and money had never been a problem—Anastasia attended the local community college, taking a few classes on creative writing.

One day she was going to do what she loved, sharing stories with others who longed for escape the way she had throughout her childhood.

"My mom was wondering if we wanted to do dinner tonight. She said she's making meatloaf."

Anastasia grinned; Elizabeth Parker's meatloaf was the best thing in the world. Many times throughout their childhood, Dakota had snuck over a plate of his mother's cooking when Anastasia was being punished for one thing or another. More often than not, that plate of food was the only thing she'd eat all day.

"They want us to come over there?" That was the only downside, their parents still lived next door to each other. So seeing the Parkers meant she might have to see her own parents too.

Dakota reached down and twined his fingers with hers in a familiar gesture that shouldn't have had her blood pounding.

But it did.

It shouldn't have made her knees weak.

But she could barely stand.

How long until she finally got the courage and told him? It was fear that kept her revelation at bay. He was the only person she had. If she lost him because didn't feel the same she'd be alone.

And loneliness was not something she could handle. Not after everything she'd already been through. So instead of leaning into him, she swallowed hard and let him guide her.

"It'll be okay, Ana. If you don't want to go, I can see if they're willing to meet us somewhere."

"No, that's okay." She smiled up at him as soon as they stopped next to the passenger door. "Honestly, I could use some meatloaf."

"You got it." He raised her hand and pressed a kiss to it. Anastasia's lips parted slightly as their gazes held.

Lust slammed into her and it took everything she had to keep from throwing herself at him on the sidewalk.

Just before it became too much, he released her hand and pulled open the door. Heart still pounding, she forced herself to look away as he came around the hood and climbed.

"Breakfast burritos here we come," he said with grin as he fired up the engine.

"Can't wait," she replied. As they made their way downtown for breakfast, Anastasia fiddled with the bottom of her shirt as she said a silent prayer that her parents wouldn't make an appearance tonight.

Unfortunately, luck was rarely—if ever—on her side.

2

ANASTASIA

"Miss Carter, I need to speak with you."

She stopped shredding paper and turned toward her boss, who stood in the doorway to his office. Anastasia swallowed hard and took a deep breath. If there was anyone in the world who scared her as much as her own father, it was this man right here.

His eyes were dark, and he had no hair on his head. The mouth that was always pulled into a tight line somehow looked even more aggravated today.

Great.

She nodded and rose to her feet, then walked into his stuffy office.

The door shut gently behind him, and Anastasia took a seat in the chair across from his desk. She folded her hands in her lap and tried to calm the nerves that clawed their way to the surface of her mind.

She hadn't done anything wrong; there shouldn't be any reason to worry.

"So, Anastasia," he began as he took a seat on the edge of his desk. "When I hired you, it was as a personal favor to your father."

"Yes, sir. I understand that."

Looking down his nose at her, he shook his head. "I've given you a flexible work schedule and as many hours as you can stand to work."

"And I appreciate that, Mr. Fraser."

"Your father and I played nine holes this morning, and he asked me to keep him apprised of your work schedule."

Years ago, her father represented Phillip Fraser when the bastard had been accused of sexual harassment by one of his employees, and ever since then, they'd been golf buddies.

Anastasia frowned. "Okay."

"I had to tell him about last week and, well, he was just as disappointed as I was."

Her pulse sped, and Anastasia folded her hands together to keep them from shaking. "About what?"

He clicked his tongue and shook his head. "About the fact that you were nearly an hour late for your shift."

Anastasia ground her teeth together. *Because you scheduled me last minute when I'd specifically asked for time off to study.* "I wasn't aware you had scheduled me."

"Is it my responsibility to make sure you check the schedule?"

"No, sir, it's not."

"I didn't think so. If you continue showing up late, I'm going to have to start docking your pay, something I'm sure your father would be none too happy to hear."

"With all due respect, Mr. Fraser, I am an adult. My business is mine, *not* my father's."

"Seeing as how he is the only reason you have this job, I will keep him apprised as I choose."

Anastasia shook her head. She'd graduated, moved out, gotten a job, started college, and yet she was *still* somehow beneath her alcoholic father's thumb.

"Are we done here?" She gripped the arms of the chair, ready to push up and leave this man's office.

He leaned back, resting his palms on the desk as he narrowed his gaze. "That depends; are you going to continue being late for work?"

Anastasia clenched her fists and tried like hell to beat back the anger desperate to claw its way to the surface. *Screw it.* She rose to her feet. "I quit."

"Excuse me?" He pushed off the desk. "You can't quit."

"Oh, I can, and I do." She turned to leave, but he gripped her arm.

"You aren't going anywhere until we call your father."

She looked at his hand around her bicep, heat rushing up her neck to her ears as adrenaline coursed through her veins, then looked up and met his gaze. "Please let me go," she said, the words pushed out through clenched teeth.

He raised an eyebrow in challenge.

Anastasia inhaled deeply. "I doubt my father will be able to get you off after *another* assault charge is placed against you."

He tightened his grip on her arm. "Is that a threat?"

As Anastasia yanked free of him, a stack of neatly shelved books crashed to the floor.

Startled, he turned toward the bookcase. "What was that?"

Anastasia closed her eyes. *Not now, please not now.* She took a deep breath to calm herself before anything else out of the ordinary happened, and without another word, she stepped onto the sales floor of the dealership and headed to clear out her desk.

If she'd had any hopes of avoiding her father tonight, that jackass in there had just shattered them all.

Mitch Carter would be on the lookout for his insolent daughter tonight.

ANASTASIA STARED BLANKLY AT THE WORDS ON THE computer screen, unable to focus on her schoolwork with the looming threat of having to answer to her father about quitting her job. Her phone buzzed, Dakota's face lighting up the screen.

She smiled, relief filling her chest with warmth. "Hey, what's up?"

"So, I just stopped by your work with a giant coffee delivery for you, and was told you no longer work there," Dakota said curiously. "Care to share?"

She sighed. "It's a long story."

"Where are you now?"

"The library."

"On my way."

"Thanks, Dakota." She hung up the phone and, after saving her document to a thumb drive and stuffing it into her pocket, Anastasia stepped outside.

Seattle was rarely sunny, especially this time of year, but as she stepped outside, a ray of sun shone down through the clouds. Anastasia turned her face toward the sky, closing her eyes as she let the sun warm her skin. Sighing deeply, she smiled. She'd finally quit that horrible job, and while it definitely made things more problematic for her in terms of paying bills, and she didn't know where to even begin looking for work, especially this close to the holidays, this decision— though impulsive—was one more step *away* from her father and the fear of his wrath.

After all, she was an adult now. There was not much he could do to her, right?

She opened her eyes, and her gaze landed on a man standing across the street from her. He wore a dark grey cloak that buttoned at the front and stared directly at her. Dark brown hair that was greying at the temples was cut short, and his mouth was slightly opened in surprise.

There was something oddly familiar about him… a feeling deep in her gut; something she knew but was just out of reach tugged at her mind. He raised his hand and waved, and she mimicked the motion, waving back at him without a second thought.

Dakota pulled his Jeep up to the curb, blocking her view of the man.

"What's up, quitter?" he joked. "Who are you waving at?" He looked out his window to the other side of the street, then back at Anastasia, his brows furrowed.

"There was a man"—she pointed to where the man had been standing only moments ago, but he was already gone—"That's weird. He's gone now."

The smile fell from Dakota's face. "Everything all right?"

"What?" She climbed inside and stuffed her backpack down at her feet. "Oh yeah, no, he just waved at me." She shrugged, unable to shake off the feeling that she'd somehow known that man.

"I guess that's what you get for being popular."

Anastasia rolled her eyes. "Yeah, okay, Mr. Popularity."

"Psht. I'm hardly popular."

"Are you kidding? We can't even go to a party at your campus without everyone stopping us to talk to you. Especially the girls," she added, trying to hide the green-eyed monster that wanted to come out whenever it came to other women with Dakota.

"What about you and Gage? You two seem pretty close lately."

Anastasia raised an eyebrow. "I'd hardly consider us close. The only time I see him is when I'm with you."

"Not according to him. He says you two have a... what did he call it? Oh yeah, a *connection*."

Anastasia's lip curled. While he was hot, Gage was also painstakingly aware of it, and she'd only ever had eyes for one guy—which definitely wasn't Gage Keesler. Because Gage was the son of Dakota's dad's partner on the police force, they'd known each other so long she'd been around the arrogant asshole more times than she cared to admit.

"Whoa, one guy who is way too full of himself thinks I'm cute. That's hardly a reason to call me popular."

Dakota shrugged as he turned down their old street. Anastasia swallowed hard; this entire neighborhood held some pretty shitty memories for her.

To her surprise, Dakota veered to the left when he should have continued going straight—and pulled into the parking lot of the park they frequented as kids.

"We're early, figured it wouldn't hurt to get some exercise in before dinner."

"How old are you?" she asked with a giggle, panic momentarily pushed aside. He had that ability, to erase her fear and give her something—anything—else to think about. "Not too old to love swinging higher than you."

"You're on."

They climbed out and made their way across the dying grass and over to three swings suspended from a rusted frame on iron chains. As they walked, Anastasia imagined it as it had been, as the place she longed to escape to.

They'd removed the merry-go-round after a kid had been thrown off and broken his arm, and it had been replaced with a seesaw. But she could still see it there, feel the wind in her face as Dakota spun her around and around.

Unfortunately, this park didn't see a whole lot of visitors anymore since the city had opened another just one block over. But for Anastasia, there was no other park quite like it. When she was here, it was as though she were walking into another world entirely. One where her problems weren't nearly as big as they seemed.

When they were kids, she and Dakota made plans to sneak out at least once a week and meet at the park. It was a nice break for her, a way to push aside the pain in her life. For a few hours, anyway.

Anastasia took a seat, and to her surprise, Dakota stepped up behind her. His hands rested on her back, the contact burning her up from the inside. He pushed her gently and already she longed to be back, pressed against him.

"So what happened at work today?" he asked as the chain started to creak with each movement.

She cleared her throat. "He called my dad."

"Your boss called your dad? Why?"

"To rat me out for showing up late to my shift. A shift I hadn't even been scheduled for, mind you."

"Why the hell would he call Mitch? You aren't a kid."

"You're telling me."

"I don't know why you took that job in the first place."

"I need money for rent, and most places weren't hiring."

"You don't have to pay rent, Ana. My parents told you that."

"I'm not going to take advantage of them, Dakota. It was nice enough of them to let me move in and pay next to nothing."

"You're family." He said it easily, and she knew it was true. The Parkers were more of a family to her than her own were. George, Dakota's dad, was a detective with the Seattle PD, and he'd tried to get her help more than once.

But she'd refused, citing the broken arm and busted lip as nothing more than an accident—she was clumsy and all that. The last thing she'd wanted was to bring Mitch

Carter's wrath raining down onto the people she loved. Not when he knew so many people high up the food chain. He could've made their lives a living hell if he'd wanted to.

Hell, she hadn't even told Dakota the truth until right before they'd graduated, and that was only because Mitch had beaten her so badly she'd barely been able to stand. She'd made her best friend promise not to say anything, though, and they'd moved out the next week while her father had been at work.

A breeze sent leaves rolling across the ground, and Anastasia closed her eyes, listening to the sound of cars driving by, and the wind as it rustled through the trees.

"So, you ready to be an old lady tomorrow?"

Anastasia laughed. "You turned twenty-one two months ago. If I'm an old lady, so are you."

"So now I'm an old lady?" Dakota chuckled.

"You know what I mean."

"We can sit on our front porch and yell at all the kids to stay off our lawn."

"Sounds like a plan to me," she said with a smile, closing her eyes again.

Minutes passed in silence, with just the feel of his hands at her back, and the breeze lifting the hair from her neck. Moments like this were why she didn't leave this town behind her the moment she turned eighteen. Life without Dakota? No way that would make sense.

"You're so beautiful." Dakota's voice was so soft she nearly missed it.

Anastasia opened her eyes, surprised that the swing

was stopped. "What?" she asked, sure she'd misheard him.

Dakota stepped in front of her, his eyes trained on her face. He swallowed hard. "I said you're beautiful."

Heat rushed to her cheeks. "I—"

"I mean it." He knelt before her, his hands on the chains so they were face-to-face. "I've always meant it."

"What are you—?"

"Just listen for a sec." He stood and started to pace, so Anastasia rose to her feet.

Was this really happening? Was he seriously going to tell her he felt the same way she did? Is it possible even? For a man like her to love someone so broken?

"I..." He stopped and faced her, his eyes searching her gaze. "Screw it." Dakota crossed the distance between them and cupped the back of her head. He pressed his lips to hers, the soft, tender kiss no match for the fire burning in her soul.

His tongue traced along the seam of her lips and she opened, groaning as she leaned into him. Dakota's hand fisted in her hair and she gripped his shoulders, terrified that if she were to let go she'd discover this was nothing more than a dream.

A wonderful, heart-pounding, lustful dream.

Heat pooled in her belly, the throbbing between her legs so damn intense she was sure she'd explode. He dropped his hands, releasing her hair and gripping her ass. The hardness agents her back was the only proof they'd moved.

The kiss turned feverish, a sweltering passion that consumed her. But too soon he pulled back and rested his forehead against hers.

"I've wanted to do that for a very long time," he whispered through ragged breaths.

"Me too," she replied, unable to stop the smile that spread across her face despite the burning in her lungs.

He slid her down his hard body, but remained pressed against her, something she was grateful for seeing as how she very much doubted she could move.

"So, uh…" He laughed as he braced both hands on the tree behind her. "What do we do now?"

"What do you want to do?"

"I want to see where this will go." He gestured between them. "I want you."

"I want that, too." She smiled widely. "But I have to ask, why now?"

Dakota stepped back and ran a hand through his hair. "Honestly? I had planned to take you to dinner next week and ask you out—officially. But seeing you on that swing and"—he shrugged—"I don't know, I guess I just didn't want to wait."

Anastasia bit her bottom lip.

"Shit, when you do that," he groaned and stepped in toward, dropping his head to his her again.

At this rate, she honestly didn't care if they never made it to dinner.

3

ANASTASIA

Anastasia woke with a smile. For the first time in nearly three months, she'd only had pleasant dreams.

She stretched and yawned, before getting to her feet. Dakota had kissed her. She pressed two fingers to her lips, giddy they still felt swollen from last night at the park.

In the driveway of his parents house.

On their couch.

Her phone pinged, and she unplugged it to check her messages.

Dakota: Thinking about you...

Anastasia grinned and hugged the phone to her chest for just a moment before pulling it back and firing off a reply.

Anastasia: Funny, I was just thinking about you too.
Dakota: Copycat.

His response was immediate, bringing another smile to her face.

The doorbell chimed, and Anastasia pulled a robe on over her shorts and tank top. Had she not been so happy, so elated with her change in relationship status, she might have checked the peep hole before pulling open the door.

"What can I—?" The words died in her throat. Her father stood on her doorstep, his freshly polished loafers looking out of place against the worn-out welcome mat. An icy chill as cold as her father's gaze tore down her spine; she tightened the belt of her robe and crossed her arms over her chest. "What are you doing here?"

Mitch Carter was a lot of things to a lot of people. He was a respected Assistant District Attorney, the husband to a trophy wife, a golf buddy, and for some strange reason, some people considered him a friend.

But to Anastasia, he was only one thing: a walking nightmare.

He lifted his hand, and she flinched, all too aware of the pain that hand could inflict.

"Oh, calm down, Anastasia." He pushed past her and stepped inside, two men she didn't recognize flanking him. "Where's Dakota?"

She swallowed hard as they entered her apartment. "School." She tightened her grip on the doorknob.

"You planning on shutting that anytime soon? I can't

imagine the Parkers want to pay a ridiculous utility bill all because you have no manners." His voice was tight, and Anastasia closed her eyes.

Calm down. You're an adult now. He can't hurt you anymore.

After closing the door but staying near enough that she could run if she had to, Anastasia turned to face him. "Why are you here?"

"Can't a man visit his daughter?"

Not you. "I wasn't expecting you or Mother for another two days."

"I'm not here for a chat." He shoved his hands into his pockets. "I need you to come with me."

"Why?"

"Your mother wants to see you."

"Why didn't she come with you?"

"Because she's ill."

"What's wrong?" Anastasia wished she felt more empathy for the woman who'd birthed her, but only curiosity fueled her question.

"Come with me and find out."

"I have things to do today."

"Like what?"

"Work," she retorted, instantly regretting the lie.

Judging by the harsh line of his mouth, and the way his eyes narrowed on her face, Anastasia knew her father had found out that she no longer worked at the dealership.

"Do I need to remind you how I feel about lying?" He stepped toward her.

"I'll call the police. You can't hurt me anymore."

He laughed. "Get dressed and let's go."

"I'm not going anywhere with you."

"Yes, you are."

She turned to open the door, but during their conversation, one of the large-framed men, this one wearing a black suit and sunglasses, had managed to make his way close enough that he slammed it closed again.

Anastasia backed into the kitchen, trying to get as far away from him as she could. "Stay back."

"Grab her."

The man reached out and grabbed her arm, hauling Anastasia up against him. She managed to slip her arm out of the sleeve of her robe, and reached for her phone, but she missed it by an inch when the other man wrapped a large arm around her waist.

"Let me go!" she screamed loudly as the man threw her over his shoulder. She kicked her legs and hit his back, trying to get free, but the man was solid.

"Shut her up." Her father ordered, and she felt a sharp pain on the back of her head right before her world went black.

4

DAKOTA

Dakota stared at the screen of his phone, waiting for a response. He hadn't wanted to leave the apartment this morning, and school was the last thing on his mind. He'd finally stopped being a damned coward, and now Ana was all he could focus on.

Her lips.

The feel of her body against his.

Shit, it had taken all his willpower to wait. But with a friendship as close as theirs, moving quickly could be a mistake. He wanted to make sure what was between them would work before moving any further.

Not that he didn't think it wouldn't. His future was with Ana, of that he had always been sure.

He smiled, not caring who saw his grin in the middle

of the lecture. Tomorrow, he could pay attention, but today, he wanted to think back on how she'd tasted.

How she'd looked bathed in light on that swing.

How her lips had been so soft against his.

Dammit, he had it bad. Looking back now, he wondered just when his feelings for her had developed into something more. As far as he could remember, he had always felt this way. She was it for him, and he was going to make sure she knew that.

Dakota: I'm excited for tonight.

When five more minutes passed and she didn't respond, unease spread through him. Was she regretting the change to their friendship? Had she changed her mind?

Dakota: You there?

She could have been showering, or maybe her phone died, but with each passing moment, a heavy feeling of trepidation grew in his stomach. Not wanting to wait any longer, he excused himself from class and made the short walk to the parking garage to get into his Jeep.

At every stoplight or stop sign, Dakota checked his phone, hoping to see a text from her, but by the time he made it home, she still hadn't responded.

Dread setting in, he pulled into his assigned spot and threw the Jeep into park, then raced up the stairs. The door was unlocked and ajar, and all hope that Ana was just in the shower or busy vanished. He raced inside, freezing momentarily when he spotted her robe tossed to the floor, her cell phone on the table.

"Ana?" he called out, running down the hall to her room. "Ana! You here?"

After checking all the rooms and bathrooms, Dakota pulled out his phone and dialed his dad.

Surely this wasn't really happening. *Please be okay, Ana.* His dad answered on the third ring.

"Hey, son, what's up?"

"Dad, it's Ana," he choked out, agony spreading through his body like a wildfire. This couldn't be happening. It had to be a nightmare.

A horrible nightmare.

"What happened?" His father's tone went from light to business in an instant.

"She's gone," he managed. "Ana is gone."

5

ANASTASIA

Anastasia's head pounded when she opened her eyes. Quickly surveying her surroundings, she realized she was lying on a floral couch in her old living room, and dread pulled her stomach into a tight knot.

Her heart thudded, how the hell had she gotten here? Memories of her father and two men coming into her apartment resurfaced and she pushed to her feet, still a little woozy from whatever had hit her in the head.

"Look who's awake, Monica! Our little girl," Mitch sneered.

Monica turned and beamed at her, her chocolate brown eyes lighting up with joy. "It's so good to see you, honey. How are you feeling? Your father said you fell and hit your head."

"I want to leave." Anastasia started for the door, but Mitch moved to block it.

Sliding his hand over the knob, he said, "You aren't going anywhere until he decides what he wants to do with you."

"What? Who?" How the hell was she going to get out of here? If she could only make it to a window, she might be able to scream.

"You're becoming more trouble than you're worth," her father said with a smile. "So, now it's time to reevaluate our situation."

"What the hell are you talking about?"

He left the door and marched over to her. She winced away when he raised his hand, but she didn't move fast enough, and it cracked against her cheek. Her eyes watered from the sting, but Anastasia bit down on the insides of her cheeks to keep from crying out. She would not give him the satisfaction.

"Watch your mouth." His phone rang, and he answered it quickly. "Hello?"

Anastasia turned her attention away from him and back to the room. Where were the two men from before? Were they waiting outside, just in case she managed to get out?

"So." Mitch hung up his phone and turned back to her. "Seems we have some time before he gets here to take you in."

"Who is he?" Anastasia eyed the door. He was far away from it now that if she was able to get around him, she might stand a chance. That was as long as the two men from earlier weren't waiting outside.

"You'll find out soon enough."

"No, I sure as hell won't." She moved for the door, and Mitch grabbed her arm.

"Get off of me!" she yelled. She pulled her free hand back and punched him in the face. The contact split her knuckle open, and she looked down in surprise as pain radiated through her hand.

Did she seriously just punch her father?

"You will pay for that, you little bitch." He charged her, and Anastasia stumbled over the coffee table. Before she could get to her feet, something struck her back, and she cried out in pain. The sharp sting surged through her body, and she tried to get to her feet again. "You will show me respect!" he yelled.

Another blow knocked her back to the ground, and Anastasia screamed. She could feel it tearing her shirt, and splitting her skin. Blood had spilled from her wounds, and she could see it staining the white carpet beneath her.

Her vision swam as he beat her, and eventually she became so dazed from the pain, it was impossible to move. *Is this how I'm going to die? Dakota and I finally move past the friend zone, and now it's all over?*

The room filled with a bright light, and Anastasia focused on the form that had appeared on the other side of the room. She couldn't make out his features, but watched curiously as he raised a hand. Her father was ripped away from her and slammed into the wall, and Anastasia tried to push to her feet.

Was this who he'd said was coming for her?

Her father stood, and Anastasia managed to crawl out of reach of him.

"You," her father growled.

The man moved across the room, and stood between Anastasia and her father, his long cloak pooling around his feet. His back was to her, but she recognized the cloak, so out of place for modern-day Seattle.

"Me," the man said. With a dramatic flick of his wrist, Mitch was thrown from the room into the hall.

He got to his feet quickly and marched back toward them, his face twisted into rage. Just as he was about to cross the threshold into the living room, he slammed into an invisible barrier and was thrown back again.

"Oh, Anastasia." The man she'd waved to on the street that afternoon turned to her. His blue eyes were kind, and in them, Anastasia witnessed a mixture of pain and fear. "I'm so sorry I was late." He knelt in front of her and closed his eyes, holding his palm toward her. The pain in her back lessened, and she stared at him wide-eyed.

His dark hair was greying at the temples and cut just below his ears so it swayed lightly when he moved. His nose was crooked, as if it had been broken a few times, but it added character to his face.

She should have been afraid, but when Anastasia

looked into his kind eyes, her pulse slowed. "Who are you?" she whispered.

"Someone who will make sure you are never harmed this way again." He stood, reaching to touch her face, but she jerked back.

"Anastasia," he began, "please don't fear me. I will protect you, but we must go now."

A gunshot rang through the room, causing Anastasia's ears to ring. Whatever had been holding Mitch out of the room disappeared, and he stepped inside. She shook her head, and the ringing faded just enough that she could hear Mitch yelling loudly.

"You are not welcome here!" He aimed the gun at the stranger.

The man moved to block Anastasia with his body. "You should be happy I don't slaughter you where you stand." He snapped his fingers and the gun disappeared from her father's hand.

Mitch stared down at his empty hand, shocked.

The man waved his arm again, flinging her father back into the hall. He tossed a vial down on the ground, and Anastasia tried to scramble to her feet as a swirling blue light appeared in the living room.

The stranger held out his hand. "Anastasia, please, we are doomed without you, and you will die if you stay."

She swallowed hard, placing her hand in his. He was her only option, and wherever he was taking her was better than the alternative, which at this point she was pretty sure would be death. Once she was away from Mitch and out of harm's way, she could go to Dakota and tell him what happened, and then maybe George could finally arrest her father.

Mitch charged into the room, and Anastasia tightened her grip on the stranger's hand. He smiled, and together, they stepped into the light.

She felt weightless as the light took her into its embrace. She could see nothing, hear nothing, and the only feeling she had was of the man's hand laced with hers. The light was so bright Anastasia had to close her eyes.

Had her father actually killed her? Was this some kind of illusion brought on by the tendrils of death?

"Am I dead?" she whispered into the emptiness.

The man laughed lightly. "No, my dear Anastasia, you are very much alive."

6

MITCH

"Fuck!" Mitch pulled the phone from his pocket. This was bad, this was so bad. How the hell was he supposed to explain this?

He tapped the contact he wanted to call, and after ringing twice, a deep voice answered. "Hello?"

"She's gone."

"What do you mean *gone*? Did you kill her?"

He took a deep breath. There was no use in lying; it wasn't like he'd get away with it. "No, sir, she is still alive. Rescued by a man who just so happened to appear in my house with a fucking portal."

"You let him take her?" the man roared on the other end of the line.

"No, I didn't *let* him! I brought her here just like you

asked me to and he used magic to subdue me! I had no choice."

"You had better hope I can eliminate this threat, Mitch. Or you will pay dearly for your mistake." The line went dead, and Mitch threw his phone across the room. It smashed against the wall, and he turned to see Monica standing in the doorway.

"What the hell are you doing in here?"

"Did she get away?" she asked, folding her arms across her chest.

"Yes," he growled.

"Good." She turned to leave, but he grabbed her arm.

"What the hell do you mean '*good*'?"

"I think it was about time she got away from here."

"Do you have any idea what this means for us?"

Monica nodded. "But it's better than having to watch you kill that poor girl."

He tightened his grip on her arm. "You had better hope things turn out okay for me after this mistake or I swear I'll drag you down with me."

She straightened. "Then do it. It's only what I deserve after what I was forced to witness for the last twenty years." She ripped her arm out of his hand and headed back down the hall.

7

TERRENIA

ANASTASIA

The weightless feeling disappeared in an instant, and Anastasia opened her eyes. She stood beside the stranger in a small room filled with light that poured in from open windows. The walls, ceiling, and floor were wooden, reminding her of the cabin she'd often visited with Dakota and his family.

A couch made of wooden logs sat in the center of the room, decorated with cushions that looked as if they'd been hand sown. The kitchen was made up of wooden countertops, a large washbasin, shelves of handcrafted dishes, and a fireplace with a Dutch oven hanging from a bar inside.

She gaped at her surroundings, feeling like she somehow stepped back in time and stood in one of the pioneer villages she'd visited on field trips as a kid.

The man pulled his hand from her grip, rubbing it with his free hand.

"Sorry," she muttered. She hadn't realized she'd been gripping his hand so hard.

"Not a problem. Portals are not easy the first few times you take them."

"Portals?"

He nodded and opened the door. "Welcome to Terrenia."

Anastasia stepped out into the fresh open air, and her mouth fell open. The tallest trees she had ever seen surrounded her. Brightly colored birds sang as they flew through the clear blue sky, and beautifully colored flowers swayed in a warm breeze.

"You must be starving. Let's go see my wife first. She can heal those nasty cuts on your back."

She'd nearly forgotten about her injuries.

"Who are you?" she asked.

"I'm sorry, I forgot to introduce myself. I'm Gregory Silvan."

"Where are we?"

"We are in Terrenia. Our village is at the center of this world, but there are others that are scattered throughout the land."

"Terrenia?"

"It's difficult to explain, but I will do my best." He folded his arms behind his back and began to lead her down the path. "You have no doubt heard of dimensions in your studies?"

She nodded. "It's theorized that there are ten separate ones."

"There are actually many more than that, but the exact numbers are unknown. Your scientists have yet to discover the others that actually contain life. Our world is in a dimension that runs parallel to yours; we are about ten hours ahead on time, which is why it's daylight here, and nighttime back in Seattle."

"How do I know any of this is real?"

"Good question." He stopped and placed his hands on her shoulders. "Listen to your heart; what is it telling you?"

She took a deep breath. "That this is real, but my head doesn't believe it just yet."

Gregory grinned. "It usually takes some time before our heads catch up with our hearts." He released her, and they continued walking.

In the distance, Anastasia heard the loud giggling of children playing, and the sound soothed her.

"So, we came here in a portal?"

"Yes. It's a way to briefly connect the worlds. The portals I use only last for a few moments before they close."

"There are different types?"

"I promise I will explain everything to you once you've had time to rest. I cannot imagine how overwhelming this must be."

"Honestly, I'm still trying to figure out how you managed to throw my father back into the hallway."

"That man deserved much more than I gave him." His voice deepened to a growl. "But, as to your question, I used magic."

"Magic is real?" She stopped, and he turned to face her.

He raised an eyebrow. "How else would you explain everything?"

"I have no clue. Head trauma?"

His eyes grew dark. "I will never let him harm you again."

"I'm sorry; I guess that was a bad joke, considering I might very well have some." She shrugged, and they continued walking. "What did you mean when you said you were doomed without me?"

"Long ago, a seer foretold of a prophecy about a woman who would be the only hope against the coming Darkness that would spread throughout the worlds. It was said that she would be more powerful than anyone would know, and although she had suffered at the hands of evil, she would rise above it with strength that would carry her into victory."

"Wait a minute." Anastasia stopped. "Please tell me you don't honestly think that was about me."

"Why do you ask?"

"Because I am no one. A girl from Seattle who likes to write and read. I've never done anything of any meaning. Shit, I'm barely passing my classes in college."

He put his hand on her shoulder. "Everyone is someone, Anastasia. Sometimes it just takes a bit of time to figure out who that person is."

They began walking again, and Anastasia winced as the pain in her back returned. She ground her teeth, refusing to give in, even though each step she took sent the pain radiating through her body. Finally, the trees cleared, revealing a large group of small cottages similar to the one they'd portaled into.

Children ran around, laughing and smiling, while adults doing various chores smiled and watched on. Tables were positioned around a large fire pit that still smoldered from the night before.

As she and Gregory approached the villagers, heads began to turn toward them and conversation slowed. Some villagers smiled gently, while others just watched intently as they passed.

Feeling self-conscious, Anastasia wrapped her arms around herself. She stuck out like a sore thumb in her sleep shorts and tank top. The women here wore long dresses, some with short sleeves, and others with longer half sleeves. The men were dressed in long pants and loose shirts.

Anastasia was someone who did her best to blend in, and now she stood out.

A young boy ran up to them and smiled brightly. He had a scrape on his chin, and his cheeks were spotted with tiny freckles that matched his light brown hair. He looked to be about twelve or thirteen, but his eyes seemed older to her.

"Hi, I'm Brady." He stuck his hand out, and she took it gently.

"Hi, Brady, I'm Anastasia. It's nice to meet you."

"Is this her?" he whispered out of the side of his mouth to Gregory.

"Yes, it is."

Brady's eyes widened, and he released her hand. "She's pretty," he whispered, and Anastasia smiled.

"Yes, she is, now go on and find your mom. Tell her Annabelle has some herbs for her."

"On it!" he called over his shoulder as he ran off.

"What a sweet boy," Anastasia said with a smile as they continued walking toward one of the houses.

"That he is, and a smart one, too. Takes good care of his mom and younger sister, Sarah, since his father died about three months back. It's so sad the number of children around here who have lost their parents recently."

Before she could ask what he meant, the door to the house in front of them opened and one of the most elegant women Anastasia had ever seen waved to them.

"There's my wife," Gregory said with pride as they stepped up onto the porch. "Hi, my love." He kissed her loudly on the cheek, and the woman blushed. "Anastasia, this is my wife, Annabelle. Wife of mine, meet Anastasia." He stepped aside, and Anastasia felt her own face flushing as Annabelle stared at her, tears filling her eyes. Not wanting to see the pity reflecting in the other woman's eyes, Anastasia stared down at her hands and began to fidget with the hem of her shirt.

Do I look that bad?

Annabelle wiped her eyes. "It is so wonderful to meet you." She reached forward and took one of Anastasia's hands in her own. "So incredibly wonderful."

Gregory cleared his throat. "Anastasia needs some healing."

"Oh, yes, of course! Come in, dear."

"I'll be just outside."

"Thank you, Gregory. I'll take good care of her."

Annabelle ushered Anastasia inside and sat her on a stool near a roaring fire. The warmth soothed her aching body, and Anastasia closed her eyes for just a moment before opening them again and watching Annabelle.

The woman's dark hair was braided down her back, and strands of silver had woven their way through her hair. She was slender, and the blue gown she wore matched the lightness of her crystal eyes.

She worked over a pot on the counter, grinding up some herbs and mixing them into a paste.

"So, how was the trip through the portal?" she asked as she stirred the paste.

"It was interesting." Anastasia tried to move, but winced when her back seized up. Whatever Gregory had done to help mask the pain back in her room was clearly starting to wear off.

"Gregory certainly has fun with them." She smiled and knelt in front of Anastasia. "This is a cream made from calendula. It will help speed up the healing process and give you some mild pain relief." She smiled and then said awkwardly, "Honey, I need you to remove your shirt so I can get to the nasty marks on your back."

"How did you…?"

"You were hunching."

"Oh, okay." Anastasia very gently lifted the shirt over her head and held it to cover her chest.

"Oh, you poor thing." The sorrow in her voice had tears stinging Anastasia's eyes. "I'm afraid these are going to scar."

Anastasia winced as the woman started to apply the salve to her back, but almost instantly, the pain began to fade to a dull ache. When she was finished, Annabelle set the bowl to the side and helped Anastasia back into her shirt.

"Come here, dear," she said once Anastasia was dressed, pulling her in for an embrace. "Who did this to you?"

"My father." Anastasia sniffled.

Annabelle went stiff and released Anastasia. "You're safe now," she said softly, and then went to work bottling the remainder of the salve.

"I'm still not entirely sure my father didn't manage to kill me and this is all some sort of afterlife."

Annabelle's face grew serious. "A father does not do the things to you that this man did. The man who did this is evil and does not deserve a name that should be filled with love."

Anastasia couldn't agree more. "Mitch. His name is Mitch."

"Atta girl." She smiled and stood. "Let's go out and meet everyone."

Annabelle held Anastasia's hand as she led her out of the small cottage. Each step Anastasia took became less pained physically, but for whatever reason, every moment that passed had dread unfurling in her belly.

Something felt wrong.

8

ANASTASIA

Anastasia stepped out into the sunshine. Where the hell was she? It looked nothing like anywhere she'd ever been. Be it nerves or cautious curiosity—if there even was such a thing—she followed Annabelle down the stairs. If anyone was able to help her get a phone so she could call Dakota, she imagined it would be the doctor or her husband.

Her eyes landed on Gregory who was holding his hand out, bouncing a ball of light in his palm. Brady and a young girl who looked a lot like him, watched, awestruck, and when Gregory closed his fist, the light burst into dozens of smaller lights that floated up and got lost in the sky.

The pair laughed wildly and ran to a woman whose dark hair was pulled up into a tight bun.

"Gregory's been working with magic for the last twenty years or so. He enchants each healing potion I use to give it a boost." Pride warmed Annabelle's voice. "Unfortunately, we've needed the medicinal aid more often nowadays."

Anastasia started to ask her why, but the villagers formed a circle around them, and she quieted, instantly feeling awkward.

"Everyone!" Annabelle called. "This is Anastasia." She looked over at Anastasia lovingly, and wrapped her arm around her shoulders much like Dakota's mother had done a time or two throughout her life. "She is going to be staying with us."

Everyone around her muttered a "Welcome" in unison, and her stomach flipped. She hated being the center of attention.

The largest man Anastasia had ever seen began moving toward them. He was shirtless, a large sword strapped to his waist. His entire torso was covered in tattoos, and his greying hair fell to his shoulders. A large jagged scar made its way down his chest.

Anastasia swallowed hard as he approached, fighting the intense urge to crawl away. That was, at least, until his eyes met hers. They were kind, as green as the leaves of the trees, and his warm smile set her mind at ease.

"This is Tony," Annabelle said.

He held out his hand. "It is absolutely wonderful to

meet you, Anastasia. We are so pleased to have you here in Terrenia."

"He and Gregory have been best friends for years," Annabelle explained.

"It's nice to meet you," Anastasia said with a smile.

Annabelle guided her down toward where people were going about their daily business.

"It's so lovely to meet you." A woman with blonde hair and dark eyes bowed her head slightly. "Isn't it, Maximus?" She lightly elbowed a boy who looked to be about Anastasia's age. When he turned to look at her, she almost jumped back.

His blonde hair was slicked back at his neck, and a deep scar curved on his cheek. It was his eyes, though, that filled her with fear. They were cold and menacing, matching the sneer on his face.

There was no amusement in his gaze, no warm welcome. "Yeah, it's great."

Annabelle must have sensed Anastasia's unease, because she dismissed them and guided Anastasia back toward the path she'd walked with Gregory earlier.

"You will meet more of our people day by day. Some are out hunting, others are away fighting."

"Fighting?"

Annabelle sighed. "The Brutes are becoming more of a problem than we ever thought they would be."

"Brutes?"

"Big, burly beasts. They stand nearly eight feet tall and their skin is so pale it's nearly translucent. No one knows where they came from. Some believe they are men who sold their souls; others believe they were brought here from another world entirely."

"What do you believe?"

"The latter. I think they were brought here by the Darkness. They've been attacking villages, taking the able bodied and killing the rest. Some of our Fighters have gone to hold the line and try to drive them back into the mountains."

Anastasia shook her head; she'd left one war zone only to be brought into another. And apparently Gregory believed she was some prophesized hero. How was she supposed to defeat beasts that an army of trained fighters couldn't stop? She hadn't even been able to escape her father. At least not permanently.

But she sure as hell had drawn some blood, hadn't she? She thought back to the murderous look in his eyes after she'd punched him.

They continued walking in silence until the cottage came into view. Once inside, Anastasia was overwhelmed with the feeling of home again. She and Annabelle made their way over to the couch, and Anastasia sat, careful to not rest her back against the cushion. While most of the pain was gone, her back still ached.

"So, tell me of your life."

Anastasia didn't make a habit of spilling her secrets to strangers. "Actually, I was hoping I might be able to borrow a phone? I need to call someone and let them know I'm all right."

"Did Gregory not tell you?"

"Not tell me what?"

"We don't have a phone. You can't contact anyone outside of our world."

Her heart dropped. "What? I have to tell my... friend that I'm okay!"

"I'm sorry, Anastasia. It's just not possible."

Anastasia stood and rushed outside. Despite the pain in her back, she pushed into a run and ran until her lungs nearly burst.

What the hell did she mean Anastasia couldn't call home? How would Dakota react when he returned home and discovered her missing? Would he think her father had finally beaten her for the last time? Would anyone even know Mitch Carter had been at their apartment?

She dropped to her knees in the dirt and covered her face with her hands. What if she never saw Dakota again?

"Anastasia?"

She didn't look up when she heard Gregory's voice. He'd brought her here; he was the reason she wouldn't see her best friend again. But he'd also saved her life.

"I need to let Dakota know I'm all right." Anastasia sat back and wrapped her arms around her knees.

"I'm afraid that's not possible. There is no way to contact the other world from ours."

Anastasia glared up at him through tears. "You didn't tell me I would never talk to Dakota again."

"I didn't have time. We had to get out of there before that bastard killed you."

"If I can't call, then I have to go back." Panic surged within her, making her heart race. "You can take me back just like you brought me here. Dakota isn't going to know where I am."

"The boy you were with today? Outside the library?"

She lifted her tear-filled eyes to his. "That really was you?"

He nodded. "I'd been looking for you for some time." He took a seat beside her. "You are very special, Anastasia, and we need you."

She shook her head. *I'm no one special.* "Why can't I go back? If you were able to open a portal there to get me and bring me here, why can't you open one again?"

His eyes darted away from hers, and he began to fidget with his hands. "Portaling to a new world takes strong magic—much stronger than I have, I'm afraid. I used my last portal vial to bring you here."

Her heart sank. "So there's no way for me to go back?"

"I'm afraid not."

She covered her face with her hands, and her shoulders shook on a sob. She was never going to see Dakota again, or hear him laugh, or see what they might have been together.

What had she done to deserve this? To deserve to

lose the one person who mattered most to her in the entire world?

Would he go on with his life? Marry someone else? Have kids? The idea was nearly too much to bear, and Anastasia pressed her hands to her chest as her heart broke into a million jagged pieces.

At least Mitch will never find me here. That was about the only sunlight in her ever-darkening world.

9

SEATTLE

DAKOTA

Dakota stepped into his childhood bedroom and stared at the closed window just opposite of his. How many times had he made the jump to the roof next door to see Ana? How many nights had she spent sleeping in his room to feel safe?

What the hell happened to her? Had she left on her own? Been taken by someone? His father had interviewed their neighbors, who described an older man who had shown up that morning, and the timing lined up to just after Ana had sent her last text.

In Dakota's mind, the man had been a perfect match for Mitch Carter. His father had agreed, and called his partner—Detective Keesler—to go interview him. That's where they were now, interviewing the father of the girl he loved. A father who very well might have killed her.

A knock on his door pulled his attention to the doorway as his mother entered the room. "Dakota?" Tears left trails down her pale cheeks.

He stood quickly, his pulse speeding. "What's wrong?"

"I need you to come downstairs."

"Mom, what's wrong?" he asked again, walking to the door.

"I need you to talk to Detective Keesler."

"Why?" Had they found her?

"Honey." She placed a hand on his forearm, stopping him in the hall just outside his bedroom.

"Mom, did they find her?"

She shook her head, and Dakota's heart dropped to the floor. What was he supposed to do without her?

He wasn't sure how he made it down the stairs. It felt as if his entire body had gone numb from the shock. Missing? How could she be missing?

"Hey, Dakota." Frank Keesler stood as Dakota entered the kitchen.

Dakota looked over to see his dad staring out through the window that faced the Carters' house.

"I'll make this quick." Detective Keesler gestured for the chair across from him. "Can you tell me everything that happened last night? From the time you arrived home to the time you left this morning?"

Dakota nodded and went over the events that had

kept him up all night. The details were easy enough to remember; it was a night he was never going to forget. He'd finally managed to summon the courage to tell her how he felt, and the taste of her lips on his was going to be forever branded into his memory.

"Where is she?"

Frank sighed and shut his notebook. "We don't know."

"He must have hurt her," Dakota growled.

"We don't know that. He has an alibi for the entire morning."

"He's lying."

"Dakota, we can't do anything if there's no proof."

"He was seen by my neighbor!"

"Your neighbor was still drunk from the night before and swears they saw *a man* arriving at the apartment. He could barely give us a description and didn't confirm with a photograph. It's possible she just took off." He put his hand on Dakota's shoulder, and Dakota moved away from it.

"She didn't just leave."

"She quit her job yesterday; maybe she was just tired of being in Seattle. Needed a fresh start."

"Frank," Dakota's dad interrupted. "She didn't just leave."

The detective shrugged. "It's out of my hands until we get more information. We will find her, Dakota."

"This is bullshit." He headed out the front door and straight to the Carter residence.

He raised his fist and banged on the door. Mitch opened it, a smug smile on his face.

"Nice to see you, Dakota." He stepped out and shut the front door behind him.

"Where the fuck is she?" He gripped the front of Mitch's shirt and slammed him back against the door. Size wise, Dakota knew he had the other man beat, and he'd been longing to kick his ass since the night he'd nearly put Ana in the hospital their senior year.

"I don't know, *boy,* why don't you tell me? You were the one sleeping with her."

Dakota slammed him hard against the door.

"Dakota!" his mother screamed, and before he could be stopped, he rammed his fist into Mitch's face. The other man's nose crunched beneath Dakota's fist. Strong hands gripped Dakota by the shoulders, hauling him backwards, and Mitch crumbled to the floor.

"You know where she is, you son of a bitch!" Dakota howled in anger and ripped his arms away from the two men holding him. "I swear, if you hurt her—"

"You'll do what, kid?" Mitch scowled as he swiped at the blood on his lip. "Come sucker punch me again?"

"Dakota, get in the house."

"Listen to your mommy, Dakota. I'd hate for you to get hurt."

"Ha! I'm over twenty-one now, old man; how about you get up and let me kick your ass like I've been wanting to do all my life?"

"Dakota, get in the fucking house!" his father

roared. "You're going to get your ass arrested, then what the hell good are you for her?" He put his hand on Dakota's chest, and Dakota fought the urge to shove him aside and attack Mitch again.

"I will find her," Dakota growled, then stalked back to the house.

AN HOUR LATER, HIS FATHER WALKED INTO HIS childhood bedroom.

"Hey, son."

Dakota said nothing, just continued staring down at the photograph in his hand. It had been taken one of the weekends Ana had stayed with them at their family cabin. She wore overalls and a white T-shirt, her hair in a messy bun while she smiled up at him.

Where the hell was she now?"

The bed dipped when his dad took a seat next to him. "That's a good picture of you two."

Dakota nodded.

"We will find her, son, and if Mitch was involved, we'll lock his ass up."

"*If* he was involved? We both know he was."

"There's nothing we can do, Dakota. Our hands are tied unless we can find more evidence. We will keep looking, though."

Dakota shook his head angrily.

"Mitch has decided not to press charges. He understands your tensions were high."

"My tensions were high? Are you fucking kidding me? *Tensions?* I'm pissed the hell off, Dad. My girlfriend is missing and her abusive father—who is behind it—gets to continue breathing."

"Sometimes roadblocks go up, Dakota, but the great thing about them is they can be taken down. I promise I will find her. No matter what it takes."

"I will too." He looked to his father, determination in his heart. "No matter what it takes."

10

TERRENIA

ANASTASIA

Anastasia stretched and opened her eyes. Light streamed in through the window, causing her swollen eyes to ache.

At some point during the night, she'd finally managed to cry herself to sleep, but her heart still ached and more tears threatened the second she thought of Dakota and what he must be feeling not knowing what happened to her.

She closed her eyes and tried to picture what their date might have been like. Would he have worn that black button-down shirt she loved so much? Would she have finally put on that red dress she splurged on three months ago?

"Dakota, I'm so sorry." She buried her face in her

pillows. Would he ever forgive her? Not that it mattered; she'd never be able to go back.

A high-pitched scream ripped her from her thoughts, and Anastasia stood as quickly as she could, wincing when her back screamed in response. *Dammit, that hurt!* Another scream sounded in the quiet morning, and Anastasia made her way outside.

Villagers screamed loudly as giant beasts thundered into the village center. They were pale, and were larger than any man Anastasia had ever seen.

"Where is she?" one howled, and Anastasia watched, heart in her throat, as Gregory faced off with them.

"I don't know what you mean."

"Don't lie to me, sorcerer. We know she is here."

"Anastasia!" Annabelle whispered.

She turned back to the house, and Annabelle motioned for her to come inside. She was crouched down in the kitchen, and Anastasia crawled over to her.

"We will tear apart this village looking for her if we have to."

"No, you won't," Gregory said.

Anastasia leaned up to look out through the window just in time to see him blast the giants backwards with a blast of light.

A group of men—Fighters, Annabelle had called them—flanked Gregory, their swords drawn.

They launched into an attack, and Anastasia watched with fascination as they fought. The beasts—or whatever they were—drew large blades from their waists, and Anastasia saw the older Fighter—Tony—barely move out of the way of one of them before burying his own blade in the things chest.

Its blood poured out, blue liquid spilling on the ground. "Its blood is blue?" she whispered, and Annabelle nodded.

"Those are Brutes."

Anastasia's eyes widened. "The things that you have been at war with?"

She nodded again. "Our Fighters are strong enough to keep them back for the most part, but we're losing at least two warriors a week now."

Anastasia crept up to look back out, and watched as the Fighters drug the bodies of the monsters away.

The door opened, and Gregory stepped inside.

"Who were they looking for?" she asked.

His eyes widened in surprise, and he swallowed hard. "You."

"Me?"

He nodded. "I told you that you were special. They want to stop you before you reach your full potential. You're a threat."

"A threat to what?"

"The Darkness."

"So, wait. You expect me to be able to defeat those things? It took seven grown men to take down four of them!"

"You were given the tools you need to fulfill your destiny," Gregory said easily.

"Yeah, okay. And what tools are those exactly? The ability to take a beating?"

Gregory's jaw clenched. "Get dressed and meet me outside," he said curtly and headed back out into the sun.

"There are clothes in the dresser in your room," Annabelle told her, then followed him out.

Curious, Anastasia made her way into the bedroom and pulled on a pair of leather pants and a brown vest made from some kind of animal hide.

After slipping into a pair of boots she found in the closet, she made her way out the front door.

Tony and Gregory stood side by side, holding the reins to three horses.

"Have you ever ridden before?"

She shook her head.

"We'll go slowly."

Tony helped her onto the back of a dark brown horse, and Anastasia felt oddly comfortable in the soft saddle on its back. When the animal began to move, she couldn't keep the smile off her face. She'd always wanted to learn to ride, had begged her parents for lessons back when she'd been seven and naïve enough to think they might have let her.

Tony and Gregory mounted their own horses and fell in line, Tony behind her and Gregory in front.

The way the horse moved, muscles bunching and

releasing below her, was more exhilarating than she could've imagined.

"Where are we going?" Anastasia asked as Gregory led them down a path lined with trees.

"To show you what's at stake," Gregory responded tightly.

They moved slowly, something she was grateful for because making an ass out of herself by falling off the horse probably wouldn't have been great for the morning.

Especially not when those *things* were looking for her. "Should we be out here? Aren't those Brutes or whatever looking for me?"

"They will have retreated for now. Possible a larger grouping will be headed our way soon, but for now we should be safe," Tony answered.

"Should be safe, that's great. *Should be*," she mumbled, earning a chuckle from Tony.

"I assure you, Anastasia, between Gregory and me we will make it back to the village in one piece."

She shot him a glance, and despite her nerves, smiled. "Thanks."

The trees surrounded them, casting a shadow over the path they traveled. Birds chirped overhead, singing various happy tunes, and a few times during their journey, a rabbit or deer crossed their path.

Most of the animals here were similar to the ones back home, except—to her delight—the butterflies, which were the size of basketballs. She'd nearly screamed when one fluttered in front of her horse, inciting another laugh from Tony.

He was getting a kick out of her, and it was only slightly annoying.

The path opened into a clearing, and Anastasia saw the remnants of what had once been a village. She covered her mouth with her hand as she looked at the charred ground and burnt buildings.

"What happened?" she asked as Tony helped her down from her horse and she stepped closer to the destruction. The homes that had once stood lay in a pile of soot and ash, and Anastasia could still smell the lingering scent from the fire.

She toed over a board, revealing a child's stuffed doll with bloodstains on its smiling face. She cried out and covered her mouth with her hands.

"This"—Gregory gestured around them at the smoldering piles of ash—"is the remnants of a village that the Brutes destroyed three days ago. We buried seventeen people. Some men, some women, and a handful of children."

"But why? Why would anyone do this?"

"Power."

Her eyes landed on Gregory's. "What power comes from this?"

He shrugged. "Your guess is as good as mine, Anastasia. But this is what will happen to the rest of our world, and if it still isn't enough, possibly yours too."

Destruction. Blood. Death. Her nightmare couldn't have been a warning, could it?

She continued to walk, hot tears burning in her eyes. At the edge of the village, near the tree line, were mounds of dirt with crosses at the end. She counted them and, just as Gregory had said, there were seventeen graves.

Seventeen innocent lives.

Sadness swirled with fear and frustration, tightening a vise around her heart. She spun to face Gregory. "This still doesn't explain what you want me to do about it. I've never even taken a self-defense class." She gestured to her back that still ached from Mitch's belt. "Obviously, I'm no good at fighting."

"Because you haven't been trained, Anastasia." Gregory took a step toward her. "There is much about you that you still need to learn. So much more than you could even imagine."

"I really doubt that."

Gregory shook his head sadly. "Then we are all doomed."

11

GREGORY

Gregory chose to ride in the back on the way home. He needed some time to gather his thoughts and decide what to do next.

Anastasia was finally here. While her presence elated him, the pain of what she'd left behind caused him great heartache. If only he'd found her sooner, perhaps it would have been less of a transition for her.

Convincing her that she was worth something was going to take more time than he'd thought. His hands tightened on the reins; the man who had raised her had sure done a number on her mind, and broken down any confidence she would have had.

The war was coming. Gregory glanced over at Anastasia; she was going to have to fight the biggest war of them all.

"Brother." The voice filled Gregory's mind, and his body went rigid. He turned slowly, knowing he wouldn't *see* the owner of the voice, but he still wanted to confirm that they were still truly alone in their journey.

"You have some nerve to show up here, Vincent," he whispered.

"Not really there, Gregory," Vincent reminded him.

"Might as well be. What do you want?" Gregory's back was straight, his body tense. He waited for an attack he knew wouldn't come, but wished it would. At least then they could finally put an end to everything.

"A man can't pop in to see how his brother is doing?" Vincent's tone was dry, but Gregory knew there was heat behind it.

"You are no brother of mine."

"And whose fault is that?" The anger in the voice sent chills down Gregory's spine.

"You tore my family apart, Vincent."

"I tried to bring us together!" he yelled into Gregory's mind.

"You lost me the moment you started delving into the dark arts." Gregory did his best to keep himself calm. It would do him no good to get riled up.

"We could have been great together, Gregory. We would have ruled, and you would have been able to raise your daughter from infancy knowing that she would be safe from everything. It's your fault I was able to take her, and your fault that she was beaten by the

man who raised her. What will she think of you when she learns that, I wonder?"

Anger rose in Gregory's chest, and his attempts to beat it back down were beginning to fail.

"I was not going to sell my soul and the souls of my family. You knew that, and you took her from me anyway."

"You could have found her, had you used even half of the magic inside of you. But instead, you use it to bless potions that your wife makes." He spat the word *wife* out as if it left a bad taste on his tongue.

"You will not speak of Annabelle or of Anastasia."

"I will take her again, Gregory, only this time I will not leave her alive. She won't stand a chance against me. That seer was foolish."

"You won't touch her, Vincent, or so help me God, you will regret the moment you were born."

"You think I fear you, brother?" Vincent laughed mockingly. *"You are afraid of the power inside of you, whereas I fully embrace it. I do not fear you."*

Gregory's heart began to pound, blood thundering through his veins, the flame inside of him building, and he thought of Annabelle. She was his light, and the only center he had for not losing control. "If you are truly unafraid, then why are you not here, Vincent?"

"Other business to attend to. This is your last chance, Gregory. If you begin her training, I will tear everything you love apart. You will lose her again, and there will be no rescuing the girl this time."

Vincent's voice faded away, and Gregory's fists tightened on the reins again. He closed his eyes and choked back the anger. He couldn't let anything show on his face; he didn't want to risk scaring Anastasia, as he could see in her eyes she was finally getting somewhat comfortable around him.

He would wait to talk to Annabelle, although he knew that she would tell him to ignore Vincent's warning. She believed Anastasia was the only hope any of them had at defeating his brother, but dammit, did it have to come at the cost of his only child? If he trained her, Vincent would go after her. Again. But if he didn't, then at some point, Vincent would come for them all.

He would never leave them alone, not as long as Gregory continued to refuse the dark magic.

So, train her or don't train her, it seemed the outcome would be the same. He looked up at her as she watched in bewilderment as another Terrenian butterfly crossed her path.

He was going to lose her either way.

12

ANASTASIA

"**A**re you hungry?" Annabelle asked when Gregory and Anastasia stepped into the cottage that night.

"Starving, thank you." The trip had taken nearly all day, and the sun was just beginning its descent when they arrived at the stables to turn the horses in for the night. Gregory had brought along some bread and water, but it had been just enough to prevent a stomach ache from the hunger, not enough to actually fill her up.

"You are more than welcome." Annabelle set the book she'd been reading aside and stood to greet Gregory.

Anastasia witnessed the look of love that passed between them. The only other place she'd seen such emotion was when she had been near Dakota's parents.

She'd always hoped to find love like them, had actually believed it might have been with Dakota someday.

"Well, isn't this a sight to come home to." Gregory pulled his wife in for an embrace and kissed her deeply.

"Hold on a second, dear, we have company." She giggled, and Anastasia blushed.

"I know we have company, but I still love you. Even more after each and every day."

"And I, you." She looked up through her lashes at him, and Anastasia looked away.

"How about you help me cut up some vegetables for this soup?" She heard Annabelle ask and turned back to see him follow her into the kitchen.

Anastasia watched, perplexed. She had never seen her father even step foot into the kitchen, let alone assist her mother with dinner. Monica had always brought him what he needed to the table—his coffee, meals, and after-dinner drinks. Everything had always been served to him.

As she watched, Gregory and Annabelle worked together as a team, helping each other and laughing as they did so. Something about this house and this couple made Anastasia feel as if she had finally arrived home.

Immediately, a twinge of guilt pinched her chest. Dakota had felt like home to her, too. She'd never been able to even imagine her world without him in it, yet she had just left him behind without so much as a note.

She'd had to leave, though, hadn't she? Mitch would have killed her if she'd stayed, and at least this way she stood a chance of seeing Dakota again. Maybe someday, anyway. If she completed whatever her so-called destiny was, maybe she could find a way back to him. Pushing the thought aside, Anastasia made her way over to the table. She was just going to have to get used to not having her best friend with her.

DINNER WAS TERRIFIC, AND THEY SPENT THE REST OF the evening laughing. Anastasia listened to stories of how Gregory and Annabelle met, and the different adventures they had been on together. He told her of his time exploring his magic, trying to learn as much as he could. She sat in awe as he spoke of the different worlds he had visited while trying to find her.

"Before we end the night, I have something for you." Annabelle got to her feet and pulled open one of the cabinets in the kitchen. She returned to the table carrying a small Bundt cake with clear glaze over the top.

Anastasia's eyes filled. Her own parents never celebrated her birthday. Monica would sneak a small gift up after dinner, but she'd leave it on Anastasia's bed and never mention it again.

She'd only ever celebrated with Dakota and his family.

"We're sorry it's not more," Gregory said, eyeing

her. "We don't have the tools available to us here that you would have had in Seattle."

"It's absolutely perfect." Anastasia wiped her cheeks. "How did you know today was my birthday?"

"We know quite a lot, my dear," Annabelle said, setting the cake in front of Anastasia. "I hope you love it."

"I know I will." Anastasia grinned.

They cut into the cake, and Anastasia savored every single bite.

When she began yawning, Annabelle smiled at her. "That's enough for tonight. The poor girl is about to fall asleep in her chair. Besides, don't you need to go check in with Tony?"

"Oh, yes. I had completely forgotten." Gregory smiled and stood to lightly kiss Annabelle on top of her head. "Anastasia, may I speak with you?"

She nodded and stood. Annabelle offered her a kind, but guarded smile, and Anastasia stepped onto the porch with Gregory.

He sighed. "It's a beautiful night tonight."

Anastasia nodded in agreement and looked up at the bright stars.

"I understand that you didn't want this responsibility," he acknowledged. "While I would need to create more portal vials, I can see about getting you back to Seattle if that is what you choose."

"You could send me back?" Hope fluttered in her chest at the idea of seeing Dakota again, but it was quickly dampened when images of the graves from earlier popped into her head.

"It would take me some time to make another portal vial, but I can do it."

"What will happen to you all here?"

He shrugged. "I'm sure we'll manage. This isn't your world, Anastasia, and I understand that. So if you truly do not want to stay, I will not hold it against you." Without letting her respond, he stepped off the porch. "Goodnight," he said, then disappeared into the dark.

She could go home! She could see Dakota. They could finally have the relationship she'd dreamt about since she'd been a teenager.

The only cost was the destruction of possibly an entire *world*.

Gee, that wasn't a steep cost.

Deciding to sleep on it, Anastasia made her way inside.

Annabelle had cleared their dishes and had stacked them neatly on the counter near the washbasin. "Everything all right?" she asked, drying her hands on her apron.

Anastasia nodded. "I'm just pretty beat."

"I can imagine. Let's put some more salve on your back and you can head to bed."

She took a seat near the fire that had died down to embers. Annabelle began to apply the healing ointment, and the contact with her broken skin had Anastasia wincing.

"These are nearly healed, but I was right before; they will scar. I'm sorry, dear."

Now she would have physical scars to match the mental scars left on her after growing up in a home where she was afraid to so much as breathe wrong.

"You're all done." Annabelle stood, and Anastasia pulled her shirt down.

"Goodnight," Anastasia said softly.

"Goodnight, honey."

Just before she got to her door, Anastasia turned. Annabelle stood at the sink, staring out the window. "Annabelle?"

The woman turned. "Yes, dear?"

"Thank you so much." She moved across the room to Annabelle and wrapped her arms around her in a gesture she had never given to either of her real parents.

"Oh, honey, you are welcome." Annabelle hugged her back, and Anastasia closed her eyes tightly. "You sleep well tonight, Anastasia." She squeezed her one last time, then released her, and Anastasia crossed the space and stepped into her own room.

Anastasia changed into the nightgown Annabelle had set out for her and crawled onto the mattress, surprised at how soft it was. She must've been too exhausted to notice last night. She pulled the blankets up over herself and held onto her last memory of Dakota. Tears welled up in her eyes as she thought of the times they'd spent together.

She said a prayer that he wouldn't hate her, that on

some level he would understand why she left, and hoped that one day she could explain to him why she didn't come back. She knew what she had to do. Even if she didn't fully believe she was capable of defeating this Darkness, or whatever it was that was coming to Terrenia, she had to try. People were counting on her, and she couldn't stand the thought of Annabelle, Gregory, Tony, or anyone else she'd met being the next to be buried.

With her last thought, she wished that Dakota would have a happy life, and then fell into a deep, dreamless sleep.

13

TERRENIA

GREGORY

When Gregory came home, Annabelle stood in the kitchen staring out the window into the night. *She is so beautiful.* How could she continue to captivate him even after all this time? He watched her a moment and then moved to where she stood.

She leaned into him when he wrapped his arms around her. "Hello, love. All is well?"

"It is. There was a little trouble with one of our outposts, but the Fighters were able to neutralize the problem."

"That's good," she replied, but her voice was distant. She wasn't really there, and he knew why.

"How's our girl?"

She smiled and turned to face him. "She's adjusting well, surprisingly." Tears filled her eyes, and he cupped her face.

"Annabelle, what's wrong?"

"They were awful to her, Greg, so incredibly awful. The marks on her back…" She covered her face with her hands, and the tears she'd fought so hard to hold back came out in a rush.

"I know, my love." He clenched his jaw. "But she is here now, and if she chooses to stay, we will make sure she has the life that she deserves, the one she should have had from the beginning."

"What do you mean if she chooses to stay?"

He sighed and released her. "I told her that if she wants to go home, I will create another portal vial to take her there."

"You would let her leave? After we've spent all these years searching for her?"

Gregory pinched the bridge of his nose. "She has family there, Annabelle. A man she spent time with. We've plucked her from the only place she's ever known and thrust her into the middle of a war. She deserves the option. Vincent will—" He stopped mid-sentence, and Annabelle put her head on his arm.

"It was good of you to give her the choice."

He nodded. "Vincent came to me today."

"What do you mean?"

"He projected himself into my mind while we were on our way back."

"What did he want?"

"To threaten me."

"What more could he do to us?"

"He threatened to kill her if I train her."

"We can protect her, my love." She leaned into him again, and he wrapped his arms around her.

"But for how long?" he asked. "You remember what the seer said. How are we supposed to protect her from her destiny?"

"We train her. We make sure that she is prepared for what she is going to have to face. You will train her to physically protect herself, and I will teach her what I know of herbs. We can prepare her," she assured him.

"How do we tell her who she is?"

"We don't, at least not at first. I think it would be a little much for her to take in at the moment. We need to let her decide whether she wants to stay or not. If she chooses to go…" Annabelle sighed. "I guess she'll never know."

He nodded in agreement.

"She is beautiful, isn't she?" Annabelle asked, looking up at him.

"She is. But I always knew she would be." He grinned down at her.

"Oh, really? And how's that?" Annabelle asked playfully.

"Because her mother is the most beautiful woman in all the worlds." He kissed her deeply.

This was the first night in twenty years that his

entire family was under one roof, and he would do anything necessary to keep it that way.

14

SEATTLE

DAKOTA

Dakota stepped into his empty apartment. Sadness cloaked him like a blanket as he looked around the space he'd shared with his best friend for nearly three years.

There were still no leads on Ana's disappearance, and he knew without being told that the police were giving up. Quitting after only three days. He blamed himself; if he'd just skipped class that morning, stayed home like he'd wanted to, none of this would have happened. He could have protected her from whoever showed up.

No, not *whoever*. He could have protected her from *Mitch*. No matter what anyone said, his gut told him that bastard did something to Ana.

His phone rang, and he checked the ID. *Shit*. He thought he'd have more time before having to face this.

"Hello?"

"Why did I hear from your mother that you dropped out of college today?"

"Probably because I did."

"What the hell, Dakota!"

"You don't need a college degree to join the police force here in Seattle."

"And since when is that the plan? You were going to be a *doctor,* Dakota! A fucking doctor!"

"Doctors don't find missing persons, do they?"

"I told you I would do everything I could to bring her home."

"And I told you so would I."

"Do you honestly believe that becoming a cop is going to lead to her?"

"Maybe not, but if I can put assholes like Mitch away, then it's more than worth it."

"So that's what this is? You're pissed off because he's getting off."

"Hell yeah I am. This is bullshit, and you know it!"

His father was silent for a moment and then let out a breath. "Fine. You want to throw your future away, then so be it."

His father ended the call, and Dakota fought the urge to throw his phone against the wall.

He really didn't care how pissed off his dad was;

this was what he wanted to do and no one was going to stop him.

Dakota made his way to her bedroom and took a deep breath before flipping the light switch. Her bed was still unmade, her backpack slung over the back of her desk chair. He took a seat on the pale purple quilt and imagined her here, in her space, smiling and sharing the stories of her day with him.

They'd been inseparable for their entire lives. What the hell was he supposed to do without her?

Mitch had informed him that since Ana lived with him, it was his responsibility to take care of her belongings. He'd told Dakota that seeing her things would be too *painful* for Monica. As if either of them actually gave a shit about Ana.

It didn't matter, though, because she was going to come home.

Ana was out there somewhere, and he was going to find her.

15

TERRENIA: THREE MONTHS LATER

GREGORY

"**M**aximus, you have to stop underestimating her. She's quick." Gregory laughed as Anastasia threw Maximus to the ground yet again.

"She caught me off guard," Maximus whined, jumping back to his feet.

"Use the lesson; don't make excuses."

Anastasia dodged Maximus's fist and then absorbed the contact of his other one in her gut. She doubled over and laughed breathlessly.

"That was a good one," she said, but he ignored the compliment as he usually did.

She straightened and got back into the fight, managing to knock him to the ground with a right hook and a kick to his gut. Afterwards, she reached her hand down to pull him to his feet, but he slapped it away and stood on his own.

"I don't need your help."

"Fine."

"All right, that's enough for today." Gregory walked toward them and patted them both on the shoulders. "You two are coming along nicely. Shake hands."

They did, and without a word, Maximus headed back to the village.

"Way to go, Anastasia!" An excited Brady came running toward her with his hand outstretched, ready for a high five.

"Thanks, Brady." She smiled and, together, the three of them headed back toward the village.

"Man, you were awesome! You are only half his size, but you were all bam bam bam!"

She laughed at his excitement and the way he mocked throwing punches. He'd become the little brother she never had. She ruffled his hair. "Maybe someday soon you'll be big enough to spar with me." She put her fists up, and he laughed.

"I'll totally win!"

"I bet you will," Gregory said on a laugh. He swallowed hard and watched Anastasia mimic fighting with Brady. He and Annabelle had made the decision to tell her the truth about their connection to her tonight, and while his wife was more than excited, he found nervous was a more applicable word to how he was feeling.

What if Anastasia was disappointed? Or angry that he hadn't come for her sooner?

"Gregory!" Tony ran toward them with half a dozen fighters on his heels. Anastasia immediately scanned the woods around them and pulled Brady in close.

"What is it?"

"We've got trouble. About three-dozen Brutes are headed this way, approaching from the north side."

"Anastasia, take Brady back to his house, and then immediately head back to ours."

"But I can help—"

"Not yet, Anastasia. Eventually, yes. But you are not yet adept enough with a sword, and I cannot risk your safety. Please, get back to the house and warn Annabelle."

16

ANASTASIA

Anastasia thought about arguing with Gregory but knew it would do no good, and it would only delay him from getting where he needed to be.

She nodded, gripped Brady's hand, then turned and ran at a sprint to the village.

When she entered the clearing, she could tell that the alert had already been issued. No one was out in the open, and even those who had been working on building a fence around the town were gone.

She knew that the Fighters must have already headed toward the north side, and she quickly ran toward Brady's house.

"Do you think they'll get in?" he asked.

"It'll be fine, Brady. You know we have the toughest

men in the world on our side. They will take care of it and still be back in time for dinner. You'll see." She smiled and knocked on the door to his house.

"Oh, thank God." Brady's mother, Selena, answered the door and pulled her son inside.

"Thank you, Anastasia. Won't you come in? We are headed for the cellar."

"No, thank you. I'm going to head to my house. You guys get inside and stay safe."

"We will." She shut the door quickly, and Anastasia ran home.

As soon as the small cottage came into view, she knew something was wrong. The door was ajar, and Annabelle never left it open.

She crept through the door and behind a counter in the kitchen. After a quick peek around the side, Anastasia saw that Annabelle was on her knees between two massive Brutes, and a man in a robe stood before her.

The man from the worst of her nightmares. *Bodies. Destruction. Death.*

Anastasia's blood iced, and her vision wavered slightly as a flash of panic took over.

Calm down, Anastasia. After taking a deep breath, she leaned back around to get another look.

"Where is she, Annabelle?" the man asked.

"Who?" Annabelle responded softly. Anastasia could hear the fear in her shaky voice as Annabelle tried to keep it steady.

A loud crack filled the room as the man slammed his fist into Annabelle's cheek. Anastasia grabbed the dagger from her waist and felt its now familiar weight in her palm.

"You will tell me where she is. Don't be stupid," the man said.

"I will never tell you where she is."

"Then you will die."

"No!" Anastasia swallowed her fear and leaped over the counter with her knife. The man smiled at her, and Anastasia ground her teeth together.

"Anastasia. You shouldn't have come." Annabelle smiled softly.

The man drove the knife into Annabelle's chest, and Anastasia screamed, lunging for him. One of the man's Brutes charged her. It was at least eight feet tall, but she threw all of her body weight into her attack, which seemed to stun the creature just enough that she was able to slice her knife across the beast's throat. It fell, and the other beast howled with rage just before charging her. She was caught off guard, and thrown back against the counter.

"Well, aren't you something," the robed man said as he stood back and watched her fend off the second Brute's attack. She did her best to fight as she'd been trained, but it slammed her down, and her vision blurred.

"I know you," Anastasia growled when the robed man knelt beside her. She still couldn't see his face, but the sound of his voice was forever branded into her memory from the nightmares.

"Yes, you do," he confirmed, using a finger to brush a stray strand of hair from her face. "This could have been avoided; if only your father had done what he was supposed to do," the robed man whispered.

Anastasia saw the glint of a blade just before the Brute slammed it down toward her; she screamed and used as much strength as she could to hold his arm back. Her arms shook with fatigue as she tried to keep the blade from its target. The blade bit into her skin, and she cried out. The room filled with light, and the beast's weight was lifted from her as he was tossed to the other side of the room.

"Yes!" The cloaked man clapped his hands in delight, and Anastasia stared down at her own in shock.

Had she just done that?

Weight slammed into her again, and Anastasia rolled across the room. Dazed, she looked up just in time to see the door fling open.

"Anastasia!" Gregory yelled as he and four bloodied Fighters charged the cabin.

She watched helplessly as the robed man faded away and Gregory ran toward her.

"Anastasia, where are you hurt?" He searched her for any wounds.

"Gregory, I'm so sorry," she cried, the tears streaming down her face. "I tried to save her." The color drained from his face. He turned slowly to face the crumpled body that lay in the center of the living area.

"Oh no." He rushed to Annabelle and fell to his knees. "Oh no, oh God, please no," he cried as he cradled her in his arms.

"I tried, I swear I tried," Anastasia cried.

Tony knelt beside her. "Hush, child. You were very brave. It's not your fault." His eyes shone with unshed tears, and he pulled Anastasia into his arms.

HOW HAD EVERYTHING GONE SO WRONG? IT SEEMED AS if she had finally gotten lucky in her life, finally found her place, and then it was ripped apart. Was she doomed to live a life of horror? Of pain? What had she done to deserve this?

Anastasia lay curled in bed, teetering on the edge of sleep, courtesy of a healing potion she was given.

They'd sat on the kitchen floor for hours after the Fighters gathered Annabelle's body and took it away. Gregory hadn't said a single word, and she feared he blamed her for not being able to protect his wife. She should have been able to. She certainly blamed herself. Had she worked harder when he trained her, she might have stood a chance. But instead, she failed, and Annabelle died.

"Tell me where she is." The man was there looking for her, she was sure of it. Even if he hadn't had a star-

ring role in her nightmares her entire life, she would have known he was there for her.

Not that it mattered now; she was going to kill him one day. Despite the exhaustion, she balled her hands into fists.

She was going to get revenge for Annabelle's death and for the pain Gregory would now live with. She would kill that robed man and every single Brute she could get her hands on. Even if she lost her own life in the process.

17

SEATTLE

DAKOTA

Dakota stared out at the Seattle skyline. Never had he seen a city so beautiful at night, and yet it all seemed so empty to him. Then again, everything was empty since Anastasia's disappearance. Ever since that day three months ago, things only continued to get worse.

His father's death just topped it all off.

He looked down at the soda in his hand, then back into the house, where the rest of the partygoers were enjoying the night as if there wasn't a thing wrong in the world.

"Is that Dakota I see out there? Dakota Parker?" The voice was slurred, but he would have recognized it anywhere.

"Gage." He turned to face the son of his dad's old partner.

"Well, how ya doing, boy?" Gage asked as he headed toward the balcony.

"Better than you are at the moment, I suppose."

"What do ya mean? I'm great." He grinned, and Dakota's stomach churned at the pungent smell of the liquor in his breath. He took a step back to put some distance between them.

"Listen." Gage inched closer to Dakota again, and he tried to slide away. "I'm sorry about your dad."

Dakota clenched his jaw. He didn't want to talk about this. Especially not now with Gage.

"What happened to his dad?" asked one of the other intoxicated partygoers who had wandered out onto the balcony.

"He died. Was killed in an alley behind old Mal's Diner two weeks ago." He held his cup up, and Dakota had to remind himself that Gage was drunk.

"Man, that's rough."

"Yeah, it was." Dakota began backing toward the door. "I've got to go now."

"It's a shame they never found that chick."

Dakota closed his eyes and took a deep breath.

"Her name is Ana," he said without turning around.

"Whatever. You knew who I was talking about."

"Who's the chick?" the same drunk asshole asked.

"Dude, she was this really hot chick who lived next to Dakota growing up. They used to be roomies, too."

"Stop it, Gage," Dakota warned.

"One day she went missing and our"—he took another drink from his cup—"dads were put on the case!" he said it as if it were some achievement of his own, as if Dakota's entire life hadn't fallen apart that night. "Anyway, her dad said she ran away, and this guy's dad didn't believe him, so blah, blah, blah, you know the end."

Dakota clenched his fists at his side and did his best to control the anger that rose in his chest.

"You ever bang her, dude?" Gage asked. "I mean, you guys lived together for what? A year?"

"Are you serious?" Dakota spun and grabbed Gage by the throat. "Who the fuck are you to come here and start spreading my life out like that? Not to mention disrespecting my father as well as my best friend, who by the way is probably dead. Who the fuck are you?" he repeated. "You haven't done a damn thing with your life other than live off mommy and daddy's dime. So, do us all a favor." He knocked the cup from Gage's hand. "Sober up and stop acting like an entitled asshole." He threw Gage back and stalked out the door, ignoring all of the 'boos' that followed.

Dakota angrily walked back to his car and then drove to his house. It was a long commute to the academy every day, but after his dad was killed, he'd moved back home. He would never have left his mother in his childhood house alone.

Especially not with Mitch still living next door.

She sat at the kitchen table looking through old photo albums when he entered the house.

"Hey, Mom."

"Oh, hi, Dakota." She shut the album quickly and wiped the tears from her cheeks. "I'm sorry; I wasn't expecting you home for another hour or so. How was the party?"

"Boring." He went to the fridge and pulled out a bottle of water. "How are you?"

"I'm fine, honey. I just wanted to see his face before I went to bed. How are you doing?"

"Sober. If that's what you were worried about."

"Dakota, I know you would never drive drunk, so no, that's not what I was worried about."

"I'm fine, Mom." He did his best to hide the anger in his voice. Lately, it was rare for him to feel anything but anger.

She nodded but didn't look convinced. "I'm gonna head to bed. Early morning."

"Are you sure you should be going back to work?"

"I need some kind of normalcy, Dakota." Her voice caught on emotion, so she cleared her throat. "I can't keep sitting around here every day waiting for him to come home." Her eyes filled, and she covered her face as her shoulders shook.

Dakota knelt beside her and wrapped his arms around her.

The sound of sirens pierced the night, and Dakota raced to the window. Three police cruisers and an ambulance pulled into the driveway at the Carter residence, and both Dakota and his mother raced out to the front yard.

When he saw them wheel in a stretcher, his heart stopped, and it was as if time stood still. He held his breath and could hear nothing but the sound of his own blood pounding in his ears.

Had they found Ana? Had she come back?

Or worse, had she never left?

His stomach twisted and bile rose in his throat. He and his mom stood in their front yard for what felt like hours until the first responders came back out.

They watched in horror as a body bag was wheeled out the front door. "Oh no!" his mom exclaimed, then covered her mouth with her hands.

Dakota's stomach twisted, and for a moment it was as if he could see her lying there. Broken by a man she should have been able to trust. He swallowed his fear and ran for the nearest officer. "Who is it?"

"It's not Anastasia, Dakota," the man replied. He'd worked with Dakota's father, so it was no mystery who Dakota thought it might be.

Mitch stepped outside. "Monica." He growled angrily. He'd known it was only a matter of time before Mitch killed someone, and he felt guilty that he was relieved it wasn't Ana.

"I've got to head to the station." The officer nodded toward Dakota's mother, who was standing with her arms wrapped around herself.

Mitch stepped from the house, grief plastered on his face for anyone to see, but Dakota saw through it, and when Mitch turned to smile toward him, Dakota promised himself that if the murdering son of a bitch didn't go down for this, then one day he was going to bring the bastard down for good.

18

TERRENIA

ANASTASIA

Days turned into weeks, and before Anastasia knew it, she was back to training. Tony had taken over for Gregory, since he was still not speaking to anyone. He stayed locked in his room, drowning his pain in Terrenian whiskey… something she desperately wished she could justify doing.

But she didn't have time. Anastasia was determined to become faster and stronger, paving the way to her revenge. Maybe then Gregory might be able to find it in his heart to forgive her.

The last time she'd laid eyes on him was at the funeral. It had ripped her apart to see the villagers saying goodbye to a woman who meant so much to them. A woman who had begun to mean so much to her.

Tony took a seat beside her on the steps to the training cottage. "You're doing well."

Despite the fact that he was twice her age, he was strong and fast, and an opponent who didn't hold back. It was also nice not having to worry he was going to snap and kill her.

Whenever she sparred with Maximus, there was always warning bells going off in her head.

"Thanks." She took a drink from her canteen and nearly groaned as the cold water slipped down the back of her throat. "I'll see you tomorrow," she said as she rose to her feet.

"Anastasia." Tony touched her shoulder gently, and she turned to face him. "You have to let go of the anger."

She remembered Gregory telling her that as well, only now it felt as if their conversation had been a lifetime ago rather than mere weeks.

"What happened was not your fault," he continued.

"How can you say that? I was there, Tony. I didn't move fast enough. I should have charged the second I got into the house, but instead, I froze. I always freeze," she added angrily, thinking back to all the times in her childhood she didn't stand up for herself.

He folded his big arms. "Then you would both be dead. They were going to kill her. They wanted you both, but because you were smart, you managed to not only single-handedly take down a Brute, but also made it out alive."

"Barely. Had you not shown up when you did, I would be dead, too."

"It still counts."

"Gregory hates me." The tears burned in the back of her throat, but she refused to let them fall.

"He does not," Tony assured her. "He could never hate you, Anastasia. You are all the family he has left."

"Annabelle was his family. I'm just some girl he brought through a portal. I'm supposed to be some big prophesized hero, and yet all I seem to do is bring pain to those around me."

"You are foolish if you believe that, and you and I both know you aren't a fool." He turned back toward the training cottage. "Now, go home and get some rest. Tomorrow will be a long day."

Anastasia headed down the path that led home. The villagers were working steadily to get the fence finished, and it was nearly completed.

She stopped just before the last turn in the path and stared up at the fading sun. What was Dakota doing right now? She closed her eyes tightly, wishing that he were beside her. She could use his support, although she wasn't sure even he would recognize the person she was becoming.

"Pondering your life? Or your guilt?" Maximus's voice cut through the quiet, and she opened her eyes to stare into his arrogant face. His eyes, if possible, seemed even colder than they ever had before.

She rolled her eyes and started to step around him

since he blocked the way to her house, but he moved and stepped in front of her again. She turned to head back toward Tony, but stopped. Maximus's two friends, Alastair and Sebastian, blocked her path.

"Where are you going? Have someone else you want to get killed?" Maximus asked with a smirk.

"What do you want, Maximus?"

"Oh, see Al, Seb, and I were just wondering how it was you slept at night knowing you ruined the lives of the only people who took pity on you. You deserved what you got growing up," he snarled.

She tightened her fists. He was looking for a fight, but she'd be damned if she gave him one. "Please. Get. Out. Of. My. Way," she spoke through gritted teeth.

He crossed his arms, puffing out his chest. "Make me."

She tried to move past him, but he blocked her again, and Anastasia felt something inside her building, growing as the anger surged through her. There was a flash of light, and Anastasia slammed him to the ground. She straddled him and pressed the blade of her sword against his throat. A tiny trickle of blood crept down his throat, and she watched it with fascination.

Maximus's eyes were wide in his pale face.

"You should be afraid," she growled. "Do you have anything else you want to say to me?" she asked, letting the blade creep across his throat. One little push and she could end his miserable existence.

The power of her strength crept through her veins, and she absorbed it like a drug.

She wasn't sure why, but Dakota's face came to her mind. She wondered what he would think if he saw her right now, and the thought of him pulled her back to reality.

"You have no right to speak of Annabelle or of Gregory, and you have no idea what the fuck it is you are talking about. Maybe you should learn to keep your mouth shut." She sheathed her sword and got to her feet to finish her walk home.

As the cabin came into view, she heard footsteps behind her, and she spun, expecting a fight. Gregory stood behind her, his arms crossed over his chest. She studied the lines of grief etched all over his face. Youthfulness was ripped away from him when his wife died. His beard had grown tremendously and now came down to his collarbone. His hair was pulled back at the nape of his neck, and he wore dark pants with a gray robe.

"You almost killed him." They were the first words he had spoken to her since Annabelle's death, and the pain in them felt like a punch to her stomach.

"I know." The guilt began to settle in, but the fact that Gregory might be disappointed in her was what hurt the worst.

"You did well."

Anastasia's jaw dropped slightly. She'd expected him to scold her, to tell her she shouldn't fight with anger. Anything but condone her actions.

The ghost of a smile crossed his lips. "He taunted you. He had no right to say what he did." The smile disappeared as quickly as it had come. "You had every right to attack, and while I am mildly disappointed that you allowed your anger to take over, I am proud that you were able to get it under control, especially under the circumstances." He walked past her, and she followed him into the cottage. "I am sorry that I have not been reachable." He rubbed his hand over his face.

"You don't need to apologize. I'm the one responsible. I wouldn't blame you if you hated me."

"Oh, Anastasia, is that what you think?" His eyes filled with tears, and he touched her face gently. "Oh, child, what happened is not your fault. Annabelle would not want you to blame yourself, and neither do I. They would have killed her whether you had given yourself over or not. Only then, I would have lost you both." He turned to stare out the window. "I should have been here for you. I've been so wrapped up in my loss that I didn't pay attention to the fact that you lost someone too. I know that you cared for Annabelle, and you must know that she loved you. You were so much more to her than you know, Anastasia. To both of us."

"Gregory, I—"

"What did you feel?" he interrupted.

"Feel?"

"Right before you attacked Maximus, what did you feel?"

"Anger."

"What else?"

She thought back. She had been so angry. Angry for what happened, for what the bastard had said, and for the fact that she believed it. But looking back on it now, it hadn't been only anger that she had felt. She'd felt power, a sort of humming building in her veins.

"I felt powerful."

He nodded and turned to face her, eyes narrowed. "As if you had control over everything at that moment, and yet... no control at all."

She nodded.

"It's time for bed now. You will start training with me again in the morning."

He headed for his room. Once in the doorway, he stopped and turned. "If you need to talk to me, Anastasia, please do. I will do my best to be here for you from now on." Gregory disappeared into his room, and the door shut gently behind him.

19

ANASTASIA

"Where's Maximus?" Anastasia asked as she entered the training room.

Gregory opened the windows to let some fresh air fill the musty space, then turned to face her. "Maximus will no longer be training with us."

"Why not?" A small twinge of guilt wrapped itself around her heart.

"He was a nuisance," Gregory said it so nonchalantly that Anastasia's guilt began to grow.

"If this is about yesterday, Gregory, I attacked him first."

"Because he cornered you. Anastasia, violence is not something that should be taken lightly. You shouldn't enjoy causing someone pain. Maximus enjoyed it, and I will not be responsible for training a monster. Truthfully, I should have stopped working with him a long time ago."

She opened her mouth to argue with him, but stopped herself. Gregory was right. Since the day she met Maximus, he'd done everything he could to antagonize her into fighting.

Still, he would only harbor an even larger grudge against her now.

Gregory moved to stand in front of Anastasia, and she began unsheathing her sword.

"No, leave it. We are going to try something new today."

Confused, she removed her hand from her sword and watched him. Something was different, he looked almost *excited*.

There was a small light in his eyes that she hadn't seen since Annabelle died.

"Last night you said that you sensed power."

"Yes, well, it's hard to explain."

"Do you recall how you ended up on top of Maximus? How you were able to take him down and have your sword pressed to his throat before either Alastair or Sebastian could get to you?"

She thought back for a moment. "No, I guess I just saw red. He had been taunting me, and the next thing I knew, I had him pinned."

"You used magic."

"Magic," she repeated.

Gregory nodded.

"I don't have any magic." What he was saying was crazy. Wasn't it?

"We are who we are, Anastasia. Dismissing it will do you no good. In fact, I would venture to guess you've been using it your entire life. Haven't you ever made anything happen before? Something that makes no logical sense? When you were angry, perhaps?"

Anastasia thought back to all the strange things Mitch had blamed her for over the years. The books falling from shelves, plates breaking whenever she'd been angry. How the night he'd nearly killed her, she'd somehow managed to throw him away from her.

"I see in your eyes that you know what I'm talking about."

"But you told me that your magic was hereditary. Neither of my parents had any."

His jaw tightened, and his eyes darkened. "There is so much more to you than you know, Anastasia. I watched you from the beginning to the end of your confrontation with Maximus. I know what I saw, and you are going to have to accept it."

"From the beginning?" His admission shocked her. She knew he had seen the end of it, but how had he been watching her the entire time?

"I have followed you home from Tony's every night. I had to make sure you were safe." He closed his eyes and turned around to face the desk. "I couldn't lose you, too." He almost whispered the words. "I just couldn't face you after what happened."

"Gregory, what are you talking about?"

"You look too much like her." His voice was shaky, cracking with emotion.

"What?"

"I'm so sorry, Anastasia."

"Sorry for what? Gregory, you're scaring me." She started toward him but stopped when he turned to face her, eyes wet with tears and full of fear.

"We should have told you the second you'd decided to stay, but she worried you still needed time to get acclimated, and before we knew it, three months had passed." He began pacing the small room. "We were going to tell you the night that... the night..." he stuttered, and she knew which night he was talking about. "We were going to tell you."

"Tell me what?"

"Annabelle and I had a daughter. Just before her first birthday, she was taken from us and sent to live in another world by her uncle—my brother—who feared her power. It was prophesized that she would be the one who would destroy him, ending the Darkness he would spread. He believed that he would be destroyed because I refused to stand by his side and use my magic to further his goals, and he believed the reason I refused was because of my daughter. When he took her, he intended to kill her, but couldn't bring himself to destroy something so powerful.

"Even as an infant, he sensed her strength. So, instead of killing her, he sent her to a nearby world, believing that doing so would force me to tap into my magic in order to find her. He believed that if I did that, if I got a taste of the power that runs in my blood, then I would turn dark and we could rule together. He believed that I would raise my daughter to be like us, to use her great power to conquer the worlds he wanted so badly to control."

Her heart had stopped. She tried to listen to everything that he explained, but it all rang so true that she couldn't believe she hadn't suspected anything before. Honestly, she wasn't even too surprised, and it didn't take long to piece everything together.

She thought back to all the times Mitch had made comments about being stuck with the "little brat" and how he wished he had said no. She had always assumed he wished they had terminated the pregnancy, but as it turned out, it must have been he wished they had never adopted her. Monica would always tell him not to worry, that it would all be worth it in the end.

She remembered looking him up on the Internet when she was ten years old, trying to see if there was anything she might be able to learn about him that would help him to like her, to want her around. She'd been confused when she found nothing. In fact, the first mention of him wasn't until just before she'd been born.

It had seemed then as if he'd come out of nowhere. Now she realized he must have struck some sort of deal that placed him where he was.

They hadn't moved next door to Dakota's family

until well after her first birthday; Dakota's mother had told her that much.

Her thoughts circled back to Terrenia when she first arrived. Annabelle told her that Mitch had been no father to her, that a father was someone who brings love to your heart, not fear. Even the genetic markers were there. Gregory had the same blue eyes, while Monica and Mitch's were both brown. She'd just been so focused on surviving that she hadn't paid it much notice.

She looked up at Gregory, who regarded her with a wary stare as if he were afraid she might scream and run away.

"I'm your daughter."

Gregory smiled widely. It was the first real smile she had seen on his face since Annabelle's death.

"Yes, you are."

"Annabelle was my mother."

"Yes."

Rather than filling with joy, Anastasia's chest tightened with anger. Why the hell had they waited so long to tell her? "You let me go three months without knowing? Time that I could have been getting to know my mother!"

Gregory's smile faltered, and his eyes filled.

"Anastasia, she insisted we give you time to get used to being here."

"I didn't need that long." She'd gotten her mother killed. *Her mother.* Anastasia covered her face with her hands. She could have been getting to know her mother, getting to know who she had come from, rather than focusing on trying to not become anything like who she'd thought her biological parents were.

"I know I can't go back," Gregory said softly. "But if I could, I would go back and tell you the truth the night I rescued you."

Anastasia ground her teeth together. They'd wanted to give her time. Time to get used to the idea that there were multiple worlds out there and she'd been taken to one. How would she have reacted if he'd told her that night?

She would have believed him. It may have taken a few minutes to come around to it, but she was desperate for anything to separate her from the monster she'd grown up with. Anastasia took a deep breath and opened her eyes. Whatever their reasoning had been, and however pissed off she was now; it paled to one simple fact: "I was wanted."

"More than you will ever know, Anastasia. I'm so sorry I didn't get to you sooner. I took my magic slowly. I knew its depths and that I could have so easily turned dark in my search for you. Annabelle convinced me that if I turned, you were lost anyway." Tears began streaming down his face.

The revelation hit her like a ton of bricks, although on some level she wasn't surprised. She had been loved by parents who wanted her, who believed she could do anything in the world if she wanted to. She hadn't been born to a cruel man, nor did his blood run through her veins. Her mother wasn't a weak doormat, but a strong, beautiful woman.

Her heart began to ache for Annabelle, a mother whom she hadn't known long enough, and she felt the anger follow closely behind the pain, for a man who had stolen her childhood away.

20

ANASTASIA

"Focus, Anastasia," Gregory said calmly.

Anastasia sat cross-legged on the floor of the training room, her eyes closed tightly.

After the revelation that she was Gregory's daughter set in, they begun trying to tap into her magic.

"You have to be easy about it. Don't think too hard; just let it come."

"You aren't worried I will turn dark?"

Gregory laughed lightly. "That is the last thing I am worried about. It's not the sensing of one's magic that will turn them dark, it's when you begin practicing the more advanced magic that there's a risk. Besides, I don't think there's a dark bone in your body."

"Isn't that what everyone believes? That they are the ones who won't turn?"

"We will cross that bridge when we come to it. I just want you to find a way to access your power without having to be angry."

"Okay." She tuned out everything around her, and did her best to focus on the task at hand. Her mind drifted back to her childhood, and how different it would have been had she not been taken as a baby. She would have had a happy life, she knew. Gregory and Annabelle would have been wonderful parents to grow up with.

Mitch and Monica had always been so cruel to her. Monica had been more passive than Mitch, but Anastasia had always felt more as a means to an end than a family member to them. At least now she knew why.

She focused on Mitch. On how he would tear her down and make her feel like she were useless. Within moments, it was there. She could feel something; a slow humming in her blood that steadily built until it nearly consumed her.

"I feel something."

"Fantastic. Hold your hand out, palm up."

She did as he said and kept the focus on the part of her she had never known existed.

"Think about light, Anastasia."

She thought about the day she arrived in Terrenia, and about how she had seen Gregory holding the ball of light in his hands, much to Brady's delight.

"Astounding," Gregory whispered.

She opened her eyes, and smiled widely. A ball of

light the size of a softball danced in the palm of her hand.

"I did it!"

"You did wonderfully, Anastasia! Even I didn't get it the first try. It took me weeks to master that, and I had known my entire life what was inside of me."

She studied the light, then did as she had seen Gregory do and closed her palm. The light expanded and then burst into tiny pieces. She laughed as they fell around her, disappearing into the ground.

"Fantastic." His eyes were wide in awe, and he studied her closely. "You are amazing, Anastasia. Your mother would have been very proud of you."

"Thank you." Her eyes filled with tears, and she smiled at him.

"Let's try something else."

LATER THAT EVENING, THEY SAT ON THE STAIRS together staring out into the night.

"So, all those times weird things happened around me, I was using magic?"

Gregory nodded. "It appears as though anger triggers your magic. That can be a good start to help you begin to access your power, but you'll need to find that control so you can control it even when you are not angry. Anger is a trigger for me as well; it's how I learned I'd inherited my mother's power."

She looked at him, wanting him to continue.

"My brother came into his magic about a year before I did. Unlike me, he didn't fear the power. Our mother had always avoided using her own and passed down the stories of those who had lost their souls to the darkness. The thought of it scared me, but Vincent was never bothered by the threat." He ran his hand through his hair. "He started bullying me. Beat me up enough times, and eventually, I snapped. I almost killed him, and he laughed about it. That's when I swore I would never use magic again—that is, until you were taken." He conjured a ball of light and sent it floating into the air.

"That night, Vincent came to tell us what he had done. 'I didn't kill her', he assured us, as if that would make what he did right. He told me that he wouldn't return you and that if I wanted you back, I would have to use my magic to find you. He found humor in the irony that the very reason I refused my magic was the reason I would need it. I flew into a rage and very nearly took the house down with me." Gregory looked up at the sky and smiled.

"Annabelle brought me back. She was the only thing I could think of, and I remembered how happy she was the day we found out we were pregnant with you. That's when I focused, and I knew that if I lost myself, I would lose her and all hope of ever finding you."

He turned to face her. "The seer told us that you would be more powerful than we could ever imagine. If you, even for a moment, begin to believe that the power is too much, you have to find a way to come back."

"I think my friend Dakota brought me back last night when I fought with Maximus. It was so strange, he just popped into my head, and it helped me to refocus. Otherwise, I might have killed Maximus before I even realized it."

"You love him."

"Dakota?"

"Yes, it's the only reason he would have come into your mind at that moment. He is your light, as Annabelle was mine."

She nodded absently. Dakota had been her light growing up, the only reason she hadn't lost her mind in that house. He'd been the one who rescued her after they'd graduated, insisting she move in with him right away. It would make sense that he would be the one to keep her grounded now. And it wasn't like she would deny her feelings for him. She did love him, and would love him until the day she died.

"He was always there for me growing up. Bringing me food when Mitch had told me I couldn't eat, celebrating my birthday when no one else seemed to care."

"It's hard for you, isn't it, him not being here?"

She nodded absently, her thoughts still on memories of her friend.

"I'm sorry you had to leave him behind. If there'd been another way—"

"Gregory, Anastasia," Tony interrupted as he ran

toward them from the direction of the village, three Fighters following closely behind him. Anastasia jumped up. The last time Tony and the Fighters had come to see Gregory was the night they'd lost Annabelle.

"Tony, what is it?" Gregory's voice was laced with fear.

"Sebastian and Alastair."

"What about them?"

"They were killed." Tony looked at Anastasia and then back at Gregory as if asking for permission to continue.

Gregory stood and walked down the stairs. "She's fine, go ahead. Killed how?"

"It looks like a Brute did it, only they were found in Maximus's bedroom. His mother found them. It's bad, Gregory, and there's something else." Tony paused, quickly looking back and forth between Anastasia and Gregory. "Maximus and Brady are both missing."

"Oh, God." Anastasia raced down the stairs to stand beside Gregory. "We have to go find them!"

"Anastasia, I need you to stay—"

"Gregory," Tony said hesitantly, "we could use her. She is quick with a sword, and another pair of eyes will help. We will send her with Patrick and Leo." He motioned to the two Fighters who stood behind him. "With nightfall approaching, we could definitely use the extra help."

Gregory stood silently for a moment, contemplating.

"Very well," he finally agreed. "You three check the fence for any way they could have gotten in. Stay out of the trees," he warned. "Tony and I will go to the village and grab more Fighters. We will check the forest. Anastasia, stay safe."

"I will." She turned and ran back toward the village with the two Fighters on her heels.

21

ANASTASIA

"I don't see any way they could have gotten in," Patrick grumbled as they walked the perimeter of the fence.

"It's strange," she agreed. They had nearly walked the entire perimeter, and there were no signs of Brutes. No footprints, broken twigs, or any damage to the fence.

A scream tore through the night, and Anastasia's hand shot to her sword.

Patrick and Leo unsheathed theirs as well, and all three turned toward the tree line. The scream sounded again, and she bolted for the trees.

"It's Brady!" Fear gripped her heart, and she plunged into the darkness.

"We were told to stay out of the trees!" Patrick yelled after her.

"We can't let them kill him!" Leo yelled back at him.

They ran through the trees, the branches pulling at Anastasia's hair as she raced in the direction of the screaming. She burst into the clearing and stopped dead in her tracks, an angry growl forming in her throat.

Brady was tied to a tree, his eyes wide and his cheeks tear-stained.

"Anastasia!" he cried out.

She narrowed her eyes on the blood dripping from a cut in his arm. "It's okay, Brady, I'm here." She started to step toward him, and Maximus appeared between a gap in the trees.

"Maximus! What happened? Where—?" The glint of a blade caught her eye, and she looked back up to his face.

He was smiling, widely, completely unafraid.

"Took you long enough," he mocked.

"You did this?"

"You catch on quick."

"But why?"

"Because I'm tired of living in your shadow. Ever since the day you arrived it's been Anastasia this and Anastasia that. Hell, even before you arrived you were all anyone ever talked about. Blah, blah, blah!" He sneered. "Do you honestly think you're the only one who's ever had it bad? My dad died when I was a kid, and my bitch mother kept me under her thumb ever since!"

"To protect you."

"Psht. That's a load of bull. She wanted to control me, Gregory wanted to control me, but I'm done with that."

"So that makes murdering your friends and torturing an innocent child right?"

"Innocent? Hardly. He's under your influence." Maximus rolled his eyes.

"So you're doing this because you think I get too much attention?" *I just have to keep him focused on me and buy enough time for Patrick and Leo to catch up.* Surely they weren't that far behind!

"I'm doing this to prove what I am capable of. To prove that you are not what they think you are."

"And what exactly do they think I am?"

Maximus eyed her. "Don't play games with me, Anastasia. I know you've heard all about the prophecy by now. Shit, it's all my mom talks about."

"You haven't liked me since day one, and I didn't even know about the prophecy then." While it wasn't entirely true since Gregory had told her of it shortly after her arrival, she still hadn't believed it until recently.

"I nothing-d you when you arrived. You were of no interest to me. A plain, weak girl who wasn't good for anything. Now you've become a nuisance."

"I thought you would have learned your lesson about taunting me after our last encounter." She circled around him, trying to get closer to Brady.

"I have much better backup this time." He motioned behind her, and she turned for the first time to see that four Brutes formed a small half-circle around her. Neither Patrick nor Leo stood behind her, and she prayed they were just lost in the trees.

"Is that why you killed them?" she asked, hoping to buy some time for either Patrick or Leo to catch up, or for Gregory and the other Fighters to find them. "Because Sebastian and Alastair let you get your ass kicked by a girl?"

"It wasn't a fair fight!" he yelled, lunging toward her but then pulling back. "They couldn't keep their noses out of my business."

"So, they didn't want to join your Brute-loving psychopathic club?"

He grinned, and she wondered how she had never seen the madness in his eyes. The ice had always been there, but she would have never predicted he would have been a traitor or that he would have been capable of something as monstrous as hurting an innocent child.

Leaves crunched behind her, and she launched into an attack as two of the four Brutes jumped toward her. She felt the satisfaction as one fell onto her sword, but before she could pull the blade out of its chest, the other three were on her. She kicked and punched, but she was no match for the three of them.

She tried to dig down and access her magic, anything that could help her, but all she felt was fear—fear for Brady and fear for herself.

The Brutes held her arms, and Maximus came to stand in front of her. He raised a fist and slammed it into her jaw. Her head jerked back from the contact, and she grunted as his other one struck her stomach.

"You don't know how long I've wanted to knock you down a few pegs!" His breaths were heavy, and she cried out when she felt a rib crack beneath his fist. Her vision swam, and her legs went weak from the pain.

A deep growl sounded behind her, and the assault stopped.

"Get it, you morons!" Maximus yelled.

She did the best she could to pull herself toward Brady, but with each movement, it felt like her body was on fire. Anastasia narrowed her eyes trying to see what was happening, but she could only make out shapes. A large form was taking the Brutes down one by one, and Anastasia could have sworn it looked like a giant cat. She shook her head, blinking furiously to try to clear her vision.

"This isn't over!" Maximus cried out.

Moments later, Anastasia felt soft fur beneath her arm. The beast's muscles bunched beneath her broken body as it tried to lift her to her feet.

"I need to get to Brady," she told it. "Please, I need to help him."

"Anastasia!" Gregory called, and she smiled slightly as relief warmed her chest. *They found us! Brady will be okay now.*

"Get Brady!" Tony ordered the other Fighters.

"What happened, Anastasia?" Gregory knelt beside her. "Thank you," he said to her rescuer.

"It was Maximus," she choked out. "He killed Alastair and Sebastian." Her breaths were ragged, and she fought for consciousness.

"We need to get them back to the village."

"Let's go," Tony said.

"Patrick and Leo?" she asked hopefully.

"We didn't find them. Let's get you back to the village. You're in bad shape."

22

ANASTASIA

Anastasia opened her eyes slowly and squinted when the light hit them. The chest of drawers and chair in the corner let her know that she was in her room, but the events that put her there were still a little foggy. She pulled herself into a sitting position and winced when her entire body screamed in protest.

Maximus. She closed her eyes as memories of the attack surfaced and pissed her off all over again. The coward had jumped her!

Anastasia took a deep breath and stood. The pain wasn't unbearable, so she walked to the mirror. Her face was still black and blue in some places, but although they were bloodshot, her eyes were no longer swollen shut. She limped to the door and very nearly tripped when she opened it.

She squealed and jumped back, wincing with pain from the quick movement. A large cat slept directly outside of her door. The cat was black except for a few lines of brown that seemed to outline spots. It yawned and stretched lazily. When it looked up at her, its eyes were a fierce green, the color of emeralds.

"I think that cat would have slept on your bed, had I let it. She hasn't left your side since the attack." Gregory stood in the kitchen holding a mug of steaming liquid. "How are you feeling?" he asked cautiously, moving toward her.

"Like I was hit by a bus, and then it backed over me."

"I've seen those buses, and I think that's a fairly accurate statement. You could have died, Anastasia. Had it not been for her"—he motioned toward the large cat —"we probably wouldn't have gotten there in time."

"Then I feel I must say a thank you." Anastasia moved to kneel, but the cat stood, so she stepped back and watched in awe as the creature stretched out to its full size. The cat was nearly as large as a male lion.

"I've never seen one in person before, only sketches," Gregory said. "She's a Terrenian Feline. They are a bit larger here than in your Seattle." He laughed. "But they are very rare, and very few have ever seen them."

"She's beautiful." Anastasia ran her hands through the cat's thick, black hair, and she began to purr.

"She's yours or, rather, you're hers." Gregory laughed. "I'm not quite sure how that works."

"I'm going to call you Kaley." Anastasia smiled, and Kaley rubbed against her. "She must be, what, at least four hundred pounds?"

"She's not even fully grown. I would estimate she is only about a year old."

Anastasia's jaw dropped. "How big do they get?"

"The largest one ever seen was estimated at twelve hundred pounds and over seven feet when standing on its hind legs."

"Oh, wow."

"She took out two Brutes by the time we got there. Maximus was gone already."

"Brady?" Anastasia's heart jumped.

"He's fine. Has a few cuts and bruises, but he's been here every day to check on you."

"Every day? How long have I been out?"

"Four days."

Four days? How had she slept that long? "Any sign of Patrick and Leo?" she asked hopefully.

"No. We've searched, but they are just gone. I fear they may have been taken by the Brutes."

"I'm so sorry, Gregory, I should have listened and stayed out of the trees."

"Anastasia, you saved Brady. While I wish would have listened, or come and gotten us first, I can't deny the fact that I might have had to tell a mother that her young son was not coming home—"

"But Leo and Patrick," she interrupted.

"Knew the risks of becoming Fighters. They put their lives on the line each time they marched into battle against those monsters. What has been done cannot be undone, and would you have done it any differently knowing the outcome? Could you have chosen in favor of losing Brady?"

"No," she admitted. She would have still gone into those woods, and Patrick and Leo would have too. After she'd charged into the trees, Leo yelled to Patrick because he wanted to go in after Brady as well. Remembering this helped to ease some of the guilt in her heart.

"It's terrible that we haven't found them, and I'm still holding out hope that they will turn up, having just gotten lost, but until then, we need to focus on the problems at hand." He sat at the table, and she walked slowly over to take a seat across from him.

"What problems? Other than Maximus," she added.

"The Brutes have taken out two of the villages within a ten-mile radius of us. The scouts found nothing but rubble."

"Is it possible that the villagers escaped?"

"It's unlikely. There was no one in the outlying woods, and the nearby villages that are still standing were scouted out for survivors. There was no one."

"What are they doing with them?"

"I don't know."

"I should have killed him."

"That's not who you are, Anastasia. You may have

to become that person someday, but had you killed Maximus, that act would have been for nothing other than taunting you. You didn't know what he was capable of."

"How did she kill the Brutes?" Anastasia motioned to the cat.

"I'm not really sure." He rubbed his hand over his chin in thought. "For us, only platinum-coated blades or decapitation will put one down. When she attacked, she went for the throats. I think it might be something in her bite." Kaley padded over and rubbed against Gregory.

"Anastasia!" Brady burst through the door, his mother and sister on his heels.

"Hey, kid." She smiled and accepted his hug, grunting with pain when he slammed into her.

"Oh, sorry!" He stepped back cautiously.

"It's okay. How are you?"

He shrugged it off. "I'm good. Mom says I'll have some scars, but that's okay because girls like scars. It means I'm tough."

Anastasia smiled. Nothing could keep this kid down. He was the most vibrant thirteen-year-old she'd ever met, and she honestly doubted there was anything that could dull the light in his eyes.

"Thank you, Anastasia." Brady's mother took Anastasia's hand in her own and squeezed lightly. "If it hadn't been for you—"

"You don't have to thank me, Selena. Besides, had it

not been for me, Maximus might not have taken him anyway." She looked down at her feet.

"Don't you blame yourself for that evil boy, Anastasia. You can no more control him and his actions than you can control the weather." She shook her head lightly. "I will thank you. Because of you, I do not have to plan a funeral for my son." She smiled. "If you need anything at all, you only have to ask. I would actually love it if you two would join us for dinner."

Anastasia's stomach grumbled.

Sarah laughed, so she looked over and saw that Kaley had rolled onto her back so that she and Brady could rub her stomach.

"I named her Kaley."

"I like her." The young girl, who had just turned eleven, laughed again.

"So how about it? Are you two hungry?" Selena asked.

"I could eat," Gregory answered. "Anastasia?"

She nodded, still watching the kids petting the giant feline.

"Wonderful, how about we head back to my house and I'll cook you both a giant dinner. We'll grab Tony on the way."

"Perhaps we should stay in," Gregory said, eyeing Anastasia.

She shook her head. "I need to get some fresh air. Dinner sounds great."

"I TRIED TO ACCESS MY MAGIC THAT NIGHT IN THE woods," Anastasia told Gregory as they sat on the steps together after returning from dinner. "No matter how hard I focused, nothing came to me."

"You were frightened. You have to be in control of the power. Until you are more adept, it may take some time to access. You have to have a clear mind."

"That's why, when I began training, you told me that fighting angry would do me no good, because I wouldn't be able to focus on the bigger picture."

"In a way, yes, although, with your magic, anger seems to be your trigger. But that night in the clearing you were afraid for Brady and for yourself. You have to be able to control that fear, use it to channel your magic, or it will cause a block."

She nodded silently and continued looking at the sky. Kaley slept lazily at the base of the stairs, but she would be ready to pounce the second any danger showed its face.

"When can we start training again?"

"You need some time to heal first, Anastasia. We can resume our training next week. I also want you to start coming to the village meetings with me. You need to become acquainted with the Fighters and be more involved in what's going on out there." He pointed to the fence.

"Okay," she agreed quietly.

"As much as I want to deny it, your destiny lies in fighting this war, and I want you to be as prepared as possible."

They continued staring out at the steadily darkening sky. Insects chirped around them, singing their nightly songs while Anastasia pondered all that had happened the last few days.

If she had any hope of living up to the prophecy, she was going to need to train a hell of a lot harder than she had been. She was already so different than the night Gregory had brought her here three months ago, but she still had a ways to go.

3

ANASTASIA

"You sure about this?" Zarina asked Anastasia cautiously.

"Absolutely. Can you do it?"

Zarina narrowed her eyes at Anastasia. "Girl, I have been tatting up the Fighters of Terrenia for nearly ten years. I can do this. I'll warn you though, a tattoo like this is going to take some time, and it's going to hurt like hell."

"I can take it." She lifted her shirt and lay down on the table in Zarina's house that also doubled as her tattoo parlor. Her black hair was braided back and then rolled into a bun, and the vest she wore revealed arms that were completely covered in tattoos.

Since there was no electricity, the artists of Terrenia

inserted ink beneath the skin using a sharpened bone shard.

Anastasia had never gotten a tattoo before, but she imagined Zarina's method was going to hurt a whole hell of a lot more than it would have back in Seattle.

"All right, let me know if it gets to be too much. You may want to bite down on this." She handed Anastasia a leather strap, and after taking it, Anastasia put it in her mouth and closed her eyes, trying to focus on anything but what was about to happen.

She opened them just in time to see Zarina dip the bone in ink, and she bit down as the pain radiated through her body.

Remember why you're doing this. She was damn tired of seeing the scars on her back every time she caught a glimpse in the mirror. The tattoo would cover them, and Anastasia could finally let go of that night, those people, and the horrors of her childhood.

She winced again, but tried her best to keep her back steady.

"You good?" Zarina asked.

Anastasia nodded, and briefly took the strap from her mouth. "Keep going."

"Look at that! You survived!" Tony greeted her when she finally stepped out after what felt like an eternity.

"Barely," Anastasia responded with an exhausted grin. Zarina had given her a loose button-up shirt to wear instead of the short-sleeved one she'd been in, and while her back screamed in pain, she didn't regret a single moment.

It felt good to do something—anything—to erase part of her past.

"Want a drink?"

"A drink?"

"I think you've earned some Terrenian whiskey," he said with a smile. "Let's head over to the town center and grab some."

Anastasia followed Tony through the cottages and back down to the village's center.

People laughed and danced, enjoying the clear night and the cool breeze.

Her dad was nowhere to be seen, probably holed up in the cottage with a book in his hand.

My dad. Damn, it felt good to say that.

Tony stopped near a group of Fighters Anastasia had met briefly during training. After pouring amber liquid into two handmade mugs, he handed her one and clinked his against hers.

Knowing he was watching to see how she reacted to the liquid, Anastasia squared her shoulders and brought the mug to her lips. The burn was instant as the whiskey made its way down her throat, but so was the warmth that spread through her body.

The liquid was strong, but had a sweet aftertaste,

and while she knew it was going to take some time to get used to it, she decided she quite liked it.

"Atta girl!" Tony laughed heartily. "That's it, though, you got it? This shit is strong, and a hangover is not what you want, trust me."

"Maybe I wouldn't get one," she taunted.

Tony laughed. "Yeah, you'd liked to think that, wouldn't you, kid?" One of the men she knew as Andrew touched Tony on the shoulder, and they stepped to the side to talk.

"Good night?"

Anastasia turned to see Shane, the only Fighter close to her age. "Yeah, got a tattoo."

"Yikes, good for you. I still haven't mustered up the courage to get more than this." He gestured to the band around his left arm; a symbol all Fighters received once they'd completed training.

"She did my back."

"What did you get?"

"A phoenix."

"That's awesome. Can I see?" Even in the dark she could see the lust reflected in his eyes and the subtle way his mouth hung open slightly.

"Maybe some other time," she responded sweetly and took another drink of her whiskey.

"I'll take you up on that." Shane smiled and headed to the group of women who were dancing to the music being played on a set of drums. The beat was fast, and between it and the whiskey, her own heart felt like it pounded in her ears.

"So, what do you think?" Tony asked once Andrew had disappeared into the crowd.

"It's good."

"I saw Shane bugging you; everything okay with that?"

She nodded. "He was just asking to see my tattoo."

Tony ground his teeth together, and she smiled. "Easy, Dad Number Two. I've got it handled."

Tony laughed. "Dad Number Two? I like it."

"I thought you would." Tony had become like a second father to her, and someone she knew she could trust with her life.

"Hey, Tony!"

"Excuse me, Daughter Number One." Tony disappeared back into the crowd, leaving Anastasia standing by herself.

"I like you," a voice whispered in her ear, and Anastasia smelled the alcohol before she even turned to see Shane standing beside her.

This could get awkward.

"I'm flattered, but I don't want to risk our friendship," she lied, knowing full and well that aspect had nothing to do with her reasoning.

She didn't want anyone but the guy she'd left behind.

"Come on, Ana. We could be good together."

She faced him. "Don't call me Ana."

He raised his hands in surrender. "Fine, fine. Anastasia."

Her name came out in a slur of words, making her wonder just how much alcohol he'd consumed this evening.

"So, what's your deal, anyway?" he asked, taking another drink.

"What do you mean?"

"You seeing someone else?"

"No, I just—"

He gripped her biceps and pulled her toward him, crushing his lips against hers.

She shoved hard against his chest, knocking him back a few steps. "What the fuck, Shane!"

Tony grabbed Shane by the back of his shirt and hauled him backward. "You get your sorry ass home, Shane, before I kick it."

Shane threw his hands in the air, looking back and forth between Tony and Anastasia, his eyes wide and his lips in a snarl. "What, man? It was just a kiss!"

"You're an ass." Anastasia slammed her fist into his jaw, the hardness of the bone bruising her knuckles.

His head snapped back, and he straightened, rubbing his jaw. "What the hell was that for?"

"I told you, *I'm not interested.*"

"Forget worrying about me," Tony barked. "You'd better get your ass home before *she* kicks it." Tony crossed his arms over his chest.

"Whatever," Shane grumbled, turning to leave.

Anastasia realized the music had stopped and everyone stared at them.

Heat filled her chest, creeping up her neck to her cheeks. "Great, now I'm the center of attention."

"You aren't, but he is." Tony laughed, pointing at Shane. "You okay?"

"Yeah." She wiped her mouth with the back of her hand and set the rest of her whiskey down. Had her senses not been dulled, she might've been able to move in time.

Music started back up, and Tony set his own cup down.

"Let's get you home."

"I can walk myself."

"No need, I'm going that way anyway."

She smiled, grateful for the company. "Thanks, Tony."

"Anytime."

24

ANASTASIA

Anastasia made her way into her apartment, ecstatic at the chance to beat Dakota home. He was almost always home before her, cooking dinner or playing Call of Duty on the Xbox after picking up take-out. But today, she was going to beat him home and try her hand at actually making something other than blue box macaroni and cheese.

After slipping her key into the lock and turning it, she pushed the door open and stepped inside. The lights were all off, so she flipped the switch next to the door. The living room lit up, displaying their bright red hand-me-down couch and mismatched tables.

Things may not match, but she loved the space. It was theirs, and it was home.

Anastasia went to work setting the table and getting

the spaghetti sauce simmering on the stove. She had just turned off the noodles, when Dakota stepped inside.

"Hey, baby." He pulled her in and kissed her deeply. "I missed you."

"I missed you, too." She smiled against his mouth, still giddy over the fact that they were finally a couple.

"That smells delicious." He stepped to the stove and leaned over the stockpot to smell the sauce.

"Thanks. I got the recipe from your mom."

Dakota turned to her and pulled her close to him. "I love you so much, you know that?"

Anastasia's heart soared, and she pushed up on her tiptoes to press a kiss to his lips.

Dakota stepped away, his brow furrowed. He looked down at his chest, and Anastasia followed his gaze. The end of a blade protruded from between his ribs.

"Dakota?" she choked out. "No, no, no," Anastasia cried, reaching for him just as he fell to the ground.

Behind him, Vincent smiled.

"I will take everything from you, Anastasia. Everything and everyone."

ANASTASIA SHOT UP IN BED, BREATHING HEAVILY. SHE pressed a hand to her heart, urging it to slow. Dakota was alive. *Dakota* is *alive.*

She got to her feet and crept into the kitchen to grab a drink of water. The soft lavender light of early morning had just started to shine through the windows, so she didn't have to use a lantern to light her way.

After filling a cup with water, she stepped onto the porch. Kaley was lying on the base of the steps, and she padded up to sit next to Anastasia.

"Morning, girl." She rubbed the big cat's soft fur. "Couldn't sleep either, huh?" Anastasia stretched, her back aching slightly with the movement. Gregory had given her some healing tonic to use on her tattoo, one he'd spelled himself, and it seemed to have all but healed her new ink overnight.

She heard the thudding of feet, and looked up just in time to see Tony, Andrew, Shane, and another Fighter she didn't know by name.

Their faces were serious, and the look had her jumping to her feet. "What's wrong?"

"We've got about two-dozen Brutes heading for Plike," Tony informed her.

Plike was only about four miles from Terrenia, and only half its size. "They don't have a Fighting force," Anastasia said, repeating this bit of information from her studies with Gregory.

Tony nodded. "Is your father awake?"

"I'll go see." Anastasia stepped into the house and knocked lightly on her father's door.

He opened it within minutes, still wiping the sleep from his eyes. "Anastasia, what is it? Is everything all right?"

"We've got a problem."

Gregory rushed outside to speak with Tony, and Anastasia quickly dressed and prepared herself for battle. When she was ready, she joined the men out front. "We need to leave immediately. Our scout only had a few hours on the army," Andrew informed the group.

"Agreed," Gregory said. "Are the horses saddled and ready to go?"

Tony nodded. "Just waiting for your order."

"Go."

Tony, Andrew, and Shane turned to leave, and Anastasia followed.

"Anastasia, wait." Gregory gripped her arm.

She turned around, mouth open to argue. He couldn't force her to stay behind, not after everything she'd been through.

"Be careful," he said, searching her gaze.

Pride warmed her chest. "I will." She kissed his cheek and ran after the men, Kaley on her heels.

"Ready?" Tony asked when she joined the group of Fighters.

She nodded. "Let's go kick some Brute ass."

25

ANASTASIA

They rode fast, the stride of their horses eating up the distance as quickly as possible. Anastasia's heart thundered in her chest, and nerves danced in her stomach. She'd fought Brutes before, but riding into actual battle—this was a first for her.

"Andrew, Jack, you two ride around the perimeter," Tony instructed. "Check to be sure they didn't circle behind!"

The two men broke away from the group.

"Anastasia, Shane, you go on in and be sure everyone gets inside their houses. We don't need anyone coming out in the middle of the fight."

Anastasia broke away and followed Shane into the small village. The only line of defense was a short fence used to keep livestock in. If the Brutes got past the Fighters, this village would fall.

For the most part, the villagers had already locked themselves away in their houses. The only people outside were half a dozen Fighters and the village's elder.

"We're here from Terrenia," Anastasia said.

"Thank you for coming. I'm Logan." He held his hand out, and Anastasia shook it.

"Anastasia."

"She's Gregory Silvan's daughter," Shane told him.

Logan's eyes widened. "It's wonderful to meet you. I didn't realize Gregory had a child."

"It's a long story." She smiled, though she had no interest in sharing it with him. "We have Fighters surrounding your village." She gestured to the men who had dismounted and were taking their stances outside the small fence. "Do you know how many are coming?"

Logan nodded. "Our scout said two dozen."

Manageable. "Okay, please get inside." She gestured to the cottage behind them.

"Good luck, Fighter," Logan said, then turned to head inside.

"You good?" Shane asked.

Anastasia nodded.

"Listen, I'm sorry about last night. I don't remember much, but what I do remember isn't great."

Anastasia unsheathed her sword. "Really not the time, Shane." She moved to stand beside Tony at the village's entrance. The Brutes were just coming into view and their feet thundered on the ground.

"I just—"

"Not the time, Shane," Tony said, repeating Anastasia's words.

She looked up at him and smiled.

"You stay near me," he told her.

"Don't worry," Anastasia teased. "I've got your back."

Tony grinned. "How about a little contest?"

She cocked her head. "What type of contest?"

"Oh, there's time for this but not an apology?" Shane said sarcastically, waving his sword to motion toward the oncoming army of Brutes.

"Let's see who has the higher number at the end."

"You're on, old man."

"You've only been at this a few months; I've been doing it my entire life." Tony pointed to his face and flashed a confident smile. "Not worried."

"We'll see." Anastasia winked, then charged into the fray.

The Brute closest to her lashed out with a large fist. As she ducked, she swung her sword, catching the beast in the abdomen, and it fell to the ground. Another was sneaking up on Tony, who was engaged with two monsters, and she decapitated it from behind.

A Fighter yelled, and Anastasia looked over to see Jack fall to the ground in a bloody heap. Fueled by rage for the loss of one of her people, Anastasia charged and threw her body weight into the beast, knocking it to the side just long enough for Shane to drive his sword down into its neck.

The beast gargled and fell to the ground.

The fight didn't last more than a few minutes, but Anastasia's body ached like it had been hours instead. The ground was covered with bodies of Brutes, and they'd lost a handful of Fighters to the monsters.

"You fought well, Anastasia." Tony stepped beside her, sheathing his bloody sword.

"Thanks." She looked sadly to where bodies of the fallen Fighters were being loaded onto a wagon.

Tony squeezed her shoulder. "Jack, Michael, and Phillip died a Fighter's death, Anastasia. That is something they can be proud of."

She swallowed hard.

Shane made his way over, his face and arms covered in dirt and blue Brute blood. "No casualties inside the fence," he reported.

"Good. Get our horses; we need to go home."

The villagers had begun to emerge from their houses, gathering at the fence line to watch the Fighters cleaning up from the battle.

She looked amongst the faces of the men, women, and children they had saved today.

Logan made his way over and held his hand out to Tony. "Thank you so much," he said. "We wouldn't have been able to hold them off had you not shown up when you did."

Tony bowed his head slightly. "I'm glad we got here in time. You should know, Terrenia has space if you want a safe haven until this is over."

Logan smiled. "I appreciate the offer, but we have much here that needs to be tended to. Leaving is just not an option at this point."

Tony's jaw tightened, but he didn't argue. He gave a curt nod. "Very well, but should you change your mind, the offer stands."

Anastasia opened her mouth to speak, but Tony placed his hand on her arm, squeezing gently.

She held her thoughts in until they reached their horses.

"Tony, if they stay here, they're going to die."

"I know that. Hell, he probably knows that. But we can't force them to leave."

"What if we made an announcement to his village? Tell all of them that they need to leave?"

"Anastasia, he is the village's leader, and he's made the decision."

"But it's bullshit. He shouldn't be allowed to decide whether they live or die!"

Tony stopped walking and faced her. He ran a hand through his greying hair. "Anastasia, if we go against his wishes, we could have a rebellion on our hands. As it stands, Terrenia only has one leader, and with it being the center of this world, we should have a team. If we go changing things now, Gregory is going to have one hell of a fall out to deal with. Especially because you're his daughter."

"Don't you think a little fall out is better than having to bury dozens of bodies?"

He sighed. "Anastasia, I am only telling you what *I've been told. I* lead the Fighters, if *I* were to let it slip that we offered their leader a safe haven and he turned it down, *I* could be reprimanded." He narrowed his eyes at her, and Anastasia nodded.

"I suppose you shouldn't do that then, huh?"

"Correct. See you in a few." He winked and headed back to the stables.

Swallowing hard, Anastasia turned on her heel and marched back to the village's center. Screw Logan and his agenda. If everyone in the village died, the crops would all die anyway. So what the hell did it matter?

She climbed onto a table that was situated next to the large stone fire pit and cleared her throat.

The men and women who had gathered to watch the Fighters leave turned to face her, Logan among them. She averted her eyes from his steely gaze and focused on the wide-eyed, fearful faces of the people before her.

"Hi, everyone. I know you don't know me, um, my name is Anastasia Silvan." At the mention of her last name, murmurs spread through the crowd, and she nodded. "Yes, Gregory Silvan is my father. I wanted to let you all know that staying put after the Brutes have already attacked is dangerous."

"Excuse me!" Logan interrupted. .

Anastasia glanced at him, then quickly continued. "They have already been here, so chances are they will be back, and they will bring more."

"Where are we supposed to go?" a woman in the front row shouted.

"Terrenia. We have plenty of space and have been working to fortify our perimeter and keep our people safe. If you come with us now, we will get you there safely and keep you safe."

"Excuse me!" Logan yelled again, silencing the whispers that had spread through the crowd again.

He climbed up beside Anastasia and glared at her. She glanced over to the stable where Tony watched, hand on his sword. He shook his head slowly, the ghost of a smile playing at his lips.

"I have assured these Fighters that we do not need to leave. The Brutes came and lost, so why would they come back? We took down thirteen beasts today!" He cheered.

"*We* took down thirteen Brutes," Anastasia corrected. "Two escaped back into the trees, which means they'll be alerting the others so they can return with more. They will be back; it's only a matter of time."

"We have managed this long." He straightened the hem of his shirt.

"Because Terrenia is so close, they hadn't risked attacking before. Those beasts have torn through much larger villages than yours, Logan. If you stay, you will die."

"My family and I will go with you!" a man called from the side, his declaration followed by about three quarters of the villagers, and Anastasia glanced over at Tony, who was grinning.

"Wonderful! Grab your things; we will leave out in an hour."

"Thank you!" a few called out as she climbed from the table.

Logan gripped her arm hard.

Anastasia glared at him. "You'll want to release me."

"Do you have any idea what you've done? My village is ruined!"

"The fact that your title and ego is more important than the lives of your people is not my problem."

"I'll make it your problem." He gripped tighter, and Anastasia put her hand on the hilt of her sword.

"Release her, or lose that hand," Shane warned, displaying his dagger.

Logan shoved her arm away and stalked off. Shane sheathed his dagger and crossed his arms over his chest.

"You all right?" he asked.

"Yeah, I'm fine. Thanks."

"Please, it's the least I could do after last night."

Anastasia smiled. "Apology accepted."

He beamed. "Thanks."

Anastasia followed him back to where Tony stood.

"Thanks, Shane," Tony said.

"Anytime." He smiled and headed back toward the stables.

"You okay?"

"Yeah, I'm happy most of them are coming with us."

"Me too. That was a good thing you did there."

"I hope so. I couldn't stomach just leaving them here to die. It's foolish of Logan to stay. A good leader should be worried about the safety of his people and nothing else."

Tony nodded in agreement. "I sent Andrew back to let Gregory know what's going on. He'll need the heads-up."

"Why was it such a big deal for them to come to Terrenia anyways?"

Tony sighed. "Things used to be quite a bit different . Each village had their own representative, but all decisions were made by four elders who oversaw the world. About fifteen years back, a group rose up against the four and attacked Terrenia. They killed about two-dozen people before they were stopped, but of those two dozen, four were the leaders."

"They killed them all?"

Tony nodded. "Gregory stepped up and declared each village would operate on its own, whether that was with a single person or a grouping that the residents elected."

"So Gregory became Terrenia's leader?"

"Yes. No one wanted to step up and help lead after the uprising, so Gregory did."

"So the fact that I just went above Logan's head and asked his people to leave—"

Tony put his hand on her shoulder. "If anything happens, we'll deal with it." He squeezed lightly.

"It's still worth it if we can keep them safe."

"Agreed." He released her and folded his arms. "You will make a great leader one day, Anastasia."

She stared after him as he made his way to talk to the Fighters, her stomach twisting. She hadn't decided if she was going to stay when all of this was over. Gregory had told her he could find a way to send her home, and even after she'd agreed to stay, it had always been in the back of her mind that she might one day go back to Seattle.

Anastasia had always believed her future was tied to Dakota.

Was it possible she'd been wrong?

26

SEATTLE

DAKOTA

Dakota stared at the man reflected in the mirror; he hardly recognized himself. His jaw was tight, set in a solid line, and the freshly pressed blue uniform he wore didn't feel like an accomplishment but more a necessary step.

His end goal was to make Detective, and this was merely a stepping-stone to that finish line, something he had to do in order to get his revenge on Mitch, because he absolutely *would* get it. One way or another.

"Dakota?" his mom called through the bathroom door. "You almost ready?"

After taking a deep breath, he pulled open the door.

His mother gasped and covered her mouth with her hands. "You look so much like him." Tears welling in her eyes, she stepped forward and touched the badge on his chest.

"Thanks, Mom."

She nodded and stepped away. Dakota followed her out of his childhood home and down to the car parked in the garage. It was graduation day for him, which meant he was moving on to advanced training before finally getting some field work in.

He pulled the car onto the street, and they made their way to the Police Academy, where Dakota had spent the better part of the last four and a half months.

Time well spent. The police had given up on ever finding Ana, making her just another face on a missing persons poster. It took everything in him to not give up, too, but he was the only one looking for her now, the only one who seemed to give a shit that she'd disappeared.

"You okay, honey?" his mom asked from the passenger's side.

Dakota offered her a smile. "Of course, it's a good day."

"Your father would be really proud of you, Dakota."

Dakota smiled tightly and swallowed the lump in his throat. Regret weighed on him like a lead vest. The last conversation he and his father had was the night George had called to confront Dakota after he'd made the decision to drop out of school to enter the Academy.

It hadn't been a pleasant conversation, and George

had given him the silent treatment all the way up until the day he died.

"Maybe."

She reached over and touched his arm. "He would have, Dakota. Your father just wanted you to be happy."

Dakota nodded, words catching in his throat. He hoped wherever his dad was he was proud, but it didn't truly matter, because at the end of the day, he wasn't doing this for himself, or for George Parker.

He was doing this for Ana, and the future Mitch Carter had taken from them.

IT WAS NEARING SUMMERTIME IN SEATTLE, AND THE SUN beat down on them for the first time in a week. Dakota sat in his chair amongst the other academy graduates, waiting for their names to be called.

"Good afternoon, everyone," the speaker began. "I'm Chief Martin Belford. It is my honor and privilege to stand here today in front of such distinguished graduates and their families. As a police officer who will be expected to present yourself with professionalism and honor each and every day, all while performing your duties in a respectable manner. "

Dakota glanced around the crowd, letting the chief's words fade into background noise, when his eyes landed on Mitch. He was sitting off to the right side, about two rows behind Dakota's mom. Their gazes locked, and Mitch smiled.

Dakota's muscles went rigid. *Keep smiling, asshole. I'm coming for you.*

The rest of the speech went by quickly, but Dakota didn't notice it. His sole focus was on getting through it without jumping from his seat and killing Ana's father.

He stood when his name was called and made his way to the stage to receive a handshake from the Chief of Police, then stood on stage with the rest of the graduates.

They were dismissed with a lot of cheering, but Dakota quickly stepped down to seek out his mother in the crowd.

She stood about ten feet away talking to none other than Mitch Carter.

"What the fuck do you want?" he asked once he reached them.

"Dakota," his mother warned.

"No." He glared at Mitch. "I want to know what the fuck you're doing here."

"I heard you were graduating and, naturally, I wanted to come offer my support."

"You and I both know that just isn't fucking true."

"You sure are in a mood for someone who just became a cop." The 'p' on the end of cop popped, and Mitch tucked his hands into his pockets. "Not very becoming for a boy in blue, wouldn't you say?"

Dakota grinned. "I'd say you'd better breathe fresh air while you can."

"That a threat?"

"It's a promise. Come on, Mom." Dakota gripped her hand and pulled her back through the crowd toward the parking lot.

"Thanks for the rescue," she said once they had climbed into the car.

"Yeah." Adrenaline pumped like lava through his veins, and his muscles tensed, geared for a fight. "I'm gonna drop you off and head to the gym."

"You don't want to grab some dinner?"

"Maybe later. I need to work off some steam."

"Oh, all right." His mom offered a small smile as they pulled out of the lot.

———

DAKOTA NURSED A GLASS OF WHISKEY AT THE BAR later that night. He'd spent nearly four hours kicking the shit out of a heavy bag and had sparred with one of the trainers. His body was sore, sweaty, and he was exhausted, but at least the anger from earlier had nearly dissipated. The bar was fairly empty tonight since it was mainly cops who frequented the establishment, and most of them were at a private graduation party downtown.

"Hey."

He looked over as an older man approached him at the bar.

"This seat taken?" he asked as he motioned to the barstool beside Dakota.

Dakota shook his head and the man sat.

"I'm Silvan." He held his hand out, and Dakota shook it.

"Dakota."

"Good to meet you. What are you having?" He gestured to the glass, and Dakota took a drink.

"Whiskey."

He raised his hand to signal Jax, the bartender. "Two whiskeys, please."

"Thanks."

"No problem," the man answered.

His hair was dark, but there was a large scattering of grey near his temples slowly working its way through the rest of his hair. His beard was trimmed short, but his blue eyes were what caught Dakota's attention.

They were the same shade as Ana's, and Dakota forced himself to look away.

"Long day?" Silvan asked.

Dakota nodded. "Graduated from the Police Academy this afternoon." He raised his glass in salute.

"That's wonderful! Congratulations!"

Dakota smiled. "Thanks."

The man narrowed his gaze. "You don't seem very happy about it."

"It wasn't my first choice of career, but you do what you've gotta do."

"Oh?" Silvan raised an eyebrow. "There a story there?"

Dakota didn't make it a habit of sharing his personal life with strangers, but something about Silvan had him feeling like the man was an old friend, rather than a stranger who happened to sit next to him at a bar.

Before he knew it, he'd damn near told the man his entire life's story.

"It sounds to me like your father would be very proud of you."

"Yeah." Dakota took a drink, grateful the alcohol had begun dulling the ache in his heart.

"I have a daughter," Silvan said with a smile. "She's about your age and as independent as they come. I think you'd like her."

"I appreciate that, but if you're looking to set us up, I have to warn ya... I'm not big on dating."

Silvan laughed. "I don't think she is at the moment either, so don't worry about that. I only meant that I can understand how your father was feeling. Seeing a plan laid out for your child—especially when it can be a dangerous one—does not help us sleep at night, and there may be days where we don't handle the information well."

Dakota nodded absently.

"Just an old man's opinion." He smiled and patted Dakota on the back. "I need to get home. Early morning." Silvan tossed some bills on the counter. "See you around."

"Thanks, Silvan."

"Always happy to lend an ear."

Dakota watched him leave, then finished his own glass before stepping out into the night air. Stars twinkled above him where they managed to sneak through clouds, and Dakota turned his face up to the sky.

Where was Ana right now? Was she happy? Was she even alive? Three questions he asked himself almost daily. But when he looked up at the stars, he had to hope that wherever she was, she was looking at them too, that maybe she really was only just out of reach.

He had to believe that, because each and every new day was a painful reminder that his world was a little less bright without her.

PART II

"I no longer feared the darkness once I knew the phoenix in me would rise from the ashes." — *William C. Hannan*

27

TERRENIA: FIVE YEARS LATER

ANASTASIA

Anastasia examined herself in the mirror. Her sword was sheathed across her back, and three small knives were tucked into the strap of leather at her waist. Her dark hair fell in loose curls to her hips. She quickly braided it back with the precision of someone who'd done so every day for years.

No trace remained of the young woman who arrived in Terrenia all those years ago. Her once soft body was now sleek and strong, and judging by the Brute body count she'd racked up only in the last few years, her training had paid off. She could be deadly if she needed to be.

"Ready, girl?" she asked Kaley as she headed for the door.

"Morning, Anastasia." Her father sat at the table, writing in a notebook.

"Good morning." She grabbed a slice of bread from the counter and sat next to him.

"What are your plans for today?" he asked as he continued writing.

"I am going to head out with Tony in a little bit; we are going to visit the last standing village that's within a ten-mile radius. We're hoping we can get them to vacate and relocate here, where they will be safe. There's power in numbers and all that."

"That would be good."

She nodded in agreement. The last two villages they had offered to help had refused to move, and now they were nothing but a smoldering pile of ash. She hoped this one would be different. *Five years and they were still playing defense.*

"Be safe," he added as he stood to walk into the kitchen. "Take Kaley with you."

"I always do." She smiled and headed for the door.

She met up with Tony and Shane on the outskirts of the village. Tony had grabbed her horse, Revenue, from the village's stable for her, and she climbed onto his back with ease. "Hey, Anastasia," Shane said.

"Hi." She smiled awkwardly at him.

Shane was tall, standing at least a foot above Anastasia, and his dark hair fell to his shoulders. Muscular and handsome, he was also a fantastic Fighter, and had all the qualities Anastasia *should* want in a potential mate. But, all these years later, she still only had room enough in her heart for Dakota Parker.

She'd tried, hadn't she? They'd seen each other for nearly a year after rescuing the Plike village. She'd tried so hard to get Dakota out of her head and move on like she was sure he would have, but to both hers and Shane's disappointment, she'd never been able to.

Now, here they were, four years after their split, and he still wouldn't move on and find someone else.

"How are you?" he asked.

"Good, just busy training."

Shane nodded. "Not that you need much more. You could kick any of our asses with your eyes closed."

"Let's head out," Tony said, ending their awkward conversation, and they nudged their animals to begin walking through the trees. "Keep your eyes peeled."

Grateful for the distance from Shane, Anastasia took lead, with Tony following and Shane behind him.

Their small search party was meant only to warn the village, not scare them into thinking an attack was on its way. Even though Anastasia was pretty damn sure it was.

They rode easily for the first three miles until smoke appeared, billowing from the trees.

"We're too late!" Anastasia called, pushing her horse into a gallop. Kaley kept up easily, and within minutes, they emerged into the village. The second they were in the clearing, Anastasia leapt from her horse.

The entire town was in ruins, and Anastasia cried

out. Houses and other buildings were burned to the ground. Debris lay strewn across the dirt, and she nudged a small, burnt toy with her boot. Anastasia covered her mouth with her hands, horrified at the carnage.

"This devastation is fresh. Look for survivors, but keep watch. The monsters that did this may not be far off." Tony leapt off his horse and began searching the debris, lifting the large pieces to search beneath them for any remaining villagers.

Anastasia and Shane did the same, leaving their animals at the entrance to the village. She headed toward a small line of houses that were badly burned and searched beneath the debris, trying her best to ignore the bodies littering the ground.

What did the Brutes have to gain from doing this? Did they just enjoy the slaughter? Where were they taking the survivors?

Anastasia heard coughing and spun in the direction of the sound. "Over here!" she yelled to Tony and Shane as she raced toward the small, half-burned cottage the noise had come from.

A woman lay in the center of the ruined house. "Help me," she choked out. Soot painted her pale skin a deep shade of gray, and blood dripped from a gash in the center of her forehead. Anastasia reached forward and helped her to her feet.

"Unbelievable," Tony muttered.

"What?" the woman asked.

Her tone was curt, and something in her eyes had Anastasia's gut wrenching. *Why was she left behind? Had the beasts missed her? Or was it to send a message?*

"You are the only person known to have survived one of these raids. You should consider yourself very lucky, miss," Tony answered.

"Ophelia. My name's Ophelia. I fear I am very dizzy." Her knees buckled, and she fell forward toward Shane, who caught her just before she hit the ground.

"Oops, I'm sorry," she said, embarrassed, and then used his arm to pull herself back up.

"Shane, you stay here with Ophelia. Anastasia, you and I need to keep looking, make sure we don't leave anyone else behind."

SITTING IN THE LIVING AREA OF THE TRAINING COTTAGE, the Fighters, Gregory, and Anastasia waited for Ophelia to emerge after giving her some time to clean herself up. As the only survivor, they had many questions for the woman.

When Ophelia entered the room, their conversation died down slowly as she joined their circle.

"Were you able to see anything from where you were hiding?" Gregory asked.

"No, I'm so sorry. It was pitch-black in my cellar. I could only hear." She closed her eyes, shaking her head.

"The screams were awful." Ophelia covered her face with her hands, and Shane reached over to put his arm around her.

Anastasia watched the easy way he comforted the woman, thankful that someone close to their age had arrived in Terrenia—maybe she would help Shane get over Anastasia. It was an inappropriate thought at a time like this, but she wanted Shane to be happy. Maybe Ophelia could give him the love Anastasia was unable to give.

Her blonde hair was loose around her face, which was badly bruised. When she looked back up at Gregory, her light blue eyes shone with tears.

"It's okay, Ophelia," Gregory assured her. "Just tell us what happened, please, from the top."

"I was sitting inside my cottage when I heard the screaming. I climbed down into my cellar and hid. I'm sorry, but that's all I know. I didn't see anything. By the time I tried to climb out, it was all—" Her voice cracked on a sob, and she hid her face in her hands.

"Where did you get the bruises on your face?" Anastasia asked.

The woman looked up at her, and for an instant, Anastasia could have sworn she'd glared at her.

The steely gaze turned somber so quickly though, that Anastasia could have sworn she'd imagined it. "I was seeing a man recently, and he—" She sighed. "He would sometimes be rough with me." Her voice broke, and the tears returned. "I'm so sorry."

"That's quite all right." Gregory stood and motioned for Tony and Anastasia to step outside with him.

"What is it?" Tony asked as they gathered on the porch.

"I'm not sure." Gregory sighed. "But there's something off here. It could be nothing, but I want you both to keep an eye on her just in case."

"What do you think it is?" Tony didn't sound surprised.

"I'm not sure, just a feeling that I have, and I've lived long enough to know that I shouldn't brush off a feeling this strong."

Anastasia and Tony both nodded. Truth be told, she wasn't entirely trusting of their guest, either.

"We need to figure something out. If the Brutes keep tearing apart villages like this, we won't have anyone left to fight this war." Anastasia turned to face the trees that surrounded her village. Even from where she stood, she heard the laughter of those she had grown to know as her family. "We cannot let those monsters come here."

"We won't," said Tony. "We will protect our people, Anastasia."

"Yes, we will," Gregory agreed.

Their words did little to soothe the icy tendrils of fear that bloomed in her soul. She feared for those she loved and for the life she made here.

Shane and Ophelia walked out, and they turned to face them.

"I'm going to take Ophelia into town and get her some food," Shane said. "Where should we set her up for the night?"

"Talk to Leigh. See if she is up for some company. We can look for a more permanent residence tomorrow."

Leigh, Maximus's mother, had become the village's proverbial mother hen since Maximus disappeared. She was one of the sweetest women Anastasia had ever known, and it was an increasing mystery as to how she had raised such a monster of a son.

Leigh no longer spoke of Maximus, and had written him off as a family member, but Anastasia knew the poor woman was lonely and that her heart was broken. You couldn't miss the pain reflected within her pale blue eyes.

Shane and Ophelia headed toward the village, but just before they disappeared from view, Ophelia turned and smiled slightly at Anastasia.

Anastasia's stomach clenched, and she tilted her head. Something was off, and she would definitely keep an eye on Ophelia.

ANASTASIA

Just before dusk, Anastasia and Kaley walked the perimeter of the fence, looking for any damage to the village's main line of protection. This was their nightly routine, even if the day had been uneventful.

She and Tony had done what they could to make sure there were no Brute camps nearby, but over the last few years, she'd learned you could never be too prepared. Not when it came to the safety of them all.

"Hey, Anastasia! Wait up!"

She smiled when she heard Brady's voice. "Hey, Brady. What are you doing out here this late?" A curfew had been put in place for the villagers, and with darkness approaching, it would begin soon.

"Just came to keep you and my favorite girl here

company." He smiled and reached down to pet Kaley. "I heard you found a survivor in one of the nearby villages, that true?"

"Yes, her name is Ophelia. Tony, Shane, and I found her this morning."

"That's insane."

He had grown up so fast. Now that he'd turned eighteen, Brady had begun training with Tony to become a Fighter—something his mother was not overly fond of.

Brady's father had died in the war with the Brutes. The idea of losing her son as well...

Brady was strong, and already had most of the girls his age following him around. He was honest and kind, and Anastasia was grateful she could call him her friend.

"I wonder why they left her alive."

"Her story is that when the attack began, she climbed down and hid in the cellar below her house."

Brady's eyes narrowed as he watched Anastasia. "Her story? It sounds like you don't believe her."

Anastasia shrugged. "Not necessarily, I just don't think we have all the facts. Why would they leave her alive? How was it that *her* cellar was the only one they didn't thoroughly check? We've found evidence of them ripping doors off and searching cellars before, so why not now?"

"Was it bad?" Her face must've reflected the horror of the day because he shook his head. "Never mind. Maybe they didn't have time." Brady reached to run a hand down Kaley's long back. She relaxed into him and began to purr.

"It's possible, I suppose." Anastasia nudged Brady's shoulder. "You keep petting her like that, and she's never going to be able to help me finish the rounds."

"Why are you walking the fence, anyway?"

"Just checking for any damage."

"We haven't had any attacks. The wall is fine."

"I just have a bad feeling, Brady. Like something is going to happen soon. Just do me a favor and keep an eye out."

"You know I will." He kicked at the dirt, then looked back up at Anastasia. "I asked Emma to go steady with me." He smiled, and for a moment, her heart ached.

Even after all this time, she still missed Dakota.

Brady and Emma had been dancing around one another for months now. Flirting, without actually taking a step toward a relationship. Anastasia had pushed Brady to make things more official, having experienced firsthand how quickly time could run out.

Anastasia still bore the heavy weight of regret, having missed out on anything more than friendship with Dakota.

"That's wonderful! I'm very happy for you two."

He blushed, focusing on the ground beneath their feet as they resumed walking together. "Do you want to talk about it?" he asked cautiously.

"Talk about what?"

"What's bugging you."

Her smile vanished. "I don't know what you're talking about."

"Come on, Anastasia, I know you better than that."

She sighed; he was right. "I was just thinking about my best friend from where I used to live."

"Oh? What was her name?" he asked.

"His name was Dakota."

"Ohhh, gotcha. Were you two in a relationship?"

"Kind of? We'd decided to move forward the night I uh—" she sighed, "The night I came here." Brady was one of the few who knew she had come from another world. Most of the villagers assumed she'd been somewhere in their world rather than a parallel one.

"Man, that's rough."

"Yeah. He was always there for me, pushing me to enjoy life rather than hide from it."

They continued walking the fence, and her mind drifted back to a night that seemed forever ago in his room, when he had told her of his plans for their future.

Anastasia stared out of her window. The sky beyond was dark, but the raindrops against the window offered her comfort. It wasn't often that she felt at peace. Her father had come home angry today, and she sported a split lip as proof of some slight she knew hadn't truly warranted his reaction, but she took solace in the fact that she only had one year until graduation. Three hundred and sixty-five measly days before she could hold her diploma in her hand while she fled from this town and everything she had ever feared.

She held her hand out of the open window and let the raindrops fall on her palm. The sensation of the drops on her skin brought a rare smile to her face. There was something so cleansing about the rain, and since she lived in Seattle, it was good that she enjoyed it. Rain was one of the things she would miss when she left.

She knew that this couldn't be all that the world had to offer her. She had to be meant for something, didn't she? Then again, if her own parents believed she was worthless, then what did that say about her? She had grown up hearing how unwanted she had been, and what a mistake it was that she had even been born. Could it be that they were right?

A light came on in the room of the house next door and jarred her from her thoughts. She waited anxiously for the occupant to come to the window, just as he did every night. A few minutes went by, and then he pulled back the curtains and lifted the glass. Dakota Parker, her best friend for as long as she could remember, was always there for her. He smiled, and even in the dark she could see the worry behind his blue eyes.

She'd always thought he was handsome, but as he got older, the way he smiled at her did funny things to her heart. His dark hair was long enough that it looked messy now, as if he'd run his hands through it repeat-

edly. Something she knew he did when he was frustrated or stressed.

"Hey, Ana."

Smiling, she climbed out to her rooftop.

He held out a hand, and being cautious because of the rain, she took it and made the quick jump through his window.

Dakota wiped a raindrop from her face and handed her a towel to dry her hair.

"Thanks." She smiled at him and immediately regretted it. He noticed the cut on her lip, and he touched it gently.

"Want to stay the night?" he asked. So many nights she had spent in his room, sleeping in the safety of knowing that she wasn't going to be attacked in the middle of the night.

She nodded and lay down. He turned off the light and lay next to her, facing her.

"How are you?" he asked, brushing a strand of hair from her face.

"I'm okay. I was late getting home today."

"You had a meeting with Mrs. Callahan, didn't you?"

"I did, but I forgot to tell my parents."

"Nothing warrants this, Ana." He gently brushed his thumb over her lip.

"How was your day?" she asked, pulling the covers up to her chin.

"Long." He laughed and rolled onto his back. "We

had dinner with dad's partner and his family tonight. Their son is just such a jerk."

Anastasia laughed. She knew how much Dakota disliked Gage Keesler.

"Oh, come on, he's not that bad," she said sarcastically.

"It's good you feel that way since he seems to have a thing for you." Dakota looked at her and winked, and she rolled her eyes.

"Not interested."

"Why not, Ana? I mean, he is a quarterback, after all." The sarcasm dripped from his voice.

"For a losing team." She laughed and propped herself up on her elbows. "Not to mention the fact that he has an ego the size of the entire field."

"He definitely does, but he seems to think he's going places."

"Still not interested."

Dakota laughed, and they sat quietly for a moment.

"Do you ever wonder what it will be like when we graduate?" Anastasia asked, her face growing serious.

"Sure. In fact, I can tell you exactly what's going to happen."

"Oh yeah? What's that?" Intrigued, Anastasia propped herself up on her elbow.

"Well, I've already decided that I'm going to go to med school and you want to be a writer, right? So, the way I see it, we are going to move further into the city and go to school."

"Together?" Her heart leaped into her throat.

"Of course. Where else would we be?"

Could life honestly work out that way? Could she be lucky enough that he might see her as more than a friend?

"We're best friends, Ana. Where you go, I go." He looked away, and she turned back to the window to watch the raindrops race to the windowsill.

Best friends. She smiled. She supposed that was pretty dang lucky in itself.

"Ana?"

"Yeah?" She turned to face him.

"I'll always be here for you, no matter what."

"I know, Dakota." She smiled and leaned forward to kiss him on the cheek. When she pulled away, the look on his face had her heart thumping in her chest.

"Ana, I—" he started, and then took a deep breath. "I'll see you in the morning."

"Goodnight, Dakota."

"Night, Ana."

A SCREAM TORE THROUGH THE NIGHT, RIPPING Anastasia from her memories. She spun toward the sound.

"Brady, get inside and lock the gate!" Anastasia took off at a sprint, and Brady started to follow.

"No way! I'm going to help you!"

"No, Brady! I need you inside, please." She stopped and faced him, her eyes wide and jaw set. She couldn't risk Brady getting hurt again. He hadn't been training long enough to put up much of a fight, and his participation would only be a distraction.

He opened his mouth to argue, but at the last minute changed his mind. "Fine, but call if you need me!"

29

ANASTASIA

Barely inside the tree line, at least a dozen Brutes marched their way toward the fence. A body lay crumpled on the ground behind them. Kaley growled deep in her throat, and Anastasia charged.

She spun, swinging her blade through the air at the one closest. It moved just out of reach, but she recovered from the miss, bringing the blade down on its neck.

The other Brutes howled in rage, and one that was nearest to her stabbed at her with a large knife held in its meaty hand. She dodged, but not fast enough, and the blade caught her arm. She felt the sharp jab of pain as the blade slice through her skin, but refocused her energy on taking the beast down.

Kaley kept a handful of the monsters occupied, so

Anastasia focused on the ones that were currently targeting her. While she still hadn't managed to conjure up anything lethal, she used what Gregory taught her and blasted one of the Brute's with a ball of light.

The magic stunned the targeted beast, and dropped it to its knees. Anastasia drove her sword into the monster's neck.

She spun just in time to slice open the abdomen of one of her assaulters, only to have her braid grabbed by another. Anastasia winced in pain as her neck jerked.

"This her?" it asked, his voice like an avalanche of rocks crashing against each other.

"It's her," the other one answered, its voice just as gravelly as the other's.

She drove her sword into the Brute that approached from the left, and then another grabbed her arm. She spun and kicked the Brute who held her hair and when it released her, brought her blade up and down on its neck.

Other Fighters burst into the clearing, taking the last of the Brutes down.

Anastasia stood for a moment staring down at the dead. Blood began to pool on the ground, and Kaley padded over next to her. Her own blood pounded in her ears, and she did what she could to steady her breathing and allow the adrenaline to dissipate.

"You okay?" Tony asked as he came to stand next to her.

"Yes, I'm fine."

"Your arm." He pulled a handkerchief from his waistband to tie it around her bloody arm.

"Just a flesh wound; I'm fine."

"You're sure?"

She nodded, kneeling beside the body of the woman who'd been in the wrong place at the wrong time. The Brutes had caved her head in with their hands, and she lay in a pool of her own blood.

Anastasia felt a pang to her heart. Jocelyn was a kind woman who helped in the medical cottage prepping salves and healing light injuries. She'd tended to a few of Anastasia's wounds more than once over the years.

"She will be missed," Tony said as he helped Anastasia to her feet.

"You okay?" Shane asked, checking her arm.

"I'm fine, Shane."

"How the hell did they get so close?" he asked. "Where was Dave? He was supposed to be on sentry duty."

"Dead," Tony commented. "Looks like someone snuck up on him."

"Fuck." Shane ran his hand over his forehead.

Anastasia turned, and winced when pain shot up her bicep.

"We need to get you looked at," Shane said, and Anastasia looked at her arm to see the blood leaking down through the temporary bandage.

"Probably not a bad idea," she agreed.

"You sure you're okay?" he asked as they made their way back to the village together.

"I really am." She offered him a smile; Shane really was kind, and she hated herself a little for breaking his heart. "How's Ophelia?"

"She's good. Seems to be settling in all right."

"That's good."

"I guess. There's something off there."

"What do you mean?" Not wanting to sway his opinion with her own, Anastasia acted as though she hadn't been thinking the exact same thing.

"Just the way she's been acting." He ran a hand through his thick hair. "I mean, she supposedly lost everyone she knew, but she doesn't act like it. She uh… came on to me pretty hard last night."

Anastasia raised an eyebrow. "Oh?"

He nodded. "It was uncomfortable."

"I'm sorry?" She laughed. "I don't really know what to say."

Shane smiled down at her. "I like it when you laugh."

Anastasia cleared her throat, and they continued walking. Once inside the village gate, she headed for the medical cottage, leaving Shane to fill the other villagers in on what happened.

AFTER HER ARM WAS PATCHED UP, ANASTASIA MADE HER way home to let Gregory know what happened. He was waiting for her, whiskey in his hand, and they took a seat on the front porch. Not long after, Kaley arrived and lay down at their feet.

"Your arm all right?"

"Yeah. It'll scar, but hey, what's one more, right?" She took a drink and thought back to Jocelyn. She was married and they had a young daughter who would now have to grow up without her mother. "We have to find a way to stop this. For years we've been playing defense; it's time we went on the offense."

Gregory lifted an eyebrow "Football?"

"Dakota loves football." The memory saddened her, and Anastasia cleared her throat. "Or, loved it, I guess."

"I'm sure he still does."

"Thanks," she said with a smile.

Gregory shrugged. "Just a guess."

"I really miss him sometimes," she said sadly.

Gregory placed a hand on her shoulder. "I know you do. I'm so sorry."

Tears in her eyes, Anastasia tried to offer him a smile. "You don't need to apologize. You saved my life and gave me a family."

"You had family with Dakota; Annabelle and I just extended it," he said with a smile.

"And Dad Number Two," Tony said from the darkness.

"Way to be creepy." Anastasia laughed.

"Sorry, I was just making my way back home and heard you talking." He took a seat on the step below them, his back to the rails.

"Want a drink?" Gregory asked, starting to stand.

Tony put his hand up. "Yes, but I'll get it." He got to his feet and made his way inside.

"Anastasia, I want to say that I am so proud of you and the woman you've become."

His words caught her off guard, not because she didn't trust the sincerity, but because they were so *final*. "Thanks."

"If anything were to ever happen to me, I hope you always know that."

"Is everything okay?"

Gregory took a drink from his cup and wrapped an arm around her shoulders. She leaned against him, as if her entire childhood was spent this way, and he pressed a kiss to the top of her head.

"Everything is perfect," he said softly. "Absolutely perfect."

30

ANASTASIA

Anastasia was making her way into town the next morning when Ophelia waved her down. The other woman crossed the distance between them with a grace that reminded Anastasia of a predator about to pounce.

She wore a smile on her petite face, but it was forced.

Great, what the hell does she want?

"Anastasia, it's a lovely morning, isn't it?"

"It is. How are you? Settling in okay?"

Ophelia nodded quickly. "We can talk between us girls, can't we? After all, I think we're the same age, and I'm sure we could be friends." She linked her arm through Anastasia's, and Kaley, who had been padding alongside her, growled low in her throat.

Interesting. Anastasia glanced at the feline. So Kaley didn't trust Ophelia either?

Looking back at Ophelia, she smiled. "Sure, what did you want to talk about?"

"Oh, you know, this and that," she said loudly, then lowered her voice to just above a whisper as she brought her head closer to Anastasia's. "Maybe we could talk about Shane?"

Anastasia sighed. "What about him?"

"Is he single? I mean, I've been dropping hints like crazy but he just keeps shooting me down." She laughed, and the cackling sound grated on Anastasia's nerves. "That, or he's just very obtuse."

"Shane is not obtuse."

"Oh?" She stopped walking and raised an eyebrow. "Are you two a thing, then?"

Anastasia couldn't make out the emotion behind Ophelia's cold eyes, but she could have sworn it was a challenge of some kind. She nearly rolled her eyes; there was no competition.

"No, we're just friends."

"Oh, good," Ophelia responded with a tight smile.

Anastasia didn't miss the way her jaw tightened, or the fact that she appeared to be more disappointed than relieved.

She looped her arm back through Anastasia's and started walking again. Anastasia nearly groaned out loud, but managed to stop herself just in time. She was never one for girl talk, *ever,* and even if she had trusted the other woman, it was doubtful she would have been more interested in what she had to say.

"So, are we safe here? In this big village?"

Anastasia fought the urge to roll her eyes at the weak way she said 'big village'. "Yes, we are perfectly safe."

"Are you sure?"

Anastasia narrowed her eyes. Ophelia's tone had Anastasia questioning the true motives behind the question. *Challenge again?*

"Absolutely, no one is going to hurt my people." Anastasia meant it as a threat, but the smile on the blonde's face said she'd missed the underlying meaning.

"I think it's wonderful how protective you are over everyone here," Ophelia said kindly. "I can't tell you how glad I am that you brought me to your home." She released Anastasia again and turned to face her. "I think we're going to have a great time together." A wide smile stretched over the bottom half of her face, and her eyes darkened.

"Yeah. See you later, Ophelia." Anastasia turned, desperate to get as far away from her as possible. There was just *something* about her that was eating at Anastasia.

Curious, Anastasia made her way to Tony's cabin. The man was already up and sitting on his porch, enjoying a hot cup of tea.

"Morning, Anastasia. You're up early."

She took a seat beside him. "You too."

He shrugged but didn't respond right away. "Want some tea?" he asked after a few moments of silence.

"No, thanks; already had some." *Damn she missed coffee. Every single day.*

"What's bothering you?"

"How can you tell?"

"Just a guess. You look a little more in thought than usual." He grinned, and Anastasia shot him an amused glance.

"I'll have you know I spend a lot of time 'in thought'."

He held up his hands in mock surrender. "I'm sure you do."

"I just—Tony, have you ever had a gut feeling that something was off? That you were missing bigger pieces of a picture?"

He nodded.

"What do you typically do?"

"Look for the pieces. What's bothering you now?"

"Ophelia."

"Ahhh, yes."

"You agree?"

"I've gotten pretty damn good at reading people over the years. I've seen sadness, fear, anger, pain, just about every emotion you can see on those who are grieving. Ophelia does not strike me as a woman who is grief stricken."

"Right!" Anastasia threw up her hands.

"Now, it is possible she's simply blocking the pain."

"But you don't think so."

"I don't know. Did you talk to Shane?"

"Why Shane?"

"She seems to have taken a liking to him—sorry." He added when he saw the tight smile she knew was on her face.

"It's not that."

"I just know you two used to—see each other."

"Four years ago."

"All right, all right. No need to get defensive and kick my ass over it."

Anastasia let out a laugh. Tony was nearly three times her size, there was no way in hell she could kick his ass, even if she wanted to.

"I really don't trust her, Tony." All humor gone from her voice, she spoke softly so no one would overhear their conversation.

"What do you want to do?"

"I want to go back to her village. I want to see for myself where she was hiding."

Tony nodded and got to his feet. "We don't have anything going on today, just some basic training with the new Fighters. Why don't you take Kaley and head out there? See what you can find."

"Really?"

"Yeah, watch your back and take someone with you if you can."

"Okay, thanks Tony." She pulled him in for a hug and stepped down off the porch.

"Be careful, Anastasia."

"I will." She smiled, then began her trek to the stables.

The more she thought about it, the more Ophelia's story just didn't line up. The day they had found her in the wreckage of her house, she told them she'd been hiding in a cellar, that she hadn't come across the Brutes, and that they had just passed by her cellar without looking in. But Ophelia had been bleeding pretty badly and was covered in cuts and bruises.

Originally, Anastasia brushed it off, believing Ophelia must have injured herself while climbing out through the wreckage, but now she wondered if they missed something. They'd been pretty distracted with the idea of a survivor, so it was possible that important details had been overlooked.

"Hey, wait up!"

Anastasia turned to see Shane headed toward her. She stopped and waited for him to catch up.

"Tony said you were heading back to Ophelia's village. Want some company?"

Damn you, Tony. I bet you're just laughing your ass off right now. "Sure." They made their way into the stable and saddled two horses.

After walking them out through the front gate, Anastasia and Shane climbed on and made their way into the tree line.

"So what do you think we're going to find?" he asked.

"Honestly, I have no clue. Either something that proves her story, or something that condemns her." She pushed her horse into a gallop, with Kaley running beside her through the trees and Shane following closely behind on the dirt path.

The air outside was cold this morning, and the chill had her using her free hand to wrap the cloak more tightly around her body. The horse's breaths were coming out in puffs of air as they moved, and the clouds overhead were doing nothing to allay her unease. Something was off.

Anastasia stopped, holding up her hand for Shane to do the same. By her best guess, they were within a one mile radius of Ophelia's village.

"What is it?" he whispered.

"Not sure." She climbed off her horse, and he followed. "I think we need to go the rest of the way on foot."

They led the horses to a stream nearby and left them to graze on the green grass.

The village looked the same as it had the day they'd discovered the wreckage. Anastasia tried her best not to focus too intently on the graves they'd dug, but instead made her way over to where she'd discovered Ophelia.

"I'll do a quick perimeter check," Shane informed her, and Anastasia nodded curtly.

Anastasia kicked a board away that would have at one point been part of the house the woman claimed to live in. When she moved it, she saw the stained fabric remnants of a small teddy bear. Could have belonged to one of the village children, but after further investigation, Anastasia found a doll and a small wooden horse.

A child lived here, but Ophelia made no mention of one.

"We're in the clear," Shane said as he moved to stand beside her.

Kaley followed, pacing the ground around them anxiously as if she sensed something no one else could.

Anastasia pulled the heavy wooden door open and the smell of death wafted up from beneath the house, smacking her in the face with a stench that made her body curl in on itself and sent a flood of saliva into her mouth. She choked, throwing her arm over her mouth to cough into her sleeve.

Ophelia lied to us.

Shane sputtered and stepped back, choking on the smell. "Fuck, man." He groaned and stepped further away.

"Keep watch." Anastasia told him, then covered her nose and mouth with a handkerchief she pulled from her pocket. Trepidation sent a chill up her spine as she descended the stairs. Daylight poured through the cracks in the wooden ceiling, giving her just enough illumination to see her surroundings.

Another lie. Ophelia had said it was pitch black in here.

Three decaying bodies lay sprawled on the ground. Anastasia noticed a tiny frame hidden beneath the woman. Her heart broke for the mother who had been trying to protect her child. Anger filled her chest, and her body began to shake. *What kind of monster did this?* There was no damage from entry, and that simple fact made her think perhaps it wasn't a monster at all, at least not the kind she was used to dealing with.

Was a human responsible for this carnage? A wave of nausea passed over her, and Anastasia swallowed hard.

Shane and Kaley jumped down into the cellar, and before Anastasia could speak, Shane put his finger up to his mouth.

She partially climbed the ladder and opened the door slightly to look outside. Three-dozen Brutes marched into the village behind—

She gasped, covering her mouth quickly.

Maximus led the monsters. He had aged, and his face was harder than before, but Anastasia would have recognized him anywhere.

"We wait here," he bellowed. "Ophelia will make her move when the sun goes down, and then we will attack." He smiled, standing taller. "Remember what the Master said. If you find the girl, she is to be taken alive. For now, at least."

Anastasia's hand moved to curl on the hilt of her sword. He would not walk away from her again. She began to push the cellar door further open, but Shane pulled her back.

She slammed against his chest, and he pulled her further into the cellar.

"You can't take on three dozen of them and walk away, Anastasia," he whispered. "Even with Kaley and I by your side, we can't do it. We have to wait, and when they head for the village, we follow."

She turned her eyes up to his and saw the same anger she was feeling reflected on his face. "We won't make it back in time, Shane."

"We won't make it back at all if we try to fight them now."

He was right, and while she may have been willing to risk her own life, she wasn't willing to risk his or Kaley's.

"Fine. We wait." But the fear that gripped her heart suffocated her more than the stench of the dead that surrounded them.

31

ANASTASIA

After what felt like an eternity, the Brutes finally marched out, and Anastasia, Shane, and Kaley climbed out of the cellar.

"Go, girl." She patted Kaley, and the feline took off into the darkness ahead of them.

"Ready?" she asked.

He spun the blade in a move that showed his advanced skill and smiled menacingly. "Let's go get these bastards."

Anastasia nodded, and they headed into the trees. They crept through the dark, trying to make it around the marching Brutes so they could reach their horses and get to the village ahead of the army. Their numbers had doubled, and they weren't even trying to be subtle.

The fear blooming in her chest nearly burst. Why

weren't they worried about being heard? Did they already have the village surrounded?

Shane crept alongside her with the same stealth she did. Kaley had yet to return to them, so Anastasia knew she must have gotten stuck behind a grouping as well.

She watched as the numbers in front of her shrunk to half a dozen as the others moved deeper into the woods to join their brothers. Anastasia recognized the tactic from her studies with Gregory. These were the lookouts.

They were nearing the stream where they'd left the horses, and she looked over at Shane, holding a finger to her lips. She gestured to the three that were on the left, and motioned for him to take the ones on the right.

After a curt nod, Anastasia lunged for them and, with her knives, managed to take down two before the others had noticed. Blue blood dripped down her arms and was splattered on her face, but she paid it no notice. Kaley showed up just as Shane dropped the last of his group.

Their horses waited, despite their nerves. They had pawed at the ground with their hooves, leaving large divots in the dirt.

"Easy, boy," she said gently, climbing onto the back of Revenue, the Appaloosa she favored.

"We need to get back as quickly as possible," Shane commented. "Which means we need to avoid any more fights."

"Agreed. They seem to be headed for the north gate;

if we head for the south entrance, we might be able to sneak around and make it in time."

"Let's go." Shane pushed his horse into a run, and they raced through the trees toward home.

When they reached the fence line, Anastasia's jaw dropped.

"Oh no, God, please no," she whispered as she took in the scene before her.

Fires had sprung up everywhere in the quiet village, and the screams of her people filled the air as Brutes tore through her home. She didn't think any further, just jumped off her horse, launched through the gate, and threw herself into the attack.

The first Brute came at her like a bullet, and she dodged, barely getting out of the way in time.

"I had hoped to see you," it growled, aiming its weapon at her. Before he could fire a shot, a blade protruded from its chest and Anastasia looked up to see the familiar face of Andrew, one of the Fighters.

He offered her a curt nod and launched back into battle.

"Anastasia, look out!"

Thanks to Shane's warning, Anastasia dodged a blade that had been meant for her chest. She spun around and shoved her own sword into the monster's abdomen, then decapitated it with one swift move.

She wasn't sure how long she fought. Her muscles screamed in protest with each new attack, but she

pushed on. These monsters were in her home, and she
was going to make them pay for it.

Anastasia sliced and jumped, praying that with each
Brute she dispatched she would get one step closer to
Maximus. She was going to put him down like she
should've done all those years ago.

She spotted him leaving his mother's cottage,
wiping blood from his blade. Anastasia growled and ran
for him, dodging Fighters as they sliced at the Brutes.
She jumped over fallen bodies with nothing but
Maximus's face in her mind. Ophelia's laugh drew her
attention down a street to her left and Anastasia turned
to follow her. With every footstep, she grew closer to
Anastasia's home.

Family was more important than revenge, and
Gregory was all the family she had left.

Revenge would wait.

She crept slowly behind Ophelia, keeping to the
shadows. Her heart pounded, and blood drummed
loudly in her ears, but she maintained her breathing as
she'd been taught to do during her Fighter training.

Ophelia paused in front of Gregory and Anastasia's
home, looking up at the small structure for a moment.
As she reached for the doorknob, Anastasia stepped out
from the shadows, gripping her blades. She crouched,
ready to pounce—

A massive hand circled her throat, cutting off her air
as her entire body lifted off the ground. She dropped her
blades as she kicked her feet and swung her arms but

connected with nothing. She clawed at the hand around her neck, desperate for air as her lungs burned in desperation, but the beast didn't loosen his grip, and before long, white spots started to dance before Anastasia's eyes. Soon, darkness claimed the edges of her vision, closing in until only a small circle of vision remained, and in that circle, she watched in horror as Ophelia stepped inside her home.

As her eyes closed, she—

"Release her!" Shane yelled.

Anastasia hit the hard ground with a thud, gasping for air and blinking as her vision cleared. Shane battled the Brute who'd captured Anastasia, swinging his sword with artful precision as though it were an extension of his own body.

She coughed, fighting to fill her lungs with oxygen. How long had she been delayed? She had to get to Gregory. She tried to stand, but wobbled, leaning against the wall for support and fighting to get her balance and her bearings back so she could fight alongside her father.

GREGORY

Gregory stepped out of his bedroom, ready to join the fray, then stopped dead in his tracks as Ophelia shut the front door of his house.

He glanced at the dagger in her hand, then met her gaze. "It seems we were right to distrust you."

She shrugged. "Not all of you felt that way." She wiped her dagger across her thigh, smearing crimson blood across her pants. "Man, it feels good to be out of that stupid dress. Do you have any idea how hard it is to take down a grown man—or rather *three*—in a skirt?"

"What do you want?"

"Your daughter." She grinned. "She and I have some things to discuss."

"Well, as you can see, Anastasia isn't here." He kept

his voice steady, but allowed the power inside his veins to grow. She would not get her hands on Anastasia.

"I guess we'll have to occupy ourselves then, won't we?"

"I guess so." He lifted his palms and conjured the light magic that, until tonight, had only been used to entertain. He formed a glowing orb in his palm and heaved it at the intruder.

Ophelia dodged the blast, laughing. "Yes! I love a good fight. Bring it on, old man."

Gregory threw another ball of light at her, and she lunged toward him, knocking him backwards. His head hit the table, stunning him briefly.

Ophelia jumped on top of him and drove the blade down into his abdomen. Sharp pain shot through his body, and he cried out. In his entire life, he never regretted not learning to conjure lethal magic —until now.

"You know, he told me not to kill you," she whispered as she stared down at him. "Told me that you would come around eventually." She laughed and rose to her feet. "But, if you knew me at all, you'd understand that I'd rather ask for forgiveness than permission."

Gregory reached for his power, but found none, his body using all of its energy to keep him alive.

The front door opened and Anastasia burst in. His eyes landed on hers, and Gregory caught the first glimpse of the fire in her eyes. She'd become the powerful woman she was destined to be, and for the first time, he truly believed the prophecy.

Anastasia, his very own daughter, would defeat his brother.

"Took you long enough." Ophelia glanced toward Anastasia as she cleaned the blood from beneath her fingernails with the blade she'd just driven through his gut.

"You bitch," Anastasia snarled. Gregory's eyes widened as Anastasia's skin began to glow, illuminated by the power running through her veins.

"Stay focused, Anastasia." He groaned and tried to sit up. *Please don't lose yourself now.*

"Shhh, this is our conversation," Ophelia scolded him. "What is it with rude people? Now, where were we? Oh, yes, there really is no need for name calling, is there?"

"Why?" Anastasia demanded. "Why would you do this?"

"Why not?"

"Those people in your village, why hurt them?"

"Why not?" she repeated. "They were weak, useless. Well, I suppose not *useless* since their deaths did gain your trust."

"I never trusted you," Anastasia growled.

"But you brought me here, didn't you?" Ophelia grinned.

"Those people in the cellar, who were they?"

Ophelia rolled her eyes. "My birth family. They

were so weak, pleading for their lives as if they meant anything to me."

"Why would you kill your own family?"

"Just because someone is blood, doesn't make them family. When the Brutes raided our village when I was a child, did my family come looking for me? No, they left me out in the streets to fend for myself while they ran into the woods. The Brutes took me with the others they captured and forced me into a cage." Ophelia growled. "Luckily, Master took a liking to me, and before long, he raised me as if I were his own flesh and blood. He made me all that I am today."

"A psychopath? Maybe he shouldn't be winning any Father of the Year awards."

"You know, you're pretty cocky for someone who's about to die."

"I heard Maximus; you aren't supposed to kill me."

"I wasn't really supposed to kill him either." She gestured to Gregory. "But we see how well that turned out, don't we?"

"Anastasia," he murmured.

Her eyes shot to him, wide and dilated. In them he saw barely leashed control. He shook his head, urging her to not use her power.

"I'm tired of talking to you." Anastasia lunged, her dagger aimed for Ophelia's chest.

Ophelia dodged the attack, bouncing on the balls of her feet. "Oh! Kitty has claws!" She laughed and stabbed at Anastasia. When she missed, she tried again, but her body whipped into the air and slammed against the wall.

When Ophelia recovered from the hit, her eyes widened.

Gregory followed her attention, gasping when his gaze landed on his daughter.

Anastasia glowed with power. Light illuminated the room, and she held her palm up to conjure a ball of light. Instead of a peaceful orb of white light, like the ones he'd taught her to create, a flame danced in her palm.

"No," he whispered. He couldn't lose her, not now.

"What are you?" Ophelia whispered.

"More powerful than your Master could ever comprehend." Anastasia whipped the flame at Ophelia, and it burned a hole through the girl's chest. She crumpled to the ground.

"Come back, Anastasia," Gregory whispered as she moved toward him. Her eyes glowed orange, her body alive with power unlike any he'd ever seen before, even in Vincent. For a moment, he was afraid of what she might become. How was he supposed to keep her safe when he knew his own life was coming to an end?

"Anastasia, think of Dakota," he urged.

Her eyes slowly faded back to their normal blue, and she fell to his side.

"There you are." He slumped against the floor.

"Dad, I'm so sorry. I should have been here."

"It's not your fault, Anastasia." Blood pooled on the

floor, and she grabbed a small blanket to put pressure on the wound in his side.

"Hold this." She stood and ran into his room, returning with the vials of healing potions Annabelle had made all those years ago. She began opening the vials and pouring them onto his wound.

"I'm afraid I've lost too much blood, Anastasia." Gregory gripped her wrist, and she set the vial down.

"No, there has to be something I can do!" she yelled, tears streaming down her face.

"I've lost too much blood. Please stop, my dear." He gently touched her cheek.

"There has to be something I can do," Anastasia repeated, her voice cracking under the weight of defeat.

"I am so proud of you, Anastasia, you must know that. You are so much more than I could have ever imagined."

"Please don't leave me," she cried, resting her face on his chest.

"I will never leave you, Anastasia. I will always be here with you—" His breath caught, and he stared up at her as the last of his life faded away. "I. Love. You."

ANASTASIA

The pale lavender light of dawn began pouring in through the windows, and she lifted her head. Her eyes were swollen from crying, and her body ached from last night's fight. The heavy emptiness of loss settled into the gaping hole where her heart once dwelled.

She gently laid Gregory back and moved to kneel beside Ophelia's body, then grabbed her by the feet and dragged her from the house, determined to not have the murderous traitor anywhere near Gregory, alive or dead.

Leaving Ophelia's body on the path outside of the house, Anastasia returned to gather the rest of Annabelle's healing potions and her knives.

With one last look at her father's dead body, Anastasia roared in anguish, and Kaley raced to her side, pressing her body against Anastasia's.

When her anger dissipated to a low hum, she and Kaley stepped from the house, gathered Ophelia's body, and walked through the trees and down the dirt path toward the center of the village.

They rounded the corner of her street, and—

Tony skidded to a stop in front of them. "Anastasia! Thank God! I was just coming to—" He searched her gaze, his eyes wide, then his attention dropped to the body at her feet. "What happened?"

"She killed Gregory," Anastasia responded tightly.

Tony's face contorted in agony. "No." He shook his head. "How did everything go so wrong?" he screamed. "How did we not see this coming? They were on us so fast we didn't even have time to shut the gate!"

"I should have been here, Tony. I'm so sorry." A lump formed in her throat.

"They would have attacked whether you'd been here or not."

"But I would have been able to help."

"From what I remember, you did help. I saw you come through that gate."

"I should have used my magic."

"You did everything you could, Anastasia."

Gregory had never taught her to use anything lethal. *Why hadn't he trained her to use that type of power?* She didn't know until faced with Ophelia that she even *could*. But still, shouldn't she have at least tried?

"I should have tried," she said, voicing her thoughts as Tony tossed Ophelia's limp body over his shoulder.

"Had you been here, you might have been caught just as off guard as the rest of us were. That little prick Maximus came in first, and we were so distracted by his return that no one was watching the gate. He killed his own mother, Anastasia."

She gasped, and then closed her mouth, her jaw clenched. "Is he dead?"

"No, the coward bailed once the fight turned to our advantage."

"I'm going to kill him," Anastasia growled.

"I think that's a damn fine plan."

They continued walking, and Tony flung Ophelia's body into a pile of dead Brutes on a wooden cart.

Good, take her away and let her ass burn just like them.

"I'm sorry about your father, Anastasia. He was a great man and a wonderful friend. He loved you very much." His eyes filled with tears, and he pulled her in for a hug.

She returned it, but stepped away after a few moments. "I'm not going to think about it now. There will be a time to grieve when all this is over, but the war needs to end." She turned to study the carnage before her. At least half the main buildings had been destroyed and still smoldered from the fires.

More than three-dozen bodies lay covered in blankets near the fire pit.

Her one mistake had led to the deaths of over thirty-six of her friends. People she thought of as family.

She searched frantically for Brady, and was relieved to see him sitting up at the base of one of the few structures that hadn't burned. In his arms, he cradled Emma's limp body.

Anastasia whimpered as pain gripped her chest, then pressed her fingers to her lips and straightened her shoulders. Brady needed strength right now, no matter how Anastasia's own heart suffered.

She walked over to him. "Brady?"

"They killed her," he whispered without looking up. He brushed a strand of hair from Emma's face. "She wasn't even fighting. She was just trying to get away and they chased her down. I should have been there, but I just didn't make it in time." He pulled her to his chest, and Anastasia placed her hand on his shoulder, squeezed gently, then left him alone to grieve.

Selena hugged Sarah against her body and stared out at the carnage. Anastasia was relieved to see that both Brady's mother and sister were alive.

"You good?" Shane asked as he approached. She shook her head. He wrapped his arm around her shoulders, and she leaned into his body, grateful for the comfort.

"Ophelia killed my father."

"Shit, Anastasia, I'm so sorry."

She swallowed the hard lump in her throat, and it burned with the need to weep. *There is no time for grieving*. She repeated what she'd told Tony, took a deep breath, and straightened.

"Are you okay?" she asked. A large gash along Shane's jaw had been hastily taped up.

"I'll survive. Maximus caught me off guard."

"I'm glad you're alive."

"I'm glad you're alive." He repeated.

She nodded and looked back out over the carnage the monsters had left in their wake.

Her father had taught her to not fight with anger in her heart. He believed doing so made the Fighter weak.

But strength rose inside Anastasia as she allowed the rage to settle into her soul. It filled each crevice, each tiny crack, replacing the pain of loss—Dakota, Annabelle, and now, Gregory—with a burning hot need for revenge.

Men, women, and children who had done nothing lay dead on the ground, all because of a man who believed he deserved to rule, simply because he had more power than others. A man who believed he was better than them.

Anastasia wanted—needed—to feel his blood run down her hands as she shoved her sword into his heart. Ophelia was the first person she had ever killed, and Anastasia felt no guilt over that death. The bitch had gotten what was coming to her. It was time she delivered the same fate to the man who kidnapped her and sent her to live a world away from her parents, with monsters that tortured her for seventeen horrific years.

Vincent was the reason she had suffered. He was the reason she had only known her real mother for a few measly months. And he was the reason she was utterly and completely alone now.

Gregory had been trying to keep the war from starting; Anastasia recognized that fact even years ago when he started training her.

But the way she saw it, this war began the day Vincent ripped her from the loving family she deserved.

And it was well past time to end it. No more sitting around. No more waiting for his armies to attack. Being on the defensive had gotten them nowhere.

Brady joined her and Shane, standing tall at her side. She turned to him and searched his gaze, finding only resolve. He would follow her into battle if she asked him to.

"Gregory?" he asked.

She shook her head.

"I'm sorry, Anastasia."

"I'm sorry about Emma."

Tony joined them, standing beside Shane.

"What is the plan?" he asked.

"We are going to end them. All of them."

She didn't have to look at the men by her side to know they agreed.

Brady's young heart had suffered the devastating loss of someone he loved, and Tony and Shane had just lost too many of their people to count, along with

Tony's best friend in the world. They were just as hungry for revenge as she was.

It was time to stop waiting around for Vincent's army of Brutes to attack.

Anastasia had a prophecy to fulfill, and she was more than ready for the task.

ANASTASIA STARED OUT AT THE FACES OF THE survivors. It had been a long twenty-four hours, but together, the villagers had begun picking up the pieces of their shattered village.

Victims had been buried, the Brutes bodies had been burned, and as she looked from person to person, Anastasia swelled with pride. Though defeat was evident in the eyes of those that gazed back at her, something else burned just below the surface.

Fire.

"We all saw what happened last night, what's going to continue happening unless we put a stop to it," Tony began, speaking loudly to be heard.

"What do you think we've been trying to do all these years?" one of the Fighters responded.

"Not enough," Tony shot back.

Anastasia put her hand on his arm. Tensions were high; infighting wasn't going to help.

She rose to her feet. "We've been doing our best to play catch up, to recover after each attack. But, other than trying to bring the other villages to us, what have we really done?"

Murmurs began, but no one spoke up.

"We have allowed these beasts to run rampant in our world long enough," she shouted. "It's time we take the fight to them! It's time we flush them out of whatever cave they're hiding in!"

Some people cheered, but still, many whispered amongst themselves.

"We've spent years trying to find them," a man in the crowd yelled. "There are dozens of those caves. It's impossible to know which ones to check."

"We'll *make* it possible," Anastasia roared. "Even if we have to scour each and every one of those dark holes. I know you're scared. I know you're tired. But these bastards came in here and *slaughtered* our family, our friends. How can you just give up after that? How can we just let them all die in vain?"

"What will you have us do?" a woman shouted. "Gregory wanted to—"

"My father is dead," Anastasia stated. "Ophelia killed him in cold blood."

More murmurs and gasps rose amongst the crowd.

Tony stepped forward again. "We have a plan, but we need a handful of Fighters to go with us. We will start our counter attack by scouting, trying to track down these beasts."

"What of the rest of us?" a woman asked. "You expect us to just send our husbands back into battle?

Send them out into what will probably be the death of them?"

People nodded agreement, and Anastasia ground her teeth together.

"How can you not?" A woman Anastasia didn't know well, stood, speaking to the crowd. "I lost my husband two years ago to a Brute, and now my son—" Her voice cracked, and she cleared her throat. "We have all lost someone." The woman's eyes glistened with unshed tears. Her jaw quivered. "Would you truly allow those lives to be lost in vain? They fought with the very last breath in their bodies; do you truly believe it was so we could lie down and give up?" She spun in a slow circle to look at everyone as she spoke. "Even if it means I have to pick up a damn sword and fight alongside her, I will do something. It's about time someone does." She continued to look around. "I mean no disrespect—I loved Gregory as a brother—but he took no preventative action toward those monsters. He wanted to protect his daughter." She glanced at Anastasia. "Which I can't blame him for. But what are we supposed to do now? We all know of the prophecy, of the darkness that comes for us. Well, I say it's already here."

"If I have to go alone," Anastasia began, raising her voice as all heads turned back toward her, "I will. Because the very thought of these bastards breathing is nearly too much to bear. I can't force you to go, but I'm begging you to come." She paused, waiting, hoping.

"I will go." Andrew stood, looking Anastasia in the eyes. He gripped his wife's hand, and she looked up with tears in her eyes as she stood beside her husband.

"I will go," she said, her voice cracking on emotion.

"I will as well," another man said.

"Me too."

Within moments, twelve men and women stood beside Anastasia. They were ready to fight, to take back their homes and lives.

They had a plan now, and this was their first step to victory.

34

ANASTASIA

The next morning, Anastasia, Tony, Shane, and twelve other Fighters set out to search for any sign of the Brute army. Horses saddled and bags packed, she hoped that they would find where Vincent and the Brutes were hiding.

Brady had stayed behind, with quite a bit of protest, to help get things back in order. Brady's mother, Selena, stepped into Gregory's place as town leader, and would not only keep the peace in Anastasia's absence, but would oversee the continued efforts to rebuild the village after such a brutal attack.

Anastasia's biggest fear was not that she would possibly lead these men and women to their deaths, but that when they returned, the town would no longer stand. She swallowed hard. *This is what needs to be done.*

If they didn't stop the Brutes at the source, there would be no home to come back to anyway.

"Where should we look first?" she asked Tony, who rode beside her.

He pointed straight ahead to the mountain range. "The last time we managed to trail Brutes, they led us to some caves leading into the mountains." He sighed. "The caverns are treacherous, though, and we lost four good men inside."

"Maybe we'll get lucky this time."

He smiled, but the motion didn't reach his eyes. "I certainly hope so. How are you holding up?"

"I'm all right; I just keep trying to stay focused on the task at hand. We need to do this. Vincent has to be hiding up there somewhere… I know it."

"I will say, that if anyone was ever prophesized to kick some serious ass, it's you, Anastasia."

She smiled. "Thanks, Tony."

WHEN THEY FINALLY STOPPED FOR THE NIGHT, DUSK cloaked the valley in a soft amber glow. Tony dismounted and looked out at the weary Fighters. "Feed and water your horses, then make camp. We'll continue at first light."

They did as he asked, gathering water from the

nearby stream. Anastasia watered her horse and unpacked some grain from her saddlebag before filling her own canteen.

She stared up at the slowly darkening sky and sent up a silent prayer that everything would go as planned, that she would somehow have the strength to defeat the darkness and bring light back to Terrenia.

"You okay?" Kalisa, one of the female Fighters Anastasia met briefly during her training, moved to stand beside her. Her blonde hair had been tied up into a tight bun, and brown eyes looked warmly at Anastasia. They had spoken a few times over the years, but to Anastasia, it had seemed that Kalisa had always had an eye for Shane. Which meant that when they started dating, Kalisa kept her distance, and it had stayed that way even after they split.

Anastasia nodded. "Just praying we'll catch a break and end this war."

"You know, it's strange. I was young when we first heard of the Brutes, and it seems like ever since then, we've been fighting to keep them at bay and protect our people. I wonder what it will be like to not have to worry about this threat anymore."

"I hope we'll find out soon." Anastasia smiled.

"I'm sorry about your father. I didn't know him well, but I did know he was a good man."

"Thanks, he was."

"I lost my parents a long time ago. They were both Fighters," she explained. "I can tell you that, while the pain never disappears, it does become easier to live with. Especially when you get the chance to kick some serious Brute ass." She nudged Anastasia with her shoulder and smiled.

"I am definitely looking forward to that."

"I'm going to finish grabbing some firewood before Tony demotes me," she said with a laugh. "Talk soon?"

"Definitely." Anastasia continued staring up at the sky for a moment longer, then headed back to help get the camp set up.

As THE GROUP GATHERED AROUND THE FIRE THAT evening, Andrew recalled stories from his early days in the war against the Brutes. Tony laughed beside him, interjecting whenever he felt the need to correct something Andrew remembered incorrectly.

All in all, the Fighters seemed to be in good spirits, which gave Anastasia a sense of peace. The battle was far from over, but hope was the most important thing in a war, and her people had it.

"Anastasia, tell us a story," Kalisa urged, pulling Anastasia from her thoughts.

"About?"

"Anything. It can even be made up. Since this is your first outing as a Fighter, it's tradition."

Anastasia looked to Tony for confirmation, and he smiled.

"Well then, can't mess up tradition, can I?" Anastasia straightened. "You all know I grew up somewhere pretty far away, but what you probably don't know, is that I was in a different world all together."

The flames danced on the faces of her comrades, and they leaned closer to listen intently.

"In my world, Seattle, we have running water, electricity, and cars that drive to take us places."

"We have running water here, too." One of the Fighters gestured to the stream beside them, and Anastasia stifled a laugh.

"Ours was a bit different. You could turn on a faucet and water would come out at whatever temperature you wanted it to."

"You didn't have to heat it up?" the man Anastasia knew as Boris asked curiously.

She shook her head. "You can turn it hot or cold."

"What's electricity?" Andrew asked.

"Lights. But instead of fire, you just flip a switch up and down to turn the light on or off."

"Fascinating," Kalisa added.

"It was." Anastasia smiled. "I grew up—"

Movement near the creek caught her eye.

A soft rustling sound drew Tony and the other Fighters to their feet. They crept toward the trees slowly, and just before they reached the edge of the clearing, a group of Brutes rushed them.

"Hold your positions!" Tony instructed, so no

Fighter would get flanked. They were outnumbered by only a few, and each Fighter flew into action.

Anastasia dodged a blade that sailed by her head, and struck out with her sword, slicing the attacking beast from neck to navel. She reached down inside herself for her power and let the rage build as she fought against another attacking Brute.

This one was more strategic than the last, and dodged her blade or blocked it with his sword each time she swung. Once she was sure she had the magic within her grasp, Anastasia conjured a ball of flame in her palm, just as she had in the cabin with Gregory and Ophelia.

Stunned, the beast stared at the magic a moment too long, and she heaved it at him, satisfied when it burrowed in his chest. Since platinum-coated blades were the only way to kill Brutes, she finished him off with her sword and moved on to the next.

The Brute numbers had thinned, and she could all but taste the victory, but as she looked around, she noticed a body crumpled in the center.

Kalisa. Anger and grief had Anastasia's magic calling to her. A silent *let me out* humming in her veins much as it had when she'd killed Ophelia.

"Anastasia!" Tony called, breaking her concentration.

She spun and ducked just in time to miss one of the beast's fists. She sliced her blade through the Brute's torso, then paused, taking in the battles around her as she caught her breath. The last two beasts were cut down, and Anastasia knelt next to Kalisa's broken body, sadness weighing her limbs.

"She was a magnificent Fighter," Andrew said as the Fighters circled the two women. Anastasia looked at Shane, who was staring down at the woman's body. Unshed tears shined his eyes, and his jaw was hard.

"She shouldn't have died tonight," Tony added.

"No, she shouldn't have," Anastasia said, placing a hand over Kalisa's open eyes. "How did they get so close?"

Boris approached from the east, running at full speed. "The Brutes must've seen Phillip and Dacklin's fire. They're dead."

"No!" Tony roared. "They were supposed to be keeping watch! There should have been no fire!" He clenched his fists, then turned to take charge of the others. "Gather the bodies. We will bury them and move on. We are no longer safe here."

Anastasia stared down at Kalisa, her eyes welling with tears as grief wrapped a cold, spindly hand around her heart. How had tonight gone so wrong, so quickly? When would her people catch a break?

35

SEATTLE

DAKOTA

Another murder.

Dakota distanced himself from the blood-soaked asphalt and broken body that made up the gruesome scene in the alley before him. He didn't need anyone to tell him who his latest victim was.

Edgar Jackson had been first in line for state senate. He had already shown quite an increase in polls and was practically uncontested. Or had been, anyway. This poor bastard had been found by a passerby who—as he says it—had stepped into the alley to make a call. Dakota knew full and well the jackass was high, but he had no interest in busting him.

Shit, after seeing the state of this victim, he imagined the guy went home and smoked a whole lot more than just one joint.

Jackson's head had been bashed in, but with what, they didn't yet know. No weapons remained at the scene. The medical examiner would need to do a full autopsy before presenting his report, but Dakota already knew what the report would read. If it was anything like the other murders plaguing the city for the past few months, the coroner would find finger marks on the skull, as if someone had crushed the man's head with their bare hands.

And, like the other unsolved homicides before it, there would be no evidence, and the case would go into the steadily growing pile of cases that had no answer in sight.

There appeared to be no pattern to the victims and, so far, the only connections he'd drawn were that three —now four—of them had been high-ranking city or state officials. The other homicides appeared to be random, as if the killer wanted to throw the force off their trail. It wasn't until this last death that Dakota had begun putting pieces together.

This recent crime made thirty-five deaths in the last sixty days. People were panicked, and the media was having a field day with it.

"This is just insane." Harry stood next to him, staring down at the body.

Dakota glanced at his partner. Stress had aged the man twenty years in the last month. His black hair had already shown signs of grey, but the bags beneath his eyes were new.

Dakota could relate. He'd only made Detective last year, and already was racking up a large list of unsolved cases. *Fuck.* He rubbed his hands over his face. His partner had about seven years of experience on him, and even he was stumped.

It was cloudy, making it seem much later in the afternoon than it was. He checked his watch; *three-forty-five* in the afternoon meant he had just enough time to go check out his first lead.

"I'm going to head downtown." He turned and headed for his car. "I'll meet you at the station."

"Yeah." Harry nodded absently. The deaths were taking a more considerable toll on the senior detective than he wanted to admit.

Dakota climbed into his car and headed downtown. Buildings passed by his window, but he paid no notice. His mind was already running through possible scenarios for this afternoon's interaction.

How was the asshole going to take being questioned? Dakota hoped like hell he put up a fight. He could already imagine ramming his fist into the prick's arrogant face.

There was only one man who stood to gain anything from these recently linked deaths, and Dakota had waited for years for a reason to bring the bastard down. On the fast track for state senate, his opponents were dropping like flies, one by one.

Damn, it was going to feel good cuffing Mitch Carter.

A leggy blonde led Dakota into Mitch Carter's office.

The asshole stood, extending his hand. "Ah, Dakota. It's nice of you to drop by."

"This isn't a social call, Carter."

"Well then." Mitch laughed and lowered his hand. "What can I help you with, *Detective*?"

"Where were you last night between the hours of midnight and four a.m.?"

"What exactly am I being accused of?"

"Nothing." *Yet*. "Just answer the question, please."

"Ask my assistant; we were working all night." The lilt of Mitch's voice made Dakota's stomach turn. *Working, my ass*.

Mitch had a well-known reputation for "working" late with his assistants—which he went through like most men went through a six pack of cheap beer.

Dakota narrowed his eyes. "I think I will." He turned to leave the office—

"Your father would be proud of you, Dakota, following in his footsteps. Don't follow too closely, though. I would hate for anything to happen to you."

Dakota's blood boiled as he turned around. The son of a bitch had balls, that was for sure. "You will never mention my father again, Carter."

"I'm only concerned for your safety, Dakota. Wouldn't want your mother to have to face the evils of the world without her perfect son to watch over her," he sneered.

Dakota fought for control over his anger. He balled his hands into fists at his sides, and he took a deep breath. *Not worth it, Parker.*

"I still don't see what Anastasia saw in you. Seems she truly was an idiot."

Dakota crossed the floor to Mitch in two long strides. Mitch's eyes widened as Dakota got so close to him their noses nearly touched. He kept his hands clenched at his sides to keep himself from grabbing the asshole by the throat and doing what he'd wished he'd done ten years ago.

"You better watch what you fucking say to me. My parents *and* Anastasia are off limits." He turned to storm out of the office. "Don't fucking leave town," he called over his shoulder, then slammed the door behind him.

"Did you get everything you needed, Detective?" Carter's assistant asked when Dakota stepped back into the reception area.

"No, actually, I have a couple questions for you."

"Oh?" She stood and leaned over the counter, showing off an impressive amount of cleavage. Dakota couldn't have cared less. At one point, during the years he tried to forget Ana, his standards may have been nonexistent, but it would be a cold day in hell before he touched anything Mitch had pawed. *Fucking bastard.*

"I needed to know where your boss was last night, between the hours of midnight and four a.m."

She grinned, showing off perfectly straight white teeth, and batted fake eyelashes at him. "Well, you see. We were working very hard last night."

Dakota felt like he was going to throw up in his mouth. "Until four o'clock this morning?"

She leaned further over the counter, and Dakota heard one of the men sitting in a navy blue waiting chair clear his throat. "I'm a *very* hard worker."

"I'm sure you are. Thank you, Miss—"

"Oh, Daniels. Clarice Daniels." She offered him a perfectly manicured hand, and he shook it lightly.

"Thank you."

"Anytime, Detective. I took the liberty of writing down my phone number and address." She handed him a pink Post-It note. "You know, in case you need to get a hold of me. Day or night." She winked, and Dakota offered a tight smile, ready to get the fuck away from this office.

"Thanks." He turned and headed out through the brightly lit hall.

He wasn't sure how, but Dakota *would* find a way to link Mitch to these murders. Everything in his gut told him the asshole was guilty, or at least tied to the crime spree in some way.

The walk to the parking garage was a short one, and it was only a few minutes before Dakota unlocked his car. He took a moment to bite back the rage he felt whenever he had to deal with Mitch Carter. Unfortunately, it was more often than he'd care to admit.

Since the murdering son of a bitch had moved on up to District Attorney, he spent a lot of time at the precinct.

Dakota checked the time; it was nearing five p.m., and he knew that even if he went back to the office, nothing else would get done today. Not many people chose to work past five anymore.

So instead of heading to work, he made his way to the bar down the street from his building in hopes that he might be able to drink himself numb enough to sleep tonight.

———

IT WAS NEARLY MIDNIGHT WHEN HE UNLOCKED THE DOOR to his apartment.

"Dakota? Is that you?"

He turned toward the sound of his mother's sleepy voice, trying his best to put a smile on his face. She stood in the doorway to her apartment across the hall, eyes puffy from sleep.

"Yeah, hi, Mom. It was a late night; I'm sorry I woke you."

"Dakota."

He let out a breath, there was no use lying to her.

"Have you been drinking?"

"I had a few."

"How many is a few?"

"It was a long day, Mom." He pushed his door open,

then turned to face her again. "I had a run-in with Mitch today."

He couldn't tell her the details, or that he suspected Mitch had been involved with one of his cases, but he could at least let her know he had seen him.

She straightened, and her jaw clenched. "I hope you find something that locks that son of a bitch up for good."

Dakota smiled and kissed her cheek. "Me too, Mom. I love you."

"I love you, too, Dakota. And no more drinking alone. Call me, I would be more than happy to have a glass or two."

"You got it." He paused, fear momentarily gripping his heart. "I'm going to drive you to work tomorrow."

And from now on. At least until they caught whoever was behind the homicides.

"Dakota, that's not necessary. The hospital is only two blocks away."

"I have an open morning," he lied. "We can leave a little early and grab some breakfast." He walked into his apartment and shut the door, not giving her the chance to decline his offer. He watched through the peephole as she closed her own door, then breathed a sigh of relief.

ANASTASIA

A week later, they were no closer to finding the Brute hideout. They had searched a dozen villages, half a dozen caves, and part of the mountainside.

Tony stood beside her, looking out at the mountains that rose above them. "We may have to go deeper into the caverns."

"I agree. We need rest first, though." She looked back at the remaining Fighters. They hadn't run across anymore ambushes, but the constant travel wore greatly on her companions.

Even Kaley, who had caught up with them the day after the attack in the clearing, was moving more slowly than usual.

"We can make camp here tonight, and then

tomorrow we will head into the mountains. We're getting close... I know it." She turned to face Tony. "We only need to know where they are. Once we figure that out, we can make a plan. We are no match for them in force, but if we can get a shot at Vincent, then we may stand a chance. If you want to stop a snake, you have to cut off its head."

"I know I've said it before, but you are a brave girl, Anastasia. I have no doubt that Gregory and Annabelle are very proud of you. Hell, I'm proud of you." He rested his hand on her shoulder. "When I helped Gregory and Annabelle escape the village after Vincent kidnapped you, I lost my wife and young son." He gazed into the mouth of a cave nestled into the side of the mountain. The other Fighters worked quickly to set up camp for the night, eager for much-needed sleep.

"I didn't know that, Tony. I'm so sorry."

He nodded, his face tightened as he relived those painful memories. "It was a dark time for me and, had it not been for Gregory, I may have never come back from such loss. He was a great man."

"Yes, he was," she agreed, pushing back the memory of her father. She had to stay focused; she couldn't afford to lose herself in grief now. "I'm going to go and scout ahead, see if I can pick up some tracks," she said, desperate for a change in subject.

"I'll come with you." He turned to Andrew. "Stay here. No one goes off alone. We are going to go check things out, and we'll be back shortly."

"Got you, Tony," he replied, then joined the others in setting up camp.

"Want some additional company?" Shane asked.

Tony looked to her for confirmation.

"Sure, if you'd like," Anastasia answered.

Tony, Anastasia, and Shane turned to walk deeper into the caverns, Kaley following closely behind, her ears erect and her gaze flicking back and forth quickly. They couldn't risk attracting unwanted attention by using a torch, so they did their best to squint in the darkness, relying on their other heightened senses and any noises to alert them of danger.

The caves were humid, and Anastasia, who had never been bothered by small space before, had to steady her breathing to keep from panicking. It was dark, and damp, and the only noises were that of their light footsteps.

The stench of sulfur surrounded them, growing stronger as they continued to push on.

Anastasia estimated they were about a mile in when Kaley growled low in her chest, and heavy footfalls echoed toward them in the caverns. They crept closer to the edge of the small hall they were in. As they neared the end, she could see light bouncing just up ahead. They ducked behind the stone wall, as the adrenaline wove its way into her system, readying her for whatever fight lay ahead.

"Gather around," Maximus called.

Anastasia froze, adrenaline pumping harder and

faster through her veins, a white heat that buzzed just below the surface of her skin. Maximus was *here*. She'd found him. She was damn well going to put an end to him once and for all.

Anastasia reached for her sword, but stopped when Tony gently touched her shoulder and put his finger to his lips, signaling her to be silent.

As they peered around the corner and into the cavern ahead, Anastasia counted nearly six-dozen Brutes standing in the dimly lit room.

Sealed crates lined the walls, and a robed man stood in front of the crowd. Maximus moved to stand beside him.

The robed man put his hands behind his back and began to pace in such a way that was her real father, bile burned the back of her throat.

Vincent, she nearly growled his name.

"It is time, my friends," he bellowed. "We are so close to reaching our goal, I can practically taste the victory."

The Brutes cheered, the roar echoing loudly through the cavern.

Vincent raised his hand to silence them. "Remember, this is a recon mission only. You are to remain hidden in the warehouse until the time comes to attack. Trust me; you don't want to risk putting the humans on alert until absolutely necessary."

Anastasia's breath caught in her throat. *Humans?*

"If their military gets involved, that will mean game

over before we even get started," he explained, receiving grunts of dissent from the beasts.

"I will cloak the city so we won't have to worry about any outside interference, but I will only do so when it is time for Phase Two of our plan. If I attempt the cloaking spell before then, I will drain myself and, well, that wouldn't be a good thing, would it?"

The Brutes let out a deep laugh, and Anastasia looked up at Tony. His eyes were wide as he looked back and forth between her and the Brute army.

"We are going to start in Seattle. My contact there will provide us with even more weapons." He gestured to the crates against the walls. "Once we are armed, the young witch and the weak people of Terrenia will be no match for us."

Anastasia tensed. Young witch? Was he talking about her?

"We will have victory, and then we will bask in the blood of those who thought to stand against us!"

The Brutes began to cheer, the din rising to a near-deafening level.

Her stomach churned as she watched the scene unfolding before her. Cheering Brutes pumped their fists in the air as her father's brother—she refused to call him her uncle—smiled in front of them.

All while they plotted to invade a city, *her city*. The idea that they were gathering weapons was more horrifying than she wanted to face right now. No one in

Terrenia had guns; if Vincent armed the Brutes, her people wouldn't stand a chance.

"You will stick to the shadows," Vincent continued. "Kill anyone who sees you."

The Brutes grunted in response.

"Now, shall we move toward our destiny?" Vincent smiled and waved his hand. The swirling blue light of a portal opened behind him, and the Brutes began pouring through.

Anastasia sucked in a breath. Goose bumps broke out over her skin. *How did Vincent open a portal without throwing a vial down? She hadn't seen him use any magic at all!*

"We wait until the numbers are thinned," Tony whispered to her and Shane, "then we go for them." He nodded toward Maximus and Vincent.

They nodded in agreement. As hordes of Brutes poured into the city she once called home, Anastasia gripped the sword at her hip. She pulled in a deep, cleansing breath and prepared for battle.

Tony touched her shoulder as he unsheathed his sword, and the three of them plunged into the cavern, Kaley roaring loudly at their heels.

"What's this, then?" Vincent asked, amusement adding a slight lilt to his voice.

Anastasia threw herself at the nearest Brute, driving her sword through its neck and smiling with a sick satisfaction as it fell to the ground. The element of surprise had worked for them; Tony had been able to take down two Brutes himself, Shane one, and Kaley stood over another one, licking blood from her paw.

Anastasia chucked her dagger and it burrowed into the eye of a beast. She conjured up a ball of flame, then quickly threw it at another Brute as Tony decapitated it.

She looked up just in time to see the crease of Vincent's eyebrows as he watched her fight. *You better be afraid, you bastard.*

"Deal with her," he said to Maximus, then headed for the portal.

"With pleasure." Maximus smiled and unsheathed his sword.

Anastasia lunged for Maximus, and their swords connected with the loud *clang* of metal crashing against metal.

"It won't stay open long!" Tony yelled.

"I know!"

She dodged from the arc of his blade, then swung, but Maximus moved out of the way.

"Isn't this interesting? That we end up back here?" Maximus grinned. "You and me, finally face to face again so I can end this once and for all."

"The interesting part will be when I bury my sword in your chest, you arrogant prick."

Maximus laughed and dodged her sword. She spun and kicked him in the chest, knocking him close to the portal. He glanced behind him at the swirling blue light, then looked back at her and smirked.

She'd slice that smirk right off his face. Anastasia

lunged, but Maximus was too quick. He somersaulted into the portal, and her sword sliced through air instead of through the skull of her enemy.

She grunted in frustration, gritting her teeth.

"Agh!" Shane cried out, and Anastasia spun to see him fall to his knees. Tony sliced the head off the beast and helped Shane back to his feet.

She started to head for them, but Tony raised his hand.

"Go! We will hold them!" Tony yelled. He and Kaley battled side by side, fighting the few remaining Brutes while Shane cradled his wounded side.

"It's okay," he told her.

With one last look at her friends, she said, "I'll come back."

"Give them hell, Anastasia," Tony called out.

With a curt nod, she stepped into the portal.

SEATTLE

DAKOTA

T hey were sitting on the ugly red couch in their living room, binge-watching Scrubs. She had a bowl of popcorn in her lap, and he reached in at the same time she did on purpose, just so his fingers could brush her skin.

This dream version of Dakota soaked in every feature... the way her hair curled softly around her cheeks, the way her blue eyes gazed so intently into his, so full of love.

Mitch burst in, and happiness morphed into terror as he ripped Ana away from him, again.

She disappeared from his sight, just as she always did.

Dakota gasped and sat up in bed. Sweat had beaded on his bare chest, and he wiped some from his brow. No matter how many years passed, or how many girls he dated, he could never forget Ana's face. He tried so hard to forget her, to forget the anger he felt at himself for not being able to save her. He tried to forgive himself for leaving her at the apartment all alone that fateful day.

Dakota stood and pulled on his jeans, then walked to his bathroom. He splashed cold water on his face and glanced at his watch. Four a.m. *Perfect*. Rather than go back to bed where his ghosts awaited him, he headed to the kitchen, made a pot of coffee, and stared out his window at the early morning sky.

There was a flash of light in the alley below him, replacing the shadows below with a bright blue glow.

His mouth dropped open as the largest men Dakota had ever seen came barreling out of a glowing blue circle on the side of the building beside his. A blade glinted in the light, and he dropped his mug.

He grabbed his gun, then checked the magazine as he bounded down the stairs and into the alley, barefoot and shirtless. After ducking behind a dumpster to avoid being seen, his stomach twisted as he got a good look at the men—or rather *monsters*—that poured into his city.

Pale as paper they came out, some with large bones sticking from their noses and other various muscled body parts, others covered head to toe in what looked to be brands. By his guess, these—*things*—were at least seven feet tall, possibly more, and stacked with the type of muscle most men only dream about.

Their large, round faces were just as pale as the rest of them. Their noses and mouths appeared to be humanoid, aside from the fact that those mouths were pulled up in sneers that showcased their ferocity.

As much as he wanted to, he couldn't take them all on himself, so he stayed put until the crowd thinned as more and more of them disappeared into the city.

Four remained, lining up just as a man exited through the pale blue circle of light.

"Get to the warehouse and wait for me there. I have some business to attend to."

The monsters began to march away.

Dakota stood, raising his arm to aim his gun at the robed man. "Stop, and order them to stop as well. You are under arrest."

The man laughed. "Lower your weapon, boy."

Dakota's gun didn't waver.

"Who do you think you are?" the man sneered.

"Detective Dakota Parker. I need you to tell them to stop." He nodded toward the beasts who were making their way toward him.

"Why, if it isn't little Dakota Parker. Isn't this coincidental? I've heard quite a bit about you… and what a giant pain in the ass you are." He bared his teeth, then flung his arm out.

Dakota's body lifted into the air, then jerked backwards, slamming against the wall.

His vision hazy, Dakota tried to scramble to his feet as two of the four remaining beasts stalked toward him.

"No, leave him. We may need him. He will prove a nice distraction if we are followed."

Still dazed, Dakota stared at the man and the beasts as they walked away. A younger man crawled from the light and scrambled to his feet, breaking into a sprint as he chased after them.

Dakota crawled toward the blue circle of light, slowly regaining his strength. He pushed up into a crouch, then began to rise to his feet—

Someone slammed into him, knocking him back to the ground. He glanced up, momentarily blinded as the blue light surged, then disappeared, leaving them in darkness tinted with the purple glow of early morning. He rolled his attacker off of him, then straddled the individual, rearing his fist back to pummel whoever just knocked him down.

Familiar blue eyes met his, and he sucked in a breath.

"Ana?" His jaw dropped.

"Dakota?" she whispered.

He jumped to his feet and stared down at her, his mind racing nearly as fast as his pulse.

Dakota blinked rapidly, fully expecting this to be some trick of the head trauma he'd surely suffered hitting the wall. But when she didn't disappear, he shook his head.

"Ana? Is that really you?"

It didn't matter that it was dark, or that the light from whatever the hell that blue glowing thing was that brought the monsters here was gone, he would have recognized her anywhere.

She jumped to her feet, retrieved a sword from the ground, and stood facing him like a woman on a mission, her eyes wild and alert. Two knives and a gun were strapped into the waistband of skintight leather pants, and she wore knee-high leather boots and a body-hugging vest.

As she quickly scanned the alley around them, her gaze flicking back and forth like an animal stalking its prey, his stomach sank. Her mission may not have been the same as his.

She came through after those—things—after all.

He lifted his gun and aimed it at her even as every ounce of his being fought against pointing a gun at the girl he'd loved his whole life. "Put the sword away, Anastasia."

"Dakota, I don't have time for this." Her gaze flicked past him to the streets beyond the alley. "They're getting away!"

"You're not going anywhere until you tell me what the hell is going on."

"Dakota, please." She bounced from one foot to another and bit down on her bottom lip in frustration.

Five years ago, he would have let her get away with not telling him everything, but not today. Especially when he wasn't sure she was real to begin with. Where the hell had she been all this time? Why was she dressed like something out of a medieval movie?

How hard had he hit his head?

Was he dreaming?

38

ANASTASIA

Anastasia sheathed her sword and placed her hands on her hips. Her chest heaved with each heavy breath as adrenaline coursed through her veins. The longer she squared off with Dakota, the more distance between her and her targets.

But…. *Dakota.* She nearly sobbed as she looked him over.

Emotions tumbled together at the sight of him. Joy, love, relief… all warring for center stage in her mind.

He'd aged in the years she'd been away. His face had a few days' worth of stubble, and his dark hair was messy from sleep. The beginnings of laugh lines circled his mouth. Tattoos climbed up his left arm, starting at his bicep and spanning over part of his chest.

A chest that was stronger, bigger than she remembered, a light coating of hair dusting the taut skin. Hard lines and deep valleys accentuating toned muscles that could only be the result of years of fighting or countless nights spent in a gym. The body of a Fighter... had he not become a doctor?

He wore blue jeans slung low on his hips, and Anastasia's heart skipped a beat as she took in the man standing before her. Gone was the boy she'd left all those years ago.

Her heart pinched with guilt—just how much of his life had she missed?—but as she looked into blue eyes more familiar to her than her own, nothing else mattered.

"Dakota," she whispered, his name a prayer on her lips.

His brow bunched as he searched her gaze, but he didn't lower his gun.

Wait. "Why do you have a gun?"

"I'm a cop."

She raised her eyebrows. "A cop? But—"

"Detective, actually."

She shook her head. That wasn't right. He was supposed to be a doctor, like Elizabeth. He'd never wanted to follow in his father's footsteps. What happened? What changed? "What happened to—?"

"*You* happened, Ana." He shook his head, searching her gaze as he lowered the gun, his eyebrows bunched. "You disappeared. You left. I had to do something, had to try to find you..." He gave his head another quick shake, then straightened his shoulders. "Who are those men? What were those... *things*?" he spat.

Remembering her reason for being in Seattle in the first place, Anastasia placed her hand on the hilt of her sword. "I have to go after them. Please let me go."

He lifted the gun back in place, straightening his arms. "No, Ana."

"Dammit, Dakota! People have died to get me this far. You have to let me go after them!"

"I don't even know who *they* are. I'm certainly not letting you go after them until I know what's going on. You can either come with me and fill me in, or I can cuff you and take you down to the station."

His jaw was set, his eyes focused intently on her, and she knew he wouldn't cave. He had always been stubborn, but the years had clearly made him more so. Frustration caused the power in her body to hum in her veins. He wouldn't be a match for her magic. She could get away if she chose to, but the thought of hurting him —even accidentally—was not something she could handle.

She looked beyond him into the darkness.

The Brutes were already gone, and it was unlikely she would find them now. Especially not in the dark city she barely knew anymore.

A rush of anger flooded Anastasia, but she fought to ignore it. She'd been so close!

But, when she looked back at Dakota, everything else faded to background noise.

Her time with Maximus and Vincent would come, of that she was sure.

But Dakota... hadn't she waited half a decade to see him again?

Anastasia ached to be near him, so much so that her fingers twitched to touch him. She had missed him beyond measure, would have given anything to see him again, and now, here she was, face to face with the man she'd loved all her life.

And he pointed a gun at her.

Something about this both thrilled and frustrated her.

"Fine. We will talk first, but not here. I don't want to be ambushed."

39

DAKOTA

"Wait here," Dakota said as they entered his apartment. He walked to his bedroom to get dressed, but left the door partially open so he could hear if she tried to leave.

Guilt pinched his chest. This was Ana, *his* Ana—could he not trust her?

Dakota stood for a moment staring at his closet absently. What in the hell had he just witnessed? What was going on in Seattle? Was it *him*? Was he finally losing the mind he had worked so hard to hold onto after Ana disappeared?

And what in the hell was she doing running through a mysterious blue light in the middle of a dead-end alleyway anyway? And with a sword? Who carried a sword these days? Where had she gotten it?

"It's official, I'm losing my mind," he muttered as he pulled his shoes on. He had half a mind to go and wake his mother up, just to verify he hadn't imagined the whole thing.

But if he did that, and Ana wasn't real, his mother would never leave him alone. On the other hand, if Ana were, in fact, standing in his living room, well, his mother would still never leave him alone.

No, he'd handle this situation on his own.

When he stepped back into the living room, he was actually surprised to see her still standing there. He had honestly believed she would be gone when he came out, and that everything he'd witnessed over the last few hours had been nothing but a dream.

Ana stood with her back to him, facing the television in the corner.

Her dark brown hair was much longer than it had been years ago, hanging in a long, thick braid that reached the top curve of her ass. Her skintight pants left little to the imagination, displaying muscular thighs and calves that dipped into tall black boots. Boots that made her legs look as if they were a mile high—and they had never needed help in that department.

She had a sword sheathed across her back, and her waistband held more knives than he'd originally counted. He should have had her remove them, but he had been too distracted by her reappearance in his life. She had a small satchel tied to her belt, and her stance was that of a warrior.

Where had she been all these years, and why was she back now, of all times?

"Where have you been?" he asked, his voice meek. He cleared his throat. "It's been..." he shook his head. "Where have you been all this time?"

She turned slowly to face him, and when she looked into his eyes, a piece of his heart slipped back into place.

"That's a long story," Anastasia answered tightly. Her eyes narrowed on his face, and he crossed his arms over his chest.

"I've got time." He moved into the kitchen to pour himself some coffee. "Want some?"

"Yes, please."

"So?" he asked again as he poured the hot liquid into the mugs. "Start talking."

His voice was rough; he couldn't help it. His mind was completely fried.

She took a deep breath. "I don't know that you will believe me if I tell you."

"You're kidding, right?" He set a cup in front of her and took a drink out of his own. "I literally just saw a blue light appear in the alley by my house, then giant beasts filed out of it, followed by a man who apparently knew my name."

"Dakota, I—"

He held his hand up. "I would also like to add that my best friend, who went missing five years ago without a trace, just so happened to come stumbling out of that same blue light and crashed directly into me right before it disappeared. I think you would be surprised at how much I might believe, Ana."

Her mouth tightened. Was she considering whether or not to tell him the truth?

His heart pounded in his chest. His arms ached to pull her to him… if only to confirm that she was really there.

She finally nodded. "Fine. For the last five years, I have been in a place called Terrenia, which is another dimension that runs parallel to this one. There, I learned that I was kidnapped as a baby from my biological parents, one of which is a sorcerer, by the way, then sent here to live with Mitch because I was prophesized to be the one who would bring down the darkness that is being spread by my evil uncle."

What in the actual fuck? He wasn't sure what he'd expected her to say, but it sure as hell wasn't that. There was a knock at the door, and he checked the time. "Shit." He'd completely forgotten about the fact that he was supposed to drive his mom to work this morning.

He glanced at Ana. "Quiet, and stay over there where she can't see you."

He ignored the way her mouth tightened in defiance, and once she was out of sight, he pulled open the door just enough to look outside.

"Hey, Mom."

Dressed in navy blue scrubs, her hair was up in a

tight bun, and she'd applied a small amount of makeup for the day.

"Are you ready to go?" she asked.

"I can't this morning, Mom, I'm not feeling well." He regretted the words the moment they left his lips. If he was looking for any reason for her to force her way into his apartment, feigning sickness was at the top of the list. "I mean, I'm tired."

"Dakota George Parker. You open this door all the way this instant." She shoved at the door, and he gently moved aside, knowing it would do no good to fight with her.

She looked into the kitchen and gasped, smiling. "Oh, I'm sorry, honey, you could have just said you had company. I can drive mys—" The words died on her lips as her eyes widened further and her jaw dropped. "It can't be," she whispered, taking a few steps toward Ana. She turned to look back at Dakota, and he nodded.

"Anastasia?" she whispered.

"Hi, Mrs. Parker."

His mom pulled Ana in for a hug, and Ana wrapped her arms around her. When she pulled away, they both had unshed tears in their eyes. "Oh, honey, are you all right? Where have you been? Did Mitch hurt you?"

"Mom." Dakota's voice was gentle, and he handed her his cell phone. "Call in sick today, please. I know you never do, but I'm begging you to make an exception for today. And then stay in my apartment, don't go to yours," he added, remembering what he had just seen coming out of the blue light in the alleyway.

"Okay," Elizabeth agreed halfheartedly. She backed away without taking her eyes off Ana as if she were afraid she would disappear.

"We are going to be in here." He gestured to his bedroom. "We have a few things to talk about. Don't leave, Mom," he reminded her.

"I won't." She dialed up the hospital.

Anastasia followed Dakota into his bedroom, and he shut the door gently behind her. She turned around in a circle, looking at all of the photos neatly set on his dresser. She stopped in front of the photograph taken the day he graduated from the academy.

"You became a cop," she whispered, as if finally accepting what he'd already told her.

"Yes," he replied curtly.

She turned to him, and he swallowed hard. *Damn, she was beautiful.*

"Why?"

"What happened to you?" he asked, changing the subject.

She shook her head. "It's not important."

"The hell it isn't. Whatever—or whoever—took you away from me, Ana... that's pretty fucking important to me."

She winced a little, and he wished he could take back the tone in his voice. But having her here in his space and not being able to touch her, was destroying him.

She closed her beautiful blue eyes, and when she opened them again, they were full of tears. He had to shove his hands into his pockets to keep from reaching for her.

"Mitch showed up at our apartment that morning. Two men were with him and I was in such a good mood, I opened the door without even looking to see who it was."

"I fucking knew it was him," Dakota growled, unable to help himself. *And the fucker had gotten away with it.*

"They knocked me out somehow and took me back to Mitch and Monica's."

Why was she calling them by their first names? Her gaze was fixated on something outside, and she looked to be a million miles away.

"When I woke up, he told me he was going to kill me."

A tear rolled down her cheek, and Dakota ached to wipe it away.

"I fought back. With magic, of all things." She laughed softly, no amusement in the sound. "He punished me." She turned around and lifted up a small part of her shirt, revealing about two inches of scarred and tattooed skin.

He reached out and ran his fingers along the jagged lines, and his heart pounded in his ears as a wave of red-hot rage rushed his system. "He fucking beat you," Dakota growled, his voice deep and full of pain.

He'd left her there alone, and Mitch fucking *beat her*.

She pulled her shirt down and turned to face him. Unable to resist touching her any longer, he reached out and brushed a tear from her cheek.

"Yes. He did. But before he could kill me, another man appeared in the living room. He threw Mitch off of me, then offered me sanctuary. A place where I would be safe and Mitch would never get his hands on me again. He told me that they needed me." She took a deep breath. "I think that was the first time anyone ever said that to me."

Her words felt like a dagger in his heart. How the hell could she say that? He'd always needed her.

"Mitch blasted in a few moments later, and the man threw him back again. They argued, but honestly, I can't even remember what it was about now. The man opened a blue light—a portal—and took me through. I've been there ever since."

"I needed you," he said softly, barely leashing the anger he felt.

"Dakota, I didn't mean—"

"You left willingly, then." Anger tightened a painful fist around his heart. "You weren't kidnapped, and you were obviously not murdered. You left of your own free will, and you couldn't have been so kind as to leave me a fucking note? Something that said 'hey, Dakota, I'm not dead, see ya around'? Something that would have let me know you were okay!"

"Dakota, I didn't have time. Mitch was going to kill me!"

"My father died for you."

She gasped. "What?" Fresh tears rolled down her cheeks, but he paid them little notice. The fact that she had left him willingly, without even bothering to put his mind at ease, was the worst type of betrayal.

"He cared enough to keep digging even when everyone else had given up on finding you. Someone—presumably Mitch—decided he was a liability and murdered him. He bled to death in a fucking alley because of you!"

She flinched. "Dakota, I'm so sorry. I—"

"Save it, Anastasia." He grabbed his jacket from the bed and marched past her. "Don't even think about leaving, or so help me God, I will hunt you to the ends of the Earth, even into whatever world it is you tried to escape to."

He slammed the door behind him.

His mom stood by the front door, and she opened her mouth to say something.

"I don't want to hear it," he growled as he pushed past her.

40

ANASTASIA

Anastasia sat on the edge of the bed, her head in her hands. She had always tried to spare Dakota and his family from any harm at the hands of Mitch Carter, and... when she'd left with Gregory that night, her only reason had been Dakota's safety.

Instead, she had gotten George killed and caused Dakota and Elizabeth a lifetime of pain.

She'd been a fool.

At least she now knew what created the Fighter he'd become. He was so different than before, no doubt because he'd been hardened by five years of pain, devastating loss, and fighting battles for others.

Where was the Dakota who used to climb through her window with plates of food? The best friend who'd sat on the couch binge-watching whatever TV show was popular at the time? Or the roommate who held her while she slept after she had a nightmare?

Anastasia rose to her feet. Regardless of what he'd said, she needed to get as far away from Dakota and his mother as possible.

People around her had a tendency to die.

She stepped from the bedroom, and Elizabeth looked up at her. "Your coffee got cold; would you like some more?"

"No, thank you." Anastasia glanced toward the door.

"He will, you know."

Anastasia looked at the woman, eyebrows raised in question.

Elizabeth shrugged. "Hunt you down. That boy has been searching for you for five years. Now that he knows you are alive and in the same city, he won't ever stop. Don't force him to start again." Elizabeth came around to sit at the small table in the kitchen, motioning to the chair beside her.

Anastasia gave in and sat down.

"So, another dimension, huh?" she asked nonchalantly, sipping her coffee like other dimensions were normal, everyday discussion.

Had she not been bordering on exhaustion, Anastasia's chin might have hit the floor.

"How much did you hear?"

"All of it. I'm a mother, honey, an excellent eavesdropper by trade."

Anastasia smiled.

"If you're worried I'm going to blame you about George, you're wrong." She lightly touched Anastasia's hand. "What happened to him wasn't your fault. Just as what happened to you that night wasn't your fault. Mitch is an evil man, and evil men will do anything they choose, regardless of the consequences and how their actions affect other people."

"How can you not blame me? If I had left a note—"

"Then George would have still gone looking for you, and things would have ended up exactly the way they are now. Anastasia, George and Dakota were my world. It got a little smaller after George passed, but my husband was a determined man, and he would have continued looking for you until he found you. He blamed himself for what happened, and he made it his mission to bring you home, for Dakota."

Anastasia stared down at the coffee mug as the steam swirled off the top. "Dakota hates me."

"Oh, honey." Elizabeth reached over and patted her hand again gently. "That boy couldn't hate you if he tried. He's just a little mixed up right now. Give him some time; he will come around."

"I'm pretty sure I hate myself."

"Anastasia. You can't focus on things that are in the past; they are already out of your control." She straightened and took a sip of her coffee. "Now, why don't you tell me a little bit about this place you've been living? Terrenia, right?"

"You are a wonderful eavesdropper."

"One of the best, I'm sure."

Anastasia had forgotten how easy it was to talk with Elizabeth.

When she'd been a teenager, Anastasia would sneak over to their house just to sit with Elizabeth. They would chat about little things that Anastasia imagined all normal mothers and daughters spoke about, and Elizabeth had helped her through more than a few tough times.

So now, over a cup of coffee, Anastasia told her of Gregory and Annabelle, and about how kind they had been to her. She told her of how beautiful Terrenia was and how the animals were a bit different there than they were here. She described her years of training and the many battles she'd been a part of.

When she'd finished, Elizabeth stared at her, jaw slack.

"You have magic, too!" she exclaimed once she'd had a minute to process.

"I do," Anastasia admitted hesitantly.

"I have to stand." Elizabeth began pacing the small apartment. "This is so exciting. And scary, of course, and sad as well," she added, turning toward Anastasia. "I am just so overwhelmed that you are back and standing before me all warrior princess like."

Anastasia laughed, the first real laugh to come out of her since long before Gregory had been killed. "Warrior princess?" she said through her laughter, and Elizabeth started giggling.

They laughed together and, eventually, Anastasia took a seat on the couch. She hadn't realized how tired she was; a week without more than an hour or two of sleep a night would do that to a person. Even a warrior princess.

"Why don't you rest for a bit, dear? We will talk again in a little while." Elizabeth pulled the curtains tight to block out the light steadily growing outside and grabbed a blanket from the back of the couch to hand to her.

Anastasia accepted it gratefully and lay back, closing her eyes.

41

DAKOTA

nother dimension? Was she serious? Dakota wished it were early enough to drink. He damn well deserved one after the night and morning he'd had.

Weird ass beasts pouring through a blue light into his world.

His best friend practically returning from the grave.

Discovering she'd left willingly.

Of everything he'd learned this morning, that was the hardest to come to terms with. He'd never believed she'd actually run away, but to learn that she had, that the police had been right, and on some level, Mitch had been telling the truth, was enough to crumble Dakota's neatly organized world.

All these years he'd held onto his anger for not only Mitch, but also the cops who had done nothing.

He spent so many nights lying in bed, kicking himself for not following his gut and staying home that day.

How many nights had he hated himself for leaving her alone?

'My father died for you,' he'd told her.

"Fuck," Dakota murmured, rubbing his palms over his eyes. What kind of an asshole said shit like that to people? She'd told him of the horrors she suffered that night, and he'd blamed her for a death that wasn't hers to carry.

He owed her one hell of an apology. A block from his apartment, his phone rang.

"Carter," he answered gruffly.

"We've got a problem," Lance Austin, his lieutenant, said from the other line.

Dakota pinched the bridge of his nose. "What kind of problem?"

"You need to come in. This isn't something we can talk about over the phone."

"On my way." Dakota ran through the early morning air until he reached the bar a few blocks down where he'd left his car last night.

His mind raced. Was it possible those beasts had been spotted? Had there been an attack?

There were a million possibilities as to why Austin

had called him in, and after he figured out why it was, he was dead set on figuring out just what was next with Ana.

42

ANASTASIA

A nastasia woke and stretched. She hadn't slept that deeply in *ages*. Her sleep addled brain panicked when she didn't recognize where she was. She shot up off the couch, a blade already in her hand.

"Easy, honey," Elizabeth stood near the door, and Anastasia relaxed as memories from the early morning came back to her.

I'm in Seattle, in Dakota's apartment.

"I'm just going to head across the hall to grab a few things," Elizabeth told her.

"Across the hall?"

Elizabeth smiled. "Yes, we're neighbors, my son and me."

Anastasia nodded. "I'll go with you."

"Oh, honey, that's not necessary," Elizabeth said with a warm smile. "Although I would enjoy the company."

Anastasia smiled back, and lifted her sword from the table to sheathe it at her back.

The door splintered, and Elizabeth screamed as three Brutes burst into the room. "Get the cop!" one ordered as he entered the room.

"Elizabeth, run! Bedroom, now!"

Anastasia jumped over the couch and dodged a large fist to drive her sword down into the first Brute. Blood dripped down her arm as she ripped her blade out of the abdomen and sliced down to remove the head.

The second Brute reached for her and managed to knock her back into the wall. She ducked just in time to miss a blow to the face and spun to kick it in the gut. Once it was stunned, she blasted it with magic, and it crumpled to the floor.

Elizabeth screamed, and Anastasia turned as the last Brute shoved the door to the bedroom open. She slammed the beast with magic, and was satisfied when it fell to the floor.

"Are you all right?" Anastasia called.

Elizabeth stepped out, staring in bewilderment at the beast on the ground. She looked back up, and her eyes widened as a sharp pain speared through Anastasia's abdomen.

"Anastasia!" Elizabeth screamed, but the sound was a mile away as searing pain spread like fire from her midsection, and her pulse sent blood roaring through her veins, the sound a deafening rhythm in her ears.

Anastasia looked down. A blood-covered blade protruded from her stomach. She turned around slowly, gasping for breath; a fourth Brute had snuck into the room and attacked from the back.

She fell to her knees, and the thing smiled at her. "I will be rewarded for killing you. Goodbye, baby *witch*," he sneered. The Brute pushed her back and knelt on her chest. Anastasia gasped, and her vision began to waver.

"Get off of her!" Elizabeth cried.

Elizabeth charged the beast, but it flung her away with a flick of his hand, sending her flying into the coffee table.

"No!" Anastasia tried to scream, but the sound came out as whisper. The pain in her abdomen started to fade as her body went numb.

"What the—?" Dakota stood in the doorway, trying to make sense of what the hell was happening.

"Dakota. My. Sword," she choked out as the Brute rose to its feet.

Dakota dodged a fist, and lunged for her sword on the ground. When he turned around, he drove the blade into the beast's gut. The Brute sunk to the ground and fell backwards, pinning Anastasia to the floor.

"Oh my God, Ana!" Dakota dropped to his knees beside her and pressed his hands against the wound on her stomach. She could feel her pulse slowing as blood poured from the wound.

"I called 9-1-1." Elizabeth knelt beside her and handed Dakota a clean cloth.

"No. Hospitals," she tried to say, but the words were garbled.

She fought to stay awake, but everything quickly faded to black.

43

DAKOTA

Dakota stared down at Ana's sleeping form. The buzzing of machines were the only sound in the room, and with each steady *blip* of the heart monitor, Dakota felt a piece of his own crumble.

She was in here because of him. Because he'd been a king-sized douche and left her alone in his apartment, *again*. This was seriously becoming a habit that he sure as shit needed to break.

Guess she was stuck with him now, because he had no intention of letting her go again. Seeing her bleeding to death on his floor was enough to snap his ass back to reality. She had not been the driving hand behind his father's death, had not purposely left him.

She'd been abducted by Mitch, and in that moment, her only way out had been a stranger offering her safety.

He honestly couldn't blame her. At least she was alive.

Unlike Harry. Dakota closed his eyes and pinched the bridge of his nose as another dizzying wave of grief passed over him.

Austin had called him in to let him know that his partner was dead, his skull crushed like the other victims. They weren't even going to let Dakota work the case. It had been passed on to someone else, and he was now on paid leave. Apparently telling his captain there were monster men running through the city had not been an appropriate reaction.

Harry had been his mentor, someone who he trusted immensely, and now he was gone.

Head in his hands, Dakota looked up at Ana again. Her eyes fluttered open, and he got to his feet just as her eyes widened with panic. She reached down to pull the IV out of her arm, and Dakota grabbed her wrist.

"Ana, you're fine. We're at my mom's hospital."

"Dakota, we have to go. No one can know I'm here," she said, her voice shaky as her eyes flicked frantically around the room.

"No one knows you are. We checked you in under a different name. Breathe." He moved some hair out of her face. "You almost bled to death. That monster used some sort of triple-edged knife on you. Had we not brought you here, you wouldn't have made it."

"Where's Elizabeth?" She tried to sit up, so Dakota pushed a button on her bed remote, propping her up slightly.

"She's fine. She just went to the cafeteria to get some coffee. I figured she was safe here since there are so many people around."

Ana nodded and leaned back against the pillows. "Do you have my stuff?"

He lowered his voice so no one else could hear him. "The weapons we left in my car, but I brought your bag up." He handed her the small leather satchel she'd tied to her belt.

Ana pulled out a vial of orange liquid and lifted her hospital gown. She winced with pain, and he leaned forward.

"I'm okay. This will help heal it." She lifted her bandage and poured some of the thick contents on her wound over her stitches.

The liquid bubbled, and Dakota's stomach churned.

"Can you get the one on my back? I'm guessing it went all the way through?"

He nodded and took the vial from her. She rolled to her side and pulled the hospital blanket to just above her waist. He pushed her gown up to get to the injury, trying like hell to not focus on the additional scars it revealed. He was going to murder Mitch. After lifting the bandage up, Dakota poured the same amount he had seen her use on the entry wound.

"It's a phoenix," she said when his fingers brushed

over her tattoo. She rolled back over and tugged the gown back down. "I wanted something that reminded me of strength, and I didn't think anything else was more fitting. It represents—"

"Rising from the ashes. Becoming something more than you were," he finished.

"Yes," she said, carefully watching him. He handed her the vial, and she replaced the cap.

"What is that stuff?" He pointed to the now empty bottle.

"It's a healing remedy made with magic."

Dakota just nodded, not wanting to hammer her with all the questions floating around in his head. At least not until she was out of the hospital.

"How long have I been here?"

"Almost twenty-four hours. You lost a lot of blood, but you got lucky; the blade missed anything vital."

"We need to go." She put her feet on the floor and yanked the IV from her arm.

He stood quickly. "Ana, you need to rest."

"Dakota, we have to go. If Vincent somehow finds out I'm here, it will be bad, very bad. Please, we have to go."

"I told you we checked you in under a different name," he insisted.

"Dakota, please."

"Leaving so soon?"

The color drained from Ana's face, and Dakota's heart sped.

He turned quickly, placing himself between Ana and the man in the doorway. "You have no business here, Mitch," he growled.

"That's where you're wrong, Parker. That's my daughter there, and seeing as how she has been missing for the last five years, I feel we have a lot to talk about." He took a step toward the bed, and Dakota stepped forward. He'd be damned if this asshole was getting anywhere near her.

The alarms on the machines Ana had yet to remove went off as her heart rate skyrocketed.

Dakota glanced behind him. She was crumpled on the floor and his heart nearly leapt from his chest. He couldn't go to her until he eliminated the threat. Turning back to Mitch, he reached for his gun, grimacing when he grasped nothing but air at his hip.

Damn paid leave.

It didn't matter. He'd take Mitch Carter down with his hands if he had to. He squared his shoulders and looked the man in the eyes. "Get out of here, Mitch. Now."

"Did you not hear me? I'm not leaving until I've had the chance to talk to my daughter."

Dakota took a step closer. "You can either leave, or I will throw your ass out of here."

"And then you would lose your job. I. Am. Not. Going. Anywhere." Mitch tried to push past Dakota, but he held firm.

"You *are* leaving," Elizabeth said as she entered the

room, two security guards by her side. "You are upsetting my patient. A patient, I might add, who is of no blood relation to you."

"Then why doesn't she turn around? Set this whole thing to rest," he said without turning to look at Elizabeth.

"She is none of your concern. Now, are you going to leave of your own accord, or am I going to have to have you arrested for harassing one of my patients?"

He turned to face Elizabeth. "No need for that. Just a misunderstanding, I'm sure." He headed for the door. "See you soon, Parker."

When he was gone, Dakota rushed to Ana's side, kneeling beside her. Shudders racked her body, and her face had lost nearly all color.

"Ana, hey, it's okay. Come back to me." Dakota cupped her face with his hands. "I'm so sorry. We should have left when you wanted to. It's okay now, he's gone, and we will leave before he has the chance to come back."

Eyes wide, she looked up at him. Nearly a decade had passed since he'd seen that look of horror on her face, and it gutted him nearly as much now as it did the night Mitch had beat her nearly to death the week before graduation.

Tears rolled down her cheeks, and Dakota wiped them away with the pads of his thumbs. "It's going to be okay." He pulled her close and wrapped his arms around her.

44

ANASTASIA

They drove through the darkening streets of Seattle in silence. Elizabeth and Dakota sat in the front seats of his sedan, while Anastasia sat in the back. Her weapons had been in his car, just as he'd promised, and he'd reluctantly handed them to her before they'd left the parking garage.

She wondered why he was so afraid of giving them back to her. Did he still not trust her? Even after yesterday's Brute attack? Was he afraid she was going to bail the second she got a chance? He couldn't have been more wrong; the Brutes had come to the apartment looking for Dakota—she'd just been a happy accident.

That meant Vincent knew where he was, and if she left now, Dakota and his mother wouldn't stand a chance.

She closed her eyes tightly and swallowed the hard lump of tears burning in the back of her throat. Mitch had caught her completely off guard, and her reaction had been so weak, so completely and utterly helpless, that shame curled around her like an old friend.

Hadn't she conquered her fear of that horrible man? Or had she merely just pushed it aside all these years?

How the hell could she take down a fully grown Brute without hesitation, but the voice of that man transformed her back into the shaking, fearful child she'd left behind all those years ago?

Dakota witnessed her fear, the way she trembled when Mitch entered the room. Shame gripped her chest again. Dakota, of all people! And it wasn't like he'd never seen her afraid before—he'd seen that and much, much worse—but this was different. *She* was different. In that moment, when she should have confronted Mitch, she'd cowered behind her best friend.

A*gain.*

"We need to grab some supplies and head out to the cabin," Dakota said as they drove. "The apartments aren't safe."

"What did you do with the bodies?" Anastasia asked.

"Bodies?"

"Of the Brutes."

"So that's what those things are called." Elizabeth clucked her tongue in disgust.

"Nothing, yet," Dakota answered. "Dragging those damn things down the stairs seemed like a bad idea."

"They won't be there tomorrow anyway. Brutes always collect their dead."

"Well that solves that problem, I suppose."

A few minutes passed, and they pulled into the parking lot of a grocery store Anastasia remembered from other trips they'd made out to the Parker Family Resort, as George had lovingly dubbed the old cabin.

The fact that he wouldn't be joining them with his stories and infectious laughter pained her. She hadn't realized just how much she missed him until she learned he was gone.

"I'll be right back." Dakota climbed out of the car, leaving Anastasia and Elizabeth alone.

"How are you feeling?" Elizabeth asked.

"Sore, but okay."

"Let me know if that changes."

Anastasia offered her a small smile, and looked back out at the entrance to the store.

Dakota emerged a few moments later, carrying a handful of plastic bags that he put into the trunk. Without a word, he climbed back into the car and pulled out onto the street.

Anastasia stared out of the window as the city faded from view, and the trees became thicker, reminding her of the home she'd left only a day ago. What was Tony doing right now? Had he, Shane, and Kaley made it back to the other Fighters?

Were they all all right?

With a quick shake of her head, she pushed the worries aside—there was nothing she could do at the moment.

After an hour of driving in silence, Dakota pulled down a familiar gravel road. Both Dakota and Elizabeth had been silent the rest of the drive, and Anastasia wondered if the two of them had visited the cabin since George's death.

When Dakota pulled to a stop, Anastasia leaned against the window to get a better look. It was exactly how she remembered it. Trees surrounded the cabin from all sides, the only breaks being from the road and the structure itself. It was composed entirely of logs, much like the way houses in Terrenia were constructed. The windows had deep green shutters on them, and the wraparound porch still held four rocking chairs.

Four. Sadness pinched her heart. They'd added one for her when she'd started joining their weekend getaways.

George would never walk through his prized cottage again. He would never kiss Elizabeth in the kitchen like he would when he thought the kids weren't watching, or hold his future grandkids. No matter what Dakota and Elizabeth told her, she knew that his death was on her shoulders.

Dakota climbed out and went around to the trunk, retrieving the supplies. He placed them on the porch and disappeared behind the house. Moments later, the flood light illuminated them in the dark.

Elizabeth stared at the house, her body rigid and eyes wide, as if it were going to sprout legs and run away. Dakota came back around and kissed his mother's forehead before they stepped inside.

After taking a deep breath, Anastasia followed them. Dakota moved around the living room, removing sheets from each piece of furniture.

"Come sit down." Dakota gestured to the recliner George typically occupied.

Instead, she moved to the couch. She would not sit in George's place. Dead or alive, it was *his* chair.

"Do you need anything?" he asked.

She shook her head. "I'm fine, Dakota. The salve helped. In a few hours, I'll be good as new."

"Ana, you almost died. Even with your magic potion or whatever the hell that is, you're gonna need time. We're all lucky the hospital believed our story of a piece of rebar you just so happened to 'fall on'. Otherwise we all know you'd still be in that bed."

She didn't have the energy to fight with him, so she just leaned back against the couch, closed her eyes, and tried to relax.

45

DAKOTA

"You okay, Mom?" Dakota asked as he made his way into the kitchen. He'd done a walk-through of the house, verifying that all windows and doors were locked up before taking a break.

His mom had busied herself in the kitchen, making the comfort food he'd grown up with. He also knew she'd chosen meatloaf and mashed potatoes because it was a favorite of their guest.

"I'm just shaken up, is all." She stopped mixing the ground beef and met his gaze. "Dakota, those things were *horrible*. All I could think was that we just got her back and now we were going to lose her again." Tears filled her eyes, and Dakota wrapped his arms around her.

"We aren't going to lose her, Mom, I promise." He meant it, but was this even a promise he could keep? How was he supposed to help Ana in a war he knew nothing about?

"I hope you're right." She used the back of her hand to brush a strand of hair from her face. "Now, leave me be. Grab a shower or something... you stink."

Dakota let out a laugh and made his way into the bedroom. He sat on the edge of the bed and put his head in his hands.

In the two days since Dakota learned of the third high-profile homicide, his best friend barreled into him, his partner had been murdered, he'd come home to find a giant beast on top of the aforementioned best friend, his mother knocked nearly unconscious into his broken coffee table, and he'd had a run-in with Mitch Carter.

The latter alone was enough to shove him into a bottle.

So how the hell was he supposed to handle everything else?

One thing at a time, Parker.

He wished his dad was there to help him make sense of everything. What would he have done?

Dakota took a deep breath. He'd start with addressing their current predicament. Vincent and those Brutes were here for a reason, and Dakota would bet his badge that Ana knew what that reason was.

As soon as she woke up, he'd get his answers.

ANASTASIA

"Elizabeth, I think this is absolutely the best meatloaf you have ever made."

Anastasia leaned back slightly in her chair and pushed her plate away. She'd helped herself to seconds, and the decadent combination made her feel infinitely better, just as it had always managed to. Elizabeth's meatloaf and mashed potatoes was comfort food at its finest.

"You are too kind, Anastasia." Elizabeth smiled and stood to clear the table.

"No, please, let me get it." Anastasia got to her feet.

"I've got it." Dakota grabbed the plates and headed for the kitchen.

"I knew I raised him right." Elizabeth winked. "I'm

headed to bed. I am exhausted and need my beauty rest."

"You don't need rest to be beautiful, Mom." Dakota smiled as he came back into the dining room to give her a hug.

"Aren't you a charmer." She hugged him back and then smiled at Anastasia. "Get some rest tonight, honey. We are going to check that dressing in the morning," she said, pointing to Anastasia's stomach.

Dakota stepped back into the kitchen and turned the water on in the sink. He lifted plate after plate, hand-washing each and setting them into the drying rack. The routine movement transfixed Anastasia, and it took her a minute before she realized she was staring.

Not wanting him to see her, she got to her feet and slipped out to sit on the porch. Crickets sang their chirpy songs, and owls hooted with the night. The stars above shone so brightly that for a moment, she could see Gregory sitting beside her in Terrenia.

He had always loved nighttime… said it was the most magical because nearly all things were at rest.

She opened her palm and closed her eyes. Her magic had been in a sleep state, and her body was so exhausted it took a minute to pull it to the surface. A tear slipped down her cheek as she conjured an orb of calming light and sent it floating into the sky.

It burst into a dozen smaller lights that disappeared into the sky, blending with the stars.

She missed Terrenia. She missed Kaley, Tony,

Andrew, Brady, and even Shane. All of her friends that she'd left like sitting ducks. She hadn't given any thought to how she was supposed to get home. She had no portal vials, and had no clue if she even possessed the power needed to conjure a portal like she'd seen Vincent do. *Is it even possible?* She might have missed him actually throwing the vial down.

What if there was no way for her to get back home? She conjured another ball of light and sent it floating into the sky.

"Well, that's not something you see every day," Dakota said, standing behind her.

She twisted around to see him, wincing as pain shot through her torso.

"Easy, Ana. Don't tear those stitches out. Mom will kill me." He sat down beside her. "Can you do that again?"

Anastasia regarded him cautiously and then obliged. He stared, amazed at the light in her palm.

"What is that?"

"Magic," she said with a smile. "My biological father was descended from a long line of sorcerers."

"Doesn't any of this seem crazy to you?" he asked as she released another ball of light.

"It certainly did at first. For the first few months, I was convinced I was going to wake up back at Mitch and Monica's house. I had even convinced myself that I was already dead." She laughed darkly. "Either option would have been equally bad."

"I'm sorry I wasn't there for you."

"What do you mean? You were always there for me."

"That morning when I woke up, I had this gut feeling that I needed to stay put. I thought it was just personal, that I didn't want to leave you after—you know."

Heat rushed into her cheeks. That kiss was not something she'd forgotten. Anastasia shook her head. "There was nothing you could've done, Dakota. Mitch would have just killed us both."

"I can't stop beating myself up, Ana, no matter how hard I try. Losing you is my biggest regret."

"But you didn't lose me. That isn't on you."

He looked her straight in the eye, and the seriousness in those blue eyes made her heart stammer in her chest. "I did lose you," he said. "For five years, and because of it, I lost myself, too."

"Dakota, I'm so sorry."

He shook his head. "I don't want an apology, Ana. I know you felt like you had no choice."

"I wanted to come back. At first there was no way for me to, and then once I saw the pain the villagers in Terrenia were suffering through, and that they were counting on me to stop it, I just couldn't bring myself to leave. At least not until it was done."

He nodded in understanding. "I would have done the same. I, uh—I'm sorry I yelled at you."

The change of subject caught her off guard. She frowned as she met his gaze.

"Back at my apartment. I had no right. It wasn't your fault what happened to my dad, Ana."

"Dakota, it's okay."

"No, it's not. The last five years I have been so wrapped up in you that when I finally did see you again, it took me a while to come around, especially given the circumstances. I mean, seriously, could we not have just bumped into each other in a coffee shop or something?" He laughed a little, and her stomach flipped, the love she had held onto beginning to bloom again. This was the Dakota who had held her heart all these years.

"Wouldn't that have been nice," she agreed, looking back up at the stars.

"Oh." He reached behind him and handed her a bottle. "I brought you some water."

"Is that scotch in your glass?" She eyed his cup eagerly, and he nodded.

"Have at it." He handed it over, and she swallowed the contents in one gulp. The liquor burned the entire way down to her stomach.

When she looked back at him, his eyebrow was raised and his mouth turned up in an amused expression.

"Never seen a girl drink before?"

"Not that amount of scotch at one time. I had a few girlfriends who tried, but they usually ended up complaining and ordering something else."

Anastasia cleared her throat and looked down at her

feet. *Girlfriends. Does he have one now?* It wasn't like she hadn't expected him to see other women—hell, she'd dated Shane for over a year—but it still hurt like hell to hear it from his mouth.

"I'll be right back." Dakota disappeared into the house, returning quickly with two glasses.

"Terrenia has something similar to scotch. Gregory and I would have a drink after a long day of training." Grief tightened its ever-present grip around her heart.

"My mom told me that he and his wife were your biological parents." He paused, searching her gaze. "She said you were kidnapped by your uncle, which is why Mitch had you."

Anastasia raised an eyebrow.

Dakota shrugged. "You were out for a while at the hospital. She filled me in on what you two talked about. She also yelled at me for a bit." He laughed and held his glass out. "To good men like our dads."

They clinked glasses and took a drink.

"What's Terrenia like?" he asked, changing the subject as though he read her thoughts. "It's Terrenia, isn't it?" he added.

She closed her eyes and did her best to refocus her mind. "Yes, it is. It's beautiful. Actually, this place reminds me of it. I hadn't realized before, but that might be why I felt so at home there. This was the safest place I had growing up."

"Mom said that there's no electricity."

Anastasia laughed. "There's not. No running water, either."

"How do you—?" He held his hand up. "Never mind, I don't want to know."

Anastasia laughed and turned toward him. He stared at her intently, his eyes a bright blue even in the dim light. "What?" she asked.

"I missed that sound."

She smiled again and tucked a strand of hair behind her ear.

"I'm sorry Mitch found you back at the hospital," Dakota said, looking away from her. "Someone must have leaked your description."

"It's not your fault. I would have died had you not taken me to the hospital. So, I suppose I should thank you for saving my life."

He nodded, and his jaw tightened. "I thought I'd lost you again."

She wanted to tell him that he had never lost her the first time, that she had always been there, even if she hadn't been nearby. She wished she had the strength to tell him how much she missed him, that she'd thought of him every single day.

But it seemed as if they kept meeting at the wrong times. Mitch ripped them apart five years ago, and now Vincent and the Brutes were getting in her way. She couldn't allow her feelings for Dakota to interfere with her mission. She had people counting on her, people who had died for her... an entire world relying on her to end this war.

"It's going to take me some time," he said.

"That's understandable."

"I'm not talking about whether or not I believe you." He looked at her, and then quickly looked away. "After everything I've seen, I would have to be certifiable to *not* believe you."

"Then what are you talking about?"

"I'm talking about you and me. About getting back to where we were." He pulled in a deep breath. "It's going to take me time."

"Oh, Dakota. I—"

"There is something you need to understand— loving like that, believing with all of your heart that you are meant to be with someone and then having it all ripped away without any warning or explanation... that's heartbreak, Ana. I loved you so much."

"Dakota, I—"

"I'm not asking for you to say anything, just please be patient with me for now." He stood and walked back into the house.

His words packed a punch, and Anastasia felt them to the depths of her soul. He'd *loved* her, and she'd left him wondering where she was for five years. She had abandoned her best friend for another world.

What the hell kind of person did that make her?

ANASTASIA

"So, give us the rundown. What is going on out there?" Elizabeth asked Anastasia as the three of them sat around the kitchen table the next morning.

"From what I know, the Brutes are collecting weapons in this world. Vincent has a contact here who has been supplying them. They're trying to take over Terrenia, and when we were in the cave, I overheard him saying they had plans for Seattle as well." She paused, considering her next words. "Possibly the rest of this world along with it."

"But how does he plan to take over the whole *world*?" Dakota asked. "I know you said Terrenia had no guns, but we have them in abundance. The military is well stocked. How does he plan to succeed here?"

"Honestly, I'm not sure. He is very powerful, but Tony suspects, as did Gregory, that he has something going on behind the scenes. That there's some bigger power at work."

"Tony?" Dakota asked tightly.

"Tony is Gregory's best friend. Or, was, anyway," she added sadly. "He is the leader of the Fighters and has been like another father to me."

"I bet I know who his contact is." Dakota's jaw clenched.

"Mitch."

Mitch had been involved from Day One.

"That would be my guess, too." Dakota rubbed his chin. "There have been numerous murders within the city lately, and although some of them appear random, others leave a blood trail back to Mitch."

"The random ones would be people who saw the Brutes. They were instructed to kill anyone who saw them," Anastasia said.

"They got my partner," Dakota said.

Elizabeth gasped, reaching over to grab her son's hand.

"Your partner?" Anastasia asked.

Dakota nodded. "He was found the morning you arrived. It's why it took me so long to get back that day; I'd been at the precinct all morning." He rubbed his free hand over his eyes.

Anastasia touched his hand gently. Her power blazed in response to the connection the moment her skin touched his, and she quickly pulled away. *What the hell was that?* Dakota's eyes widened, and he met her gaze.

Had he felt it too?

"I have been hunting them for years now. There are very few weapons that can actually kill a Brute easily. Otherwise, you have to decapitate one to take it down."

"What weapons?"

"Blades must be coated with platinum. For some reason, the Brutes cannot tolerate that particular alloy. All weapons in Terrenia are forged from steel and then coated in platinum."

"But you can kill one without the platinum?"

"Yes. If you can manage to injure one fatally, it will eventually die, but will probably take you with it. They are incredibly strong and surprisingly quick for their size. Decapitation is the best method if you don't have any special weapons."

Elizabeth gasped, and Anastasia offered her an understanding smile. *Nothing like starting the day off by discussing decapitated heads.*

Anastasia pulled the two blades from her waistband and handed one to Dakota and the other to Elizabeth. "Carry these."

Elizabeth eyed the weapon warily. "Maybe I should leave the fighting up to the two of you."

"Carry it, Mom," Dakota urged. "Just in case you need one."

She nodded and looked back at Anastasia.

"This alone won't kill them. The platinum will hurt them, and they will slow, but it won't kill them unless you cause some damage with it."

"How many have you killed?" Elizabeth asked her.

"I honestly have no clue."

ANASTASIA WALKED THE PERIMETER OF THE CABIN, searching for anything that would compromise their safety.

Dakota approached, keeping pace beside her.

"How's your side?" he asked.

"I feel fine. Your mom opened the stitches slightly, and once I was able to get more of the healing salve inside, it started feeling much better."

He nodded and continued walking beside her. "You know, had I not seen what I did that night in the alley, I might not have believed you." He laughed, but there was no humor in the sound.

"I can't blame you. When my dad first came for me, I thought I was dead. Or that I was just dreaming."

"It's just a lot to wrap my head around."

"It is," she agreed.

They continued walking around the cabin, enjoying the sounds of nature. Just as they reached the stairs, the hairs on the back of her neck stood, and she got the overwhelming feeling she was being watched.

"Well, isn't this sweet?"

Anastasia's body went rigid as Mitch appeared in front of her on the porch. He looked just as she remembered him, the only sign of aging the slight graying at his temples.

"You still look like the little whore you always were. Running around, screwing the younger Parker all over again. I suppose times don't change, do they, Anastasia?"

"Ana, come back to me." Dakota's voice was muffled and far away.

"Still weak." Mitch scoffed and stepped down the steps until he stood right in front of her. *"I don't know why he even bothered keeping you alive. You are nothing but a powerless little slut."*

His breath came out in a hot wave, and she felt it on her face. The stench of the alcohol he'd been drinking filled her lungs and made her gag.

"Ana." Dakota gripped her hand, and his touch helped her focus a little.

"He's going to come for you. He's already slaughtered all your friends in Terrenia."

She gasped, and he laughed.

"What the hell did you think was going to happen? You've been here fucking him." He gestured to Dakota. *"And left everyone else to fend for themselves."*

"Ana," Dakota repeated, squeezing her hand again.

"There is nothing Parker is going to be able to do to protect you. He can't even see me now." Mitch laughed and stepped toward her. *"You are going to die, Anasta-*

sia. Just as your birth parents did. Only your death won't be so humane." He lunged for her, and she fell backward onto the ground.

She shook violently as fear surged like ice through her veins, chilling her to the core.

Dakota came into focus, and she blinked rapidly, quickly searching the area for Mitch.

"Ana!" Dakota yelled as he cupped her face with his hands and stared into her eyes.

"He killed everyone."

"What are you talking about? Who killed who?"

"Vincent. Mitch said he killed everyone." Her heart felt like someone had shoved a blade through it. *Was he telling the truth? Are they all dead?*

Tears streamed down her cheeks and fell to the dirt beside her.

"What happened?" Elizabeth ran out and crouched beside them.

"I don't know; she's not making any fucking sense." He turned her face to look at him. "Ana, what happened?"

"Mitch was here."

"No, he wasn't. It was only us."

She shook her head. "No. I'm not sure how, but he projected himself here." Could Mitch have magic as well? Or had Vincent projected him here to deliver the message? She shut her eyes as another wave of pain crushed over her. She wanted to die; she deserved to die with her friends. She'd left them behind and now they were all gone.

"They can't be dead."

"I see you got the message."

Dakota jumped up, moving quickly to position himself between Maximus and Anastasia. Elizabeth gripped Anastasia's arm and helped her to her feet.

Anastasia stepped beside Dakota. "Maximus," she said, his name practically a snarl.

His blond hair was slicked back, his mouth smirking with victory. *Keep fucking smiling.* She couldn't *wait* to wipe that smug grin from his face—permanently.

Dakota gripped her hand, and she looked down to see her skin was glowing. The contact of his skin against hers sent a ripple through her, making her feel even more powerful.

"Oh, this must be your bestie, huh? The one you were always hung up on." Maximus laughed and looked at Dakota. "Tell me, Anastasia, how would he feel about knowing you murdered someone?" He bared his teeth.

"She deserved to die," she said to Maximus. "Ophelia was a psychopath. Which, I suppose, is why the two of you got along so well."

"You will not say her name!" he screamed.

"Oh, I'm sorry, does that bother you, Maximus?" she taunted. If battling him all those years had taught her anything, it was that maximus was a loose cannon. Anger was his weakness. She held her palm up and watched the orb form on her palm. "Tell me, would you like to die like her?"

"I wouldn't do that if I were you, Anastasia. Would end badly for your boy and his mother." Maximus pointed behind her, and she turned.

They were completely surrounded by Brutes. Instead of panic, her magic burned in response. She felt every single strand of power as it weaved its way to the surface.

For Gregory.

For Annabelle.

For Tony.

For Brady.

For Shane.

For Andrew.

For George.

The list grew on and on in her mind as each face flashed through her memory. If Mitch had been telling the truth—and he had no reason to lie—they were all *dead.* Every single last member of her family except for the two standing beside her now.

What the hell did light or dark magic matter now? She looked over at Dakota who stood beside her, a pillar of strength even now during what might turn out to be her darkest hour.

There was only one way out of this. She possessed one tool she knew wouldn't fail her. The only problem was, it could also be the one choice that would change her forever.

"Put it out, Anastasia!" Maximus screamed, and she opened her eyes. Whatever was reflected in them must have scared the shit out of him because he took a step back.

"Ana," Dakota called for her, but she pushed his voice aside, needing to focus. For the first time, she pushed away her fear, and succumbed to the dark.

Power surged through her veins, and she felt it hammer into her body, nearly knocking her over. Dakota's grip tightened on her hand, and she used him to anchor her in the present.

She breathed deeply and stared into the face of her enemy. "You don't stand a chance against me, Maximus."

"Maybe not." He raised the gun to Dakota. "But I have other ways of dropping you to your knees."

"No!" Elizabeth screamed.

"You killed Ophelia, and now I'm going to take your precious Dakota away from you."

Anastasia stared at him, no worry in her mind; he wouldn't get the chance to kill anyone today. She released Dakota's hand and opened her palms to reveal two glowing orbs. They were no longer the bright white lights that she'd conjured before, but rather twin balls of swirling green power.

Maximus sneered. "I've seen that trick before."

The balls exploded, and Dakota dove on top of his mother as each tiny shard buried itself into the chests of the Brutes that flanked them.

Maximus stared at her and then looked back to the bodies behind her in shock as they disappeared into piles of ash.

"Ever seen *that* trick before?" she asked, her voice dripping with anger.

The Brutes behind him charged her, and as each one drew close, she threw her palm out, sending a ball of magic through their chests. They fell, one by one, until all that remained was Anastasia and Maximus standing in the center of a pile of ash.

Lightning split the sky above, and she wasn't sure whether it was a storm or an effect of the magic surging through the air.

Maximus lifted his gun and aimed it at her heart, but before he pulled the trigger, he froze. His head tilted as though he listened to something she couldn't quite hear. Anastasia spun to search for Dakota, and saw he and Elizabeth were both frozen as well.

"My dear child. What have we here?" Vincent appeared in the clearing beside Maximus.

ANASTASIA

"You," she growled.

"You *are* fascinating."

"I'm going to kill you."

He laughed. "No, you won't."

She conjured up another ball of light and heaved it at Vincent, but he put up his hand, and the ball crashed to the ground, leaving nothing but a small scorch mark in the grass.

Anastasia's mouth fell open.

"My brother trained you well, but not well enough, it seems." He waved his hand, and something ripped her backward. Her back hit the side of Dakota's car, pain momentarily blurring her vision. Fear surged through her; how the hell was she supposed to defeat him?

"You are capable of so much, Anastasia. I knew it

from the second I laid eyes on you. It's why I only *relocated* you when I'd originally set out to kill you."

"I'm supposed to thank you for placing me at the hands of someone who beat me?" She rose to her feet quickly.

"It's unfortunate that Mitch treated you the way he did, but it seems as if it only benefited you in the long run. Wouldn't you agree?"

She stared at him, blood pumping like lava through her veins. Her pulse roared in her ears.

"If you come with me, I will spare them, and I will train you to become so much more than you are."

"Why the fuck would I come with you? You killed them all!" She charged him, but he flung her aside again.

"*You* abandoned them, Anastasia. So who is really the murderer? You may not have raised a hand against them, but you sure as hell didn't help." His eyes were silver, his pupils twin pools of darkness. "I am giving you a second chance to save someone other than yourself."

"I won't turn dark," she cried as she tried to push up from the ground. Her movement was futile, as his magic just pressed down on her harder, an invisible barrier pinning her to the ground.

He shook his head, annoyance twisting his features. "There is so much more than light and dark, Anastasia. One day, you will see that."

"My father wouldn't join you, and neither will I."

His jaw tightened at the memory of his brother, and for a moment, his eyes flashed blue. He shook his head, and they were silver again, so quickly she was sure she must've imagined it. "Gregory was weak. It's unfortunate that things ended the way they did with him."

"You had him killed," she snapped, the grief sending a fresh wave of pain over her.

"He was weak," he repeated, all traces of the momentary pain erased from his hard face. "So afraid of his own power that he left his innocent daughter unprotected."

His words cut through her like a knife. "He was not weak!" She blasted out of his hold and sent a ball of light flying toward him.

"Everything that has happened, everything that I've done, has been because he wouldn't be who I needed him to be." Vincent growled and slammed her back again.

"What the hell does that mean?"

Not answering her question, he continued. "He even lied to you. Spent five years trying to dampen your power knowing it would lead to your death. *He was a coward.*"

"No! You're lying!" she cried, and although she felt the strain on her mind and body from the magic she'd used, she sent another blast aimed directly at him.

It smacked into an invisible barrier, and she crumbled to her knees. Her body shook, she could still feel the depths of her power, beckoning her closer, but the

idea of diving into the swirling pool had her terrified.
What if she didn't come back?

"Am I? Tell me, did my brother teach you about the
portals?" He paused only briefly. "I'm guessing he
didn't. I'm sure it was just an oversight and not a way to
keep you from leaving." He knelt in front of her and
gripped her by the throat. Her lungs burned from the
lack of oxygen as he lifted her from the ground. "If you
won't join me, then you must die." He squeezed tighter,
and his silver eyes flashed back to blue.

"Anastasia." He dropped her and stepped back as if
she were toxic.

She stared up at him, her breaths coming in
wheezing gasps.

"I'm sorry." He shook his head, and Anastasia stared
at him, more confused than anything.

"For what? Kidnapping me? Or killing my parents?"

"I—" He shook his head again, and when he refocused on her, his eyes were blazing silver. "I'm done with
you!" He flung his hand out, and Anastasia slammed back
into the ground. Although he wasn't touching her, she felt
his hand around her throat and she struggled to breathe.

She fought to get free from his invisible hold, and
black spots swam in her vision. If she didn't get free
soon, she would die.

She knew it.

"No!" Vincent screamed, and the hold released.
Gasping for air, Anastasia pushed to her feet. He was

staring at her, eyes blazing blue. "You will pay." He roared and disappeared. She crumbled to the ground and gasped for breath. *What the fuck was that?*

"Anastasia!" Maximus screamed.

She looked up as a gunshot rang through the trees. Maximus crumbled to the ground. Dakota stood behind him, gun raised, his eyes wide. When their gazes locked, he lowered the gun and rushed to her.

"What the hell happened?" He slid to his knees, Elizabeth right beside him.

Anastasia stared past them at the trees. What was she supposed to do now? Why hadn't Vincent killed her? It wasn't like she'd been able to do much to stop him.

"Anastasia," Elizabeth's voice was soft.

"I bet he didn't even teach you about the portals." Vincent's words rang in her mind, and she wondered if it were possible to return without a vial. It had to be, didn't it? She hadn't seen him use one in the cavern. She had to try, even if it meant risking using too much power.

"I have to go home," Anastasia finally said. She had to see if what they'd said was true, needed to witness the destruction with her own eyes before she could move forward.

"To Terrenia?" Dakota asked, his brow furrowed.

She nodded.

He pulled her to her feet, and she gripped his hand

like a lifeline, her body still shaking uncontrollably. *Did she even have enough power left?*

Dakota took a deep breath and squared his shoulders, tightening his grip on her hand. "Then let's go."

Exhausted, Anastasia closed her eyes and searched for any trace of power left. She imagined Terrenia, much like she did when she pictured the orbs of light to summon them.

Elizabeth gasped. "Oh my."

Anastasia opened her eyes. A portal glowed brightly in front of them. The swirling blue light called to her, a beacon beckoning her home.

What would she find when she stepped through?

Elizabeth grabbed her other hand, and Anastasia swallowed hard, looking at her two remaining loved ones. "Are you sure you want to come with me?"

"Yes," they said in unison.

Dakota squeezed her hand, and their connection gave her the strength she needed to move forward.

If her friends in Terrenia were all dead, Vincent would pay for it just like he was going to pay for the other deaths he was responsible for.

Somehow, she would make him pay for every single pain-filled moment he had caused her and those she loved.

Taking one last deep breath and gripping the hands of Dakota and Elizabeth, Anastasia stepped into the swirling blue light.

49

ANASTASIA

They emerged from the light just outside the training cottage.

She had done it! And better yet, she didn't feel as if the excess magic had changed her.

Anastasia looked around, scanning the area for damage, but there was none. She felt the first wave of hope surge through her. Maybe they'd been lying!

Breaking into a run, she raced down the path toward the village's center. As she rounded the last corner, her body impacted with something hard, sending her flying back to the ground.

"What the hell?"

"Tony!" she screamed, jumping to her feet. She wrapped her arms around him, relief surging through her as she held onto the man who'd been so much more than a friend to her.

"It's about damn time! I was so worried." He squeezed her fiercely, then set her down on her feet.

"Everyone else?" she asked, searching the area.

"What about them?"

"Are they alive?"

Tony nodded, and Anastasia let out a cry.

"What's wrong?"

"I'm fine," she sniffled. "Vincent told me he killed you all. Tony, I thought you were dead."

"You saw Vincent?"

She nodded.

Dakota cleared his throat behind her, and Tony looked over her shoulder. His eyes widened, and Anastasia stepped to the side.

"Tony, this is Dakota Parker, and his mother, Elizabeth. Dakota, Elizabeth, this is Tony."

Tony extended his hand to Dakota. "I've heard many things about you, Dakota."

"Same."

"Elizabeth, it is lovely to meet you." Tony took her hand and held it for a breadth longer than he had Dakota's. "Did your husband not accompany you?" he asked.

Elizabeth shook her head. "He passed away a few years back," she answered sadly.

"I'm sorry to hear that. Anastasia told me wonderful stories about him."

"Anastasia!" Brady rounded the corner and made a

beeline for her. He lifted her in a hug and set her back to the ground. He lifted his eyes to Dakota and Elizabeth.

"Brady, this is—"

"The infamous Dakota Parker." Brady smiled and extended his hand.

Dakota glanced at Anastasia and heat rushed to her cheeks.

"She talked about you a time or two." Brady shrugged.

"Oh, did she?" Elizabeth asked as she smiled and nudged Anastasia. "Hi, I'm Elizabeth, the infamous Dakota's mother."

"It's nice to meet you, Mrs. Parker. Anastasia spoke fondly of you and your husband as well." Brady smiled and turned back to Anastasia.

"What's been going on?" Anastasia turned her attention back to Tony. "Anymore attacks?"

"No. The others and I made it back this morning. Come on, Selena will want to see you."

They started down the path and a giant ball of fur slammed into Anastasia, knocking her to the ground.

Elizabeth screamed. "Ana!"

"It's all right." She laughed as a rough tongue scratched the side of her face. "Hey girl," she greeted Kaley, sitting up to wrap her arms around the feline's neck. "I missed you, too, girl."

"She's been miserable without you," Tony said. "Following me everywhere. I was worried she might eat me one day out of anger if you never returned." He laughed, and Kaley turned her intelligent eyes to Dakota.

"This," Anastasia said as she stood. "Is Kaley."

"What is she?" Elizabeth asked in wonder.

"A Terrenian Feline. She's my protector," Anastasia explained.

"She's beautiful." Elizabeth held her hand out, and Kaley nuzzled it in response. "And so soft!"

Kaley turned her head back to Dakota, and he stared at her. A moment later, Kaley bowed to him, surprising them all.

"What's she doing?" he asked.

Anastasia stared. "I don't know. She's never done that before." She looked up, her heart freezing momentarily in her chest.

Shane stood at the end of the path, his eyes fixated on her face. *Shit.*

Three heartbeats passed before he stepped toward them. "Anastasia, I'm glad to see you've returned." His jaw was set, his mouth in a tight line. He wore a loose shirt, and Anastasia wondered how the wound in his abdomen was healing.

She cleared her throat. "I'm happy to see you're alive."

He smiled. "Takes more than that to get rid of me." His eyes traveled to Dakota, who stood taller, arms crossed over his chest.

Well, this is just great, isn't it?

"Dakota, this is my friend, Shane."

"Dakota?" Shane's green eyes shot to her face, and she nodded. He knew exactly who Dakota was since Anastasia had told him her best friend was the reason they couldn't be together.

Dakota held out his hand, and Shane stepped forward to take it. "Nice to meet you."

"Yeah, you too," Shane said, quickly releasing Dakota's hand.

Brady let out an awkward laugh, and Anastasia glared at him.

He shrugged. "Should we go see my mom now?"

They made their way toward the village together. The buildings were still in the process of being rebuilt, and her heart ached seeing the look of defeat on her people's faces.

At least they were alive.

They stepped into Selena's cabin, and she turned.

"Anastasia!" Sarah greeted her with a hug, and Anastasia released the sixteen-year-old with a smile.

"I missed you."

"I missed you, too." Sarah grinned.

"Honey, why don't you go see if you can help Zarina?"

"Yes, momma." Sarah bounded from the house.

"I'm happy to see you're back." Selena embraced Anastasia. "We feared the worst when you didn't return right away."

"I'm happy to be back." She introduced Elizabeth and Dakota, and looked at the large map hanging on the wall. Small, sharpened pieces of branches had been painted red, and were scattered around the map.

"Those are known Brute attacks," Selena explained. "As Tony and the others made their way back, they took note of where the destruction was. We were trying to determine a pattern, but so far it just seems random."

"There has to be a bigger picture," Anastasia said as she searched the map. "After seeing him in person, and hearing what he plans, I just don't see how he can pull it off alone. Even with the amount of power he has on his side."

"I agree, but preparing is all we can do right now. We were getting ready to put together a larger team and flush out the caves, but if they leave right now, we will be left defenseless."

"I'm willing to bet they've already moved on." Tony crossed his arms. "Would be foolish to stay after we found them. They went through a lot of trouble to hide."

"What did you learn, Anastasia?" Selena asked.

Anastasia leaned against the counter. "He is planning on taking over Seattle and, by my best guess, the rest of the world with it. I don't know exactly what his motives are, other than he wants more power."

"That could be his singular motive," Tony commented. "I've seen a lot of horrible things done in the name of power."

"Agreed," Dakota said.

Shane glanced up briefly, and then looked back at the map.

"What is the next step?" Selena asked.

"I want to go through my dad's stuff. He kept a journal, and I'm hoping there's something in there that we can use."

"You don't think he would have told you about it if there was?" Tony asked.

"He spent five years trying to dampen your power, knowing it would lead to your death." Vincent's voice popped into her head again.

"I don't want to risk an oversight," she told him.

Tony nodded. "I need to get back to the medical cottage. I'm afraid we lost Melody that night they attacked, so I've been doing what I can with field dressings." Tony turned to leave. "I can help," Elizabeth offered. "Doctor." She pointed to herself.

Tony smiled. "That would be wonderful, thank you."

"Be careful," Dakota told his mom.

"I will take care of her." Tony nodded at Dakota, and he and Elizabeth stepped from the cottage.

"Do you need help going through anything?" Shane asked tightly. "I know how difficult it will be for you." He looked at Dakota, who stared back unwavering.

"I will let you know. Thanks for the offer." She turned to leave.

"Anastasia, wait."

She turned back, and Shane crossed the room to pull her in for a tight hug. "I missed you," he whispered just before he released her and stepped from the room.

"Shall we?" Anastasia asked awkwardly. She looked up at Dakota, whose face was unreadable.

"Sure," he responded.

"I'll let you know if we find anything," she told Selena, grabbing Dakota's hand to lead him back outside.

50

DAKOTA

Dakota studied Anastasia as she looked up at the looming façade of a small cabin. It was built using logs, just as the other places in town had been, and was secluded from the others.

His restraint was barely leashed as he watched her, his mind a jealous mess after her confrontation with Shane.

He had never thought of her with another man, so the idea that she had cared—possibly loved—someone else was a dagger to his heart.

A muscle in Dakota's jaw jumped, and he decided he wanted—no, *he needed*—to tell her how he felt. "After my dad was killed, I entered the Academy. I wanted to become a cop as soon as I could so that I could go after Mitch."

She turned to face him, and he let out a deep breath.

"I worked my ass off and made detective within two years. When I was promoted, and Harry and I became partners, I knew that I had to do whatever I could to keep what happened to you from happening to anyone else." He rubbed his hands over his face. "My first year, I was put on a case where a young mom had died. Her husband told us that she had simply fallen off a stool while she was cleaning." He ground his teeth together as the memory took form in his mind.

"He was so good at pretending he was upset. Had I not known the signs of abuse, I might have believed him. They had a young daughter, six years old. He had a good lawyer, though, and he got off. There was no reason he shouldn't have been locked up. They even gave custody of his daughter back to him." Dakota stood and began pacing in front of her. "I wanted to beat the shit out of him. I followed him one night after he dropped his daughter off at his mother's house and went to a bar. He was walking out with a leggy brunette. Had it not been for her, I probably would have jumped on the opportunity. He was drunk, and more than likely wouldn't have remembered it anyway." He turned to face her now.

"I went home angry with myself for what I had almost done. Three hours later, I got the call that his daughter had been brought to the hospital. Her father had told the nurses that she tripped and fell onto the coffee table. She had to get two stitches in her forehead, and I lost it. Had it not been for Harry, I probably would have killed him that night in the hospital."

"What happened to the little girl?"

"We were finally able to put him away for the abuse, and she went to live with her maternal grandparents."

"Good."

He nodded in agreement. "I saw you in every single victim's face, Ana. I searched for you in every Jane Doe they brought into the morgue. I made every single abuse case that came in my personal mission to try and make up for the fact that I hadn't been able to save you."

"Dakota." She reached up and cupped his face, the contact sending a shock through his system. "You *did* save me. Every single day I woke up was because of you. Knowing you were there for me is what made my life worth something. You pulled me out of hell more times than you can even imagine."

"You have always been it for me," he said tightly. "I was young, and I was stupid, or I would have told you long before that night in the park."

"Dakota," she whispered.

"Please just tell me you feel the same. Forget about everything else going on right now and just tell me that I'm not crazy."

"You're not. You were always it for me, too."

"Thank God." He cupped the back of her neck and pulled her in, crushing his mouth to hers and knocking the breath from his lungs. Her hands gripped his shoulders, and he buried his own in her hair. She was so fucking perfect, and he'd be damned if he lost her again.

She was his. He was staking his claim and, based on her response, she was accepting. Her mouth opened beneath his, their tongues meeting in a frenzied dance that had his blood boiling within his veins.

He pulled away and leaned his forehead against hers. Her breath was ragged, mimicking his own.

"Fuck. I've missed you." He groaned.

"I missed you, too."

"I need you, Ana. I've always needed you." He pulled away and looked into those eyes he knew so well.

"I have a war to fight."

"I know."

"I have to stay focused."

"*We* have a war to fight. *We* will stay focused." She was pulling away from him, and he had no intention of letting her go. He reached forward and cupped her cheek.

Her bottom lip quivered, and she turned to face the house again. He linked his fingers with hers, and pulled her up onto the porch.

"You are my strength, Ana. Let me be yours."

ANASTASIA

Anastasia stepped into the house and swallowed hard. It looked exactly the same, the damage from Ophelia's attack still present with the disheveled furniture and the blood-stained wood floor.

She averted her eyes and, using the hand Dakota wasn't holding, closed the door behind her.

"So, this is where you've been?" Dakota asked as he looked around the room.

She nodded tightly, not ready to speak yet.

"You okay?" he asked, squeezing her hand.

"It's just hard. The last time I was here was the night—"

"Your father died?"

"Yes. How did you know?"

He shrugged. "It was just a guess. Do you need to leave?"

"No. I want to do this." She released his hand and walked over to Gregory's room; if she was going to find his journal anywhere, it would be in there.

"If you need me, I'm here."

She offered him a smile, grateful he was letting her face this part alone. Anastasia pushed the door open, and Gregory's scent filled her lungs. The lump in her throat grew, and she beat back the tears that were fighting their way to the surface.

She stood in the doorway a moment, staring into the place where her father had slept. His bed was turned down as if simply waiting for him to climb into it come nightfall. As if his bed never got the memo that he was never going to slip beneath the blankets again.

His robe was slung over a chair, his boots set neatly beside it. She moved further in and turned to face his dresser. The last remaining vials of the healing potion were lined up on the wooden surface

Anastasia would collect them before they went after Vincent.

She looked at the small portrait of Gregory and Annabelle that they'd had painted years before Anastasia's arrival in Terrenia. They had been so happy together. She hoped that they had found each other again in the afterlife.

Anastasia gently opened the top drawer of his dresser, and there, nestled in between some clothing, was his leather-bound journal. Her pulse began to race when she lifted it.

After taking a seat on the edge of his bed, Anastasia opened the journal to the first page and took a step into Gregory's mind.

My Dearest Annabelle,

I fear I may not make it without you. I have been trying so hard to focus on the good that is still in the world, just as you taught me to, but I have been finding it so difficult to see past the evil. Are you still here with me, love? Sometimes it's as if I can feel you standing next to me. I keep waiting for you to walk through that door with your smile, and for your laughter to fill the room, and then, when I remember you're gone, I just want to crawl into a hole and die with you.

I know I cannot. I know that our daughter needs me, but I am finding it so hard to make myself move from this bed. You were my light; how am I supposed to stay away from the dark now?

Anastasia's fingers trembled on the page. She closed her eyes, and the tears that she worked so hard to hold back began to fall. When she opened her eyes, she continued reading.

Why didn't I listen to his warning? I could have stopped her training, and we could have lived our lives as a family, the way we never were able to before. Why was I so stubborn? Please forgive me, my love.

Gregory

His warning? Had Vincent warned Gregory that he would come for Annabelle? She quickly turned the page.

Annabelle,

I am trying to move forward. I have been watching Anastasia in her training with Tony. She is magnificent. You would be so proud of her. Our daughter shines with a brighter light than I have ever seen before. She moves with speed and purpose when she fights, and I know she will make a formidable enemy to any who dare to cross her. I am tempted to keep her with me. To not allow her to go into war with him. It's selfish, I know, but she is all I have left. All that I have left to remind me of you.

I have not seen the spark in her yet, but I know that when it comes, she will be more powerful than we ever imagined. At times I worry it may be too much for her, but then I look at her, and I know she will be able to handle it. Never has there been a brighter star than our Anastasia.

Gregory

Anastasia gripped the journal to her chest. He had

always believed in her. What had she done to deserve such unwavering faith?

She opened the journal to the next page.

Annabelle,

I saw it today. Maximus cornered and taunted Anastasia. Had I not seen it in her eyes, I may have intervened and made him a mute for the things he said to her.

She used her magic without even realizing it. With no prior knowledge of her abilities, she managed to take him down without so much as a fight from him or his two accomplices.

I spoke with her afterward. She told me that Dakota was the one who brought her back. He is her light, and while it thrills me that she has someone who, even after all this time, is able to bring her back from the brink of darkness, it saddens me a little because I know she will need to one day go back to him.

I am not ready to lose her.

Gregory

She wiped a tear from her cheek and turned the page.

Anastasia,

My dear child. If you are reading this, then I fear I am no longer with you. There are so many things I have not yet told you! First and foremost, you must know that I am so proud of you. You have blossomed into the most wonderful young woman I have ever known. You have been a light in my life since the moment you were born, and although you were taken from us, you continued to be our world until the day we both stopped breathing and even beyond that.

Please do not mourn me. Know that I am watching over you, just as your mother is, and we will always be here with you. You will never be alone, Anastasia. I will try now to tell you the things I did not have the courage to tell you in life.

Your magic will continue to grow into something that may frighten you at first; don't let it. You will always be in control. I have never seen anyone whose light burned brighter than yours. Do not fear the power—embrace it. Vincent's downfall was that he had no light because he never loved anyone except himself. I had your mother; it's why I never strayed. You have Dakota and, Anastasia, you must make it back to him. He is a wonderful man. I spoke to him quite a few times when I visited. I was always watching over him because I knew how much he meant to you.

You need to know that you don't have to have a vial to open a portal. You only need to conjure the power, much in the way you call upon the light in your palm. I used the vials because I was afraid I might not be able to pull myself away. I am sorry that

I never told you about the ability to revisit your world; I fear I was selfish in worrying that you may never return to me.

In order to defeat Vincent, you are going to need to embrace everything inside of you.

You will succeed. I know that you will bring peace to our world once again.

Do not fear the dark, Anastasia. Without it, there would be no place for light, and that's what you are, my dear child, light in an ever darkening world.

You must trust Tony; he has been the best friend I could have ever asked for, and the brother I always wished for. He will never lead you astray.

The battles that we fight silently are sometimes the most difficult, and I know that you have fought plenty. Know now that the ones you have faced have not made you weaker—you are a stronger person for the way you survived. Never give up, my daughter. You are the strongest Fighter I have ever had the pleasure to know.

I will always love you, and I will always be with you, even though you may not see me.

Your father

Anastasia quickly flipped through the rest of the pages, but they were blank. Nothing had been written in the journal after his letter to her. Ophelia must have gotten to him before he could write more. How had he known he was going to die?

Her thoughts drifted back to the night on the porch when he'd told her that if anything was ever to happen to him, he wanted her to know how much she was loved, and how proud he was.

Was it possible the same seer who spoke of her destiny had foretold his death?

She shut the journal and curled her legs up underneath her. All of the pain and grief she had been fighting came crashing down on her as her mind continued to replay scenes from her time with Gregory.

Eventually, Dakota's arms surrounded her as he pulled her into his lap and cradled her against his chest.

"It's okay, Ana, I'm here." He kissed her forehead and held her while she cried.

52

ANASTASIA

When she opened her swollen eyes, the only light came from the embers in the fireplace. She sat up quickly, searching the living room. Relief filled her when her gaze landed on Dakota beside her.

"It was getting cold, so I started a fire and brought you out here."

"I'm sorry I fell asleep."

"Don't be."

The power she'd used back in Seattle must have drained her more than she'd considered.

"How are you?"

"Better." She was surprised that she did actually feel better, as if a weight had finally been lifted off of her chest. "And like I need a drink."

He laughed. "That's my girl." He leaned over and kissed her lightly, then got to his feet. "Why don't we get one and then you can tell me what you found out? If you want to, that is."

"Sounds good to me." She set the journal down on the table to retrieve two cups and the bottle of liquor Gregory kept tucked away in the cabinet.

"So, is this your dad?" Dakota asked as he lifted the portrait that had been in Gregory's room from the table. "I brought it out after I carried you to the couch," he explained.

"Yes, that's him and my mother, Annabelle."

"I met him," Dakota told her.

"He said that he visited you."

Dakota's brow furrowed.

"In the notebook. He said that he kept an eye on you because of how much you meant to me."

"He did. Except he called himself Silvan."

She smiled. "That was his last name."

"That sneaky bastard." Dakota laughed. "I mean that lovingly, of course."

"I know you do." She handed him a cup and took a drink from her own.

"He always sat at the same spot in the bar down the street from my apartment. We became friends. I told him things I never felt comfortable telling another person."

"He had that effect on people," she said, nodding. "As did my mother."

"Damn." He took a long drink from his cup. "I'm going to miss talking to him."

"To Gregory." She held out her cup, and Dakota clinked his against hers.

"To Gregory Silvan."

They sipped their liquor in silence, listening to the crackling embers in the dying fire.

Once they finished their drinks, Anastasia led Dakota back down toward the village. As they walked, she absorbed the sounds of the insects and animals moving through the trees in the night air.

All was calm in Terrenia—for now.

There was no telling what would happen tomorrow, or the next day for that matter. Not while Vincent still walked any of the worlds.

As they neared the village, Anastasia heard the faint sound of someone strumming a guitar and wondered who was playing tonight. Her thoughts were interrupted when Kaley padded over. Anastasia stifled a laugh when Dakota jolted. He glared at her, and she shrugged.

"That is a big ass cat," he said defensively.

"She's not even fully grown yet." Anastasia rubbed the feline's soft black fur as they walked.

"Seriously?"

"My dad said they can get to about seven feet if they stand on their feet."

"Fuck," he said, and Anastasia grinned again.

"Don't be afraid; I'll protect you." She smiled up at him, and his blue eyes held her own again. The corner of his mouth was turned up in a knowing smile, and he leaned down to press a gentle kiss to her lips.

Her legs went weak, and he tightened his arm around her waist.

Someone cleared their throat, and Anastasia pulled back.

"Selena sent me to find you," Shane said tightly, his eyes boring into Dakota's.

"Is everything okay?" she asked.

He stared at Dakota for a few more seconds, and then turned slowly to her. "She wants to know what your next move is." Shane spun and marched back toward the village.

"Well that was awkward," Dakota murmured.

"Sorry about that."

"What the hell is his deal?"

"Well," Anastasia began, "we… saw each other for a while."

Dakota's eyebrows rose. "Oh?"

Anastasia nodded. "I was trying to move on."

"Move on?"

"From you," she said, ripping the Band-Aid off. No sense in keeping secrets. "I knew you probably had a girlfriend—or five—and I was tired of pining for someone I may never see again."

"Gotcha," he said as he resumed walking back down the path.

"Gotcha?"

Dakota let out a laugh. "Look, Ana." He stopped

and turned to face her. "Am I thrilled that you dated Fighter boy over there? Hell no, but we were apart for five years. I was hardly celibate." His words were logical, but they sent a small pang through her heart. Dakota brushed a stray hair behind her ear. "The past doesn't matter right now. Not when we've finally got another chance." He stepped closer to her, and kissed the top of her head. "So don't let it get in the way."

Anastasia offered him a smile. "Okay."

They entered the clearing, and Anastasia smiled. Nearly the entire village had gathered in its center to hear Andrew plucking away at a guitar. Children and couples danced around the fire pit, laughing and smiling as if they didn't have a care in the world.

She spotted Elizabeth and Tony standing on the front porch of the medical cottage, Tony leaning down to say something to her and Elizabeth laughing heartily. It was nice, this vision of peace.

But her gut told her it wasn't going to last long.

They headed for Selena's house, where Shane waited on the porch steps. His jaw was tight, his mouth set in a humorless line. He opened the door for her, and she turned to Dakota.

"I'll be right in," she said.

He raised an eyebrow and looked at Shane before nodding and stepping inside.

The door shut, and Shane crossed his muscular arms over his chest.

"Want to tell me why you're acting like an ass?" Anastasia snapped.

He let out a breath. "Oh, I don't know, *Ana*. How about the fact that he shows up and now all of a sudden his opinion matters when it comes to *Terrenian business*."

"Dakota is smart, Shane. He can help us."

Shane rolled his eyes.

"Look, I get that you're pissed off because we didn't work out. But that was *four* years ago, Shane. Don't you think it might be time to move the hell on? If you remember, I told you when we split that the feelings I still had for Dakota were the reason why. I was honest with you about it, and how do you repay me? By being an ass to us both when I come home."

"I never thought you'd see him again!"

She glared at him. "So you believed I would, what, get over him eventually and get back with you?"

Shane looked away angrily, then back at her. "I had hoped so."

"Well, I'm sorry, but I just don't see you as anything but a friend." She headed into the cabin, and shut the door behind her.

Dakota and Selena stood talking in the living area, and she made her way over to them. Part of her felt incredibly guilty for letting Shane down. But wasn't that better than leading him on? Letting him think she loved him when every night, whether they were sharing a bed or not, her thoughts drifted to Dakota?

She looked up at him as he focused on the map hanging on the wall. His jaw was covered in a few days' growth, his eyes narrowed on the markings. As if he sensed her, he looked back at her and smiled.

Warmth filled her chest. So he felt it too. That humming in the blood that screamed *that's the one*.

"So, what's our next step?" Selena said, interrupting her thoughts. "Did you find anything in Gregory's journal?"

Anastasia shook her head sadly. "It was just a journal. Nothing in there about stopping Vincent or healing Terrenia."

"Dammit," she cursed. "What are we supposed to do?"

"We know he's in Seattle now," Dakota added. "And that he probably won't be leaving until he's done with whatever the hell it is he's planning."

"True," Selena agreed.

"We also know that he has to be more cautious there, seeing as he has the military to go up against if things go sour."

Anastasia nodded. "Here, he could hit us with everything he's got and we could do little to defend."

"So I say we hit him in Seattle. I know the city well and have enough contacts that I should be able to find out where he's hiding."

Anastasia's heart pounded in her chest as a plan took form. "That's a wonderful idea." She smiled. "Attack where he least expects it. After all, he knows we came back here."

"Exactly." Dakota nodded.

Selena nodded. "How many Fighters do you want to take?"

"I don't think we need to take any," Anastasia told her. "Right now, stealth is going to be our greatest weapon. If we go in there taking a bunch of large men who've never seen a car, we'll stick out like a sore thumb."

The other woman raised an eyebrow. "Car?"

Exactly. Anastasia shrugged, not wanting to explain at the moment. The door opened, and Tony and Elizabeth entered on a laugh.

"I thought I saw you two come in here." Elizabeth wrapped an arm around her son.

"What's going on?" Tony asked.

"We think we've got a plan," Anastasia told him with a grin. "One that will give us the advantage we've been lacking."

53

ANASTASIA

"I don't like it." Tony commented once they'd finished filling him in. "You two going up against Vincent alone? Sounds like suicide to me."

"Not if we don't get caught," Anastasia said.

"And if you do get caught?" His brown eyes shot to hers. "You will die."

Shane, who'd snuck in halfway through the idea, fumed, his cheeks red with anger. She saw his anger in the way his jaw was hard, his body stiff against the wall. "This is fucking idiotic."

"And why is that?" Dakota asked.

"Because you don't know what the hell you're doing," he snapped. "You may be a cop—or whatever the hell your kind calls Fighters—but you sure as hell are no warrior. Vincent will slaughter you, and you'll get Anastasia killed."

She folded her arms over her chest. "I'm more than capable of taking care of myself." Letting the power build in her veins, she held open her palm.

Shane's eyes widened slightly at the floating orb.

"I always knew you were stubborn, Anastasia." He narrowed his eyes on her face, "But I would never have added stupid to that list."

"You better watch your damn mouth," Dakota warned.

"Or what, *cop?* You honestly think you can take me on?"

Tony stepped between them. "I think I can kick both your asses if you don't knock it off. Shane, you ever call Anastasia stupid again and I'll break your fucking face. Dakota, you have to understand that Shane has been fighting against Vincent for years. As far as enemies go, we know what you're fighting against better than anyone."

"Agreed," Dakota admitted. "But I know Seattle."

"Agreed," Tony responded with a nod.

Anastasia pinched the bridge of her nose. "Look, this is not a debate. This is the best possible plan, and if it fails, I will portal us back here."

"And if you can't?" Selena asked. "That's the big hiccup here, isn't it? If you can't come back, we will lose."

"If I stay and he kills us all, we'll lose then, too. At least this way we have a chance of sneaking up on him."

They all stood quietly for a moment, processing the plan. She knew she was right; they had to get back to Seattle and at the very least *try* to find a way to get to him. Even if it meant hightailing it back here if things went wrong. At least they'd be doing *something*.

Selena finally nodded. As acting town elder with Tony, they were the ones to make the final decisions regarding anything having to do with Terrenia.

Not that it mattered much to Anastasia; she'd have portaled her and Dakota back to Seattle with or without their permission.

"We will ready Terrenia for a counter-attack, should one come," Selena said softly. "Shane, get Brady and the rest of the recruits ready for war. We will need everyone we have on hand in case Anastasia and Dakota are forced to retreat."

Shane scoffed and shook his head. "This will fail." He left the cabin without another word.

"Elizabeth, would you mind staying behind and helping with the injured?"

"Not at all. I'm not much in a fight, but I can sure as hell stitch up an injury."

"You most certainly can," Tony agreed.

Anastasia caught the grin on his face as he looked down at Elizabeth. *He likes her.* She smiled. Good for him.

"When will you leave?" Elizabeth asked Anastasia.

"First thing in the morning." She wanted to practice her battle magic a bit longer. Now that she knew she had it, she wanted to make sure it was perfected for when she went up against Vincent. He may have years on her, but she hoped she had power enough to take him out.

Even if it meant killing them both.

***

"YOU'RE GOING TO NEED TO LEARN TO FIGHT WITH ONE of these." She handed Dakota a sword later that morning. They'd made their way back to the cabin where Anastasia had taken some time to pack up the healing potions and other various items they might need in their assault.

He smirked. "I know how to use a sword."

"Then let's see." She held her blade firmly and took her stance. He lunged, and she blocked, then she lunged, and he blocked.

"Not bad." She grinned.

"I had some time on my hands in college, so I took up fencing. Well, that and boxing."

She spun, and he moved away quickly. Impressed, she regarded him a moment. When he attacked, she was ready. She laughed and moved, knocking the sword from his hand and pointing hers at him.

"I've got to admit, Ana, this is doing something for me." He laughed and bent to retrieve his sword.

"Wait until we get to the hand-to-hand."

"That sounds interesting."

Her face flushed, and he laughed. She lunged for him again, and this time he caught her around the waist and kissed her deeply.

"But I'm okay to go there now, if you want." He set his sword down and moved away from her.

"If you think you can handle me," she taunted as she set her sword to the side as well.

Again, she took her stance as he took his. He lunged, and she dodged. He threw a punch, and she blocked. "You holding back on me, Parker?"

"Possibly."

"Don't." When she spun, her right hook came into contact with his side, and he bent at the waist, laughing.

"Well, well, Anastasia. It seems there is more to you than I ever knew."

She threw another punch, and he blocked it, then pinned her to the ground. She laughed and rolled him over, and when she twisted around him, so his head was between her legs in a headlock, he tapped. She stood and smiled down at him. "Want to go again?" she asked playfully.

"Of course. What kind of man would I be if I didn't want another round of that?" He winked, and she laughed.

He charged toward her, wrapping his arms around her and lifting her off the ground. Anastasia squealed, banging her fists against his back, and he lowered himself to his knees, tossing her onto the grass. She threw her legs up, wrapping them around his waist in an attempt to subdue him. She began to alligator roll, but he collapsed on top of her, his body limp and heavy, pressing her into the ground.

He nuzzled his nose in her neck, then reached up and began tickling her sides—

Elizabeth cleared her throat.

They froze, holding each other's gazes, their lips twitching. In unison, they slowly turned their heads to look up

Elizabeth's lips twitched, then she burst into laughter.

Tony stood beside her, a sparkle of amusement in his eyes as he shook his head.

"Well, isn't this a sight," Elizabeth said when she finished laughing.

"I let her win." Dakota chuckled, tapping Ana's leg, so she would release him.

"Don't take it too personally, Dakota." Tony laughed. "Anastasia here has been giving some of our best Fighters a run for their money over the last few years. She sure is something."

"She definitely is," Dakota said, eyeing her. He pushed up, and then reached to pull Anastasia to her feet.

"We were coming to see if you needed any help getting ready," Elizabeth said, stifling a smile. "But we can always come back if you two are preoccupied."

Anastasia blushed. "Everything's ready to go."

"You found Gregory's journal, then?" Tony asked. "I assume since you didn't tell us about it this morning, there wasn't anything pertinent in there?"

"Come see for yourselves." Ana brushed dirt and grass from her clothing. "You two are more than welcome to read it."

They followed a dirty Dakota and Anastasia into the house. Together, Elizabeth and Tony sat at the table and read Gregory's final journal entry.

By the time they were finished, Elizabeth wiped a tear from her cheek. Even Tony's eyes glistened.

"He was the most wonderful man I have ever known." Tony set the journal down. "I will always watch over you as if you were my own, Anastasia. Trust in that."

"I do." She smiled and touched his arm gently.

"He seems like he was quite the man. Dakota, he was right about you." Elizabeth beamed. "You never told me that you met him, though."

"I didn't know it was him. To me, he was just Silvan."

"The man you used to drink with at the bar?" she asked, surprised.

Dakota nodded.

"Well, isn't that the darnedest thing."

Dakota nodded. "You're okay staying behind?" he asked his mother.

"Of course. I would only be another distraction for

the two of you. Besides, I think I can be of some help here."

Dakota turned to Tony. "You will keep her safe?"

"I will protect her with my life." Tony placed his fist over his heart.

Dakota nodded and turned to Anastasia. "What's our first step when we get there?"

"I think I know who has been supplying Vincent with his weapons, and I am looking forward to paying that asshole a visit."

"Mitch," Dakota clarified, grinning widely.

"Yes," Anastasia said. "I'm done being afraid of him. It's time he knows who he is dealing with."

54

ANASTASIA

They spent the rest of the afternoon and evening gathering weapons, and Anastasia spent some time conjuring her power. It was coming much quicker to her now, no longer needing anger to trigger the magic.

She hadn't used much, not wanting to drain herself before the morning. They were going to need every tool at their disposal if they wanted to succeed.

What would life be like then? If they succeeded and had nothing more to fight about?

Would she finally be able to actually enjoy *living*?

Anastasia's eyes traveled over the faces of her people as they sat around the fire. Although her parents and Dakota's father were not with them in the flesh, she knew they watched over them all.

They had lost the last few battles, but as long as they didn't quit, they would be victorious in the war.

Tony sat next to Elizabeth, and he said something to her that made her laugh. Brady was with his mother, who fussed over him as she usually did, and the familiar routine made Anastasia smile. Sarah laughed with three other girls about her age, and they pointed at one of the younger Fighters before breaking into a fit of giggles when Sarah blushed.

Shane stood in the corner, a glass of whiskey in his hand, watching it all. Her heart hurt for him.

"I'll be right back." Anastasia stood and made her way over to where he stood. "Hey."

He didn't return her greeting, just took another drink.

"I'm sorry, Shane."

"For what? Getting yourself killed?"

"I'm not going to get killed."

"Why aren't you letting me go? Surely two pairs of hands are better than one."

Anastasia folded her arms, not missing the jab he'd taken at Dakota. "Dakota is going, Shane."

He rolled his eyes. "Yeah, perfect fucking Dakota."

"What the hell is your problem? I know you liked me but—"

"Loved you."

Anastasia's mouth hung low, and her eyes widened.

"Yeah, I *love* you, Anastasia. Have since the moment I met you. So don't come at me with that *like* bullshit. You don't feel the same? Fine, whatever. But don't you dare try and lessen how I feel."

"Shane—"

"Not interested. Just don't die." He turned and left, leaving her staring after him. "Hey," Brady said as he approached her from behind.

Anastasia turned to him and forced a smile. "Hey, you."

"Mom says you're going back to try and kill Vincent."

She nodded.

"Are you going to be all right? I know I'm not fully trained yet, but I really think I could help."

"Dakota and I will be fine," she promised.

"I just, I think of you like a sister, you know?"

She smiled and wrapped her arms around him. "I know. And you're the little brother I always wanted to annoy." She messed his hair up and stepped away.

"Just be careful."

"You too. Help your mom keep things going around here."

"I will. And Anastasia?"

"Hmm?"

"Don't worry about Shane. He'll come around. I'm just happy that you have Dakota back."

She smiled at the boy who had been forced to grow into a man way too soon. Eighteen and going on thirty. "Thanks, Brady."

Anastasia made her way back to sit next to Dakota.

He wrapped an arm around her waist and pressed a kiss to her temple. She studied the faces around her again with new strength.

This is what she would fight for. These people. Her family. She glanced at Dakota, who watched her, flames reflected in his fierce blue eyes. He was her center, her focal point, and with him beside her, she would walk through the fires of hell without flinching. He was the very strength inside of her, and for the first time in her life, she believed she had all she needed to defeat Vincent and get their lives back.

These people, this laughter and love that surrounded her, were what made it all worthwhile. She closed her eyes and nuzzled closer to Dakota, her light in a war against darkness.

She had finally made peace with her past and, in doing so, had secured her victory over the future.

Or so she hoped.

55

ANASTASIA

*S*urrounded by devastation, Anastasia surveyed
what was left of Terrenia. Death and destruction
marred the once green landscape, now a resting
place for the dead.

*No one was left. Not a single friend or loved one
remained in this village she'd once called home.*

*She felt herself smile, although inside, she felt
nothing but emptiness. Why was she smiling? She
wanted to scream in horror, to beat her fists against
whatever had done this until skin hung in bloody
ribbons from her knuckles.*

Where was everyone?

"Ana."

She spun toward Dakota's voice and felt the first

flash of light within her heart as it fought to push back against the blackness.

Dakota disappeared before she could get to him, quickly replaced with Vincent. His eyes were blue again, and he looked so much like her father her heart pinched with grief.

"Now you know what it's like," he said simply, a tear rolling down his cheek.

"What do you mean?" she asked, feeling nothing toward the man that she knew she should hate.

"Look around, Anastasia. You did this."

She circled slowly, studying the destruction once again. He was wrong; he had to be wrong. She lifted her hands and saw the blood still dripping from her shaking limbs. "No," she croaked.

Vincent nodded sadly. "You did this," he repeated. "But you didn't wish for it to happen."

"This wasn't me!"

"It was you. And now you know what it's like."

"What the hell are you talking about?" she screamed, tears burning in her throat.

"I didn't want any of this to happen," Vincent said. "But it has, and now it must be dealt with."

"You are the one. You caused this! You killed them all!"

He shook his head. "Not this time, niece."

Anastasia's mind went blank again, erasing all emotion. She blinked. How strange.

She held up her hand and a glowing orb of white

light danced within her palm. She thrust the orb at Vincent, who cried out as he evaporated into dust.

She smiled as he disappeared on the breeze, and Gregory appeared in front of her.

"Do not fear the dark, Anastasia," he said.

"I don't."

"But beware the cost of your victory." He gestured around him, and Anastasia's cool façade shattered, dropping her to her knees.

ANASTASIA SCREAMED AND SHOT UP IN BED. MOMENTS later, Dakota burst in, gun drawn.

She pressed a hand to her chest, her heart thumping wildly against her palm. It was just a nightmare, nothing but a nightmare.

"You okay?" Dakota knelt in front of her.

She nodded, unable to speak.

How many times had he come to her rescue because of a nightmare? Nearly all her life she'd suffered from them, and when they'd lived together, she'd been unable to keep the dreams from him.

"Can you stay with me?" she asked.

Dakota nodded.

Anastasia leaned back against the pillows as the bed dipped with his weight. He'd done this before, too, slept beside her when she'd suffered a bad dream.

But tonight's nightmare had been so much more; it felt like a warning, but from whom, she wasn't sure.

She laid her head on Dakota's chest and focused on the sound of his heart beating.

Thump, thump.

Thump, thump.

In the worst of her nightmares, that heart flat-lined.

AS REMNANTS OF HER NIGHTMARE STILL BURNED IN HER memory, Anastasia stood beside Dakota in the living room of Elizabeth's cottage.

"Are you sure this is a good idea?"

Anastasia turned to Elizabeth and offered her a hopeful smile. "I really do." Kaley stepped forward and rubbed her head against Anastasia's stomach, so she knelt and rubbed her soft fur affectionately. "I'll miss you, girl. Watch over them for me." She smiled and stood to face Tony and Brady. "We will be back soon."

They both nodded, and Brady pulled her in for a hug. "Be careful out there."

Elizabeth hugged Dakota with tears in her eyes, then gripped Anastasia's arms. "Take care of him," she said, then she turned to Dakota. "And you take care of her. I love you both so much."

"I love you, too," they said in unison.

Anastasia conjured a portal, and the swirling blue light appeared within seconds. They took one last look at those they loved, twined their fingers together, and stepped through.

Within seconds, the acrid punch of sulfur assaulted them as they gazed upon a sea of destruction.

"Holy shit," Dakota whispered. "It's all gone." He turned to Anastasia, ash falling into his dark hair. "Seattle is gone."

Find out what happens next in Blood of the Phoenix! Available now! Click here to download!

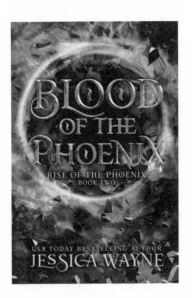

FOR MY GRANDMOTHER

My Grandmother with my oldest kiddo 2012

Without my Grandmother introducing me to her love of reading, none of this would be possible. It started with Highlights magazine and other small books, which turned into me obsessing over GooseBumps and Harry Potter.

When I turned sixteen, she introduced me to romance through Nora Roberts' world, and ever since then I haven't looked back!

She'd find a new author or series she loved and would tell me, and I would do the same. I can't tell you how many times we read and re-read JR Wards Black Dagger Brotherhood Series, or Karen Marie Moning's Fever Series.

In fact, when I went into the hospital to have my first kiddo, she brought me a hardback copy of Iced by KMM, which had just released.

Even though she's gone, I still make notes of my favorite authors and new books I find out of habit. It's been nearly three years since she passed, and I still reach for the phone every time I want to share something.

So this is for all those times she shared stories with me-

All those times we stayed up drinking home made Kahlua-

All those phone calls-

And the text message that was never returned.

I love you Grandma Carme, this book was for you and I hope you know how much it meant to me that we shared so many worlds together.

ALSO BY JESSICA WAYNE

FAE WAR CHRONICLES

EMBER IS DYING.

BUT AS SHE WILL SOON DISCOVER, SOME FATES ARE WORSE THAN DEATH.

ACCIDENTAL FAE

VAMPIRE HUNTRESS CHRONICLES

SHE'S SPENT HER ENTIRE LIFE ERADICATING THE IMMORTALS. NOW, SHE FINDS HERSELF PROTECTING ONE.

WITCH HUNTER: FREE READ

BLOOD HUNT

BLOOD CAPTIVE

BLOOD CURE

CURSE OF THE WITCH

BLOOD OF THE WITCH

RISE OF THE WITCH

BLOOD MAGIC

BLOOD BOND

BLOOD UNION

CAMBREXIAN REALM : THE COMPLETE SERIES

THE REALM'S DEADLIEST ASSASSIN HAS MET HER MATCH.

The Last Ward: FREE READ

Warrior Of Magick

Guardian Of Magick

Shades Of Magick

RISE OF THE PHOENIX: THE COMPLETE SERIES

ANA HAS SPENT HER ENTIRE LIFE AT THE CLUTCHES OF HER ENEMY. NOW, IT'S TIME FOR WAR.

Birth of the Phoenix

Blood of the Phoenix

Vengeance of the Phoenix

Tears of the Phoenix

Rise of the Phoenix

Tethered

SOMETIMES, OUR DREAMS DO COME TRUE. THE TROUBLE IS, OUR NIGHTMARES CAN AS WELL.

Tethered Souls

Collateral Damage

FOR MORE INFORMATION, VISIT WWW.JESSICAWAYNE.COM

ABOUT THE AUTHOR

Photo Credit Mandi Rose Photography

Jessica Wayne is the author of over thirty fantasy and contemporary romance novels. The latter of which she writes as J.W. Ashley. During the day, she slays laundry and dishes as a stay at home mom of three, and at night her worlds come to life on paper.

She runs on coffee and wine (as well as the occasional whiskey!) and if you ever catch her wearing matching socks, it's probably because she grabbed them in the dark.

She is a believer of dragons, unicorns, and the power of love, so each of her stories contain one of those elements (and in some cases all three).

You can usually find her in her Facebook group, Jessica's Whiskey Thieves, or keep in touch by subscribing to her newsletter.

Stay Updated:

Newsletter: https://www.jessicawayne.com/free-books-by-jessica-wayne
Website: https://www.jessicawayne.com
Readers Group: https://www.facebook.com/groups/jessicaswhiskeythieves

facebook.com/AuthorJessicaWayne
twitter.com/jessmccauthor
instagram.com/authorjessicawayne

CONTEMPORARY ROMANCE BY J.W. ASHLEY

THE CORRUPTED TRILOGY

They're being hunted and the only way to come out of it alive, is to put their badges aside.

RESCUING NORAH

SHIELDING JEMMA

TARGETING CELESTE

OLIVE YOU: *Six best friends and their hunt for true love (or something like it anyway).*

LONG ROAD HOME: *Coming home was always part of the plan. He was not.*

HOME FOR SUMMER: *He thinks she's a spoiled brat. She thinks he's a stick in the mud. Turns out, they're both wrong.*

WAY BACK HOME: *Facing your past is always the hardest part of moving forward. Especially when you've kept a secret for five years.*

HOME AT LAST: *Rule #1: Never get tied down. Leo smashed through that like it was a pane of sugar glass and he's an action star whose mission is to take me down...repeatedly.*